Lock Down Publications and Ca$h
Presents

I0655141

A THUG'S STREET PRINCESS 3

Written By
MEESHA

First Edition 2024

Printed in the United States of America

This is a work of fiction. Names, characters, places, and incidents either are products of the author's imagination or are used fictitiously. Any similarity to actual events or locales or persons, living or dead, is entirely coincidental.

Lock Down Publications
P.O. Box 944
Stockbridge, GA 30281
www.lockdownpublications.com

Like our page on Facebook: Lock Down Publications
www.facebook.com/lockdownpublications.ldp

Stay Connected with Us!

Text **LOCKDOWN** to 22828 to stay up-to-date with new releases, sneak peaks, contests and more...

Like our page on Facebook:
Lock Down Publications

Join Lock Down Publications/The New Era Reading Group

Visit our website:
www.lockdownpublications.com

Follow us on Instagram:
Lock Down Publications

Email Us: We want to hear from you!

Chapter 1

Breeze

I took off running with my gun in-hand. The nigga who had just shot my people was hauling ass down Sawyer Avenue. I was keeping up with him for the most part then he upped his speed and bent the corner on 78th. He turned into an Olympic track champion before my eyes. A sharp pain traveled across my chest, causing me to pause at the corner. My pursuit ended at that point, but I kept my eyes on the target. Struggling to catch my breath, I followed his every move as I leaned against a fence and was disappointed as I watched the black luxury car speed around the corner. Whoever the nigga was definitely had a lucky charm around his neck.

"Where did he go?" Honey asked, coming up behind me.

"He's gone. I couldn't get a shot off. Plus, my chest started hurting and I fell behind while chasing him. The nigga was too fast. He jumped in a black Beamer. If I see it again, I'll know it's that muthafucka." I said securing my Glock behind my back.

"Come on. G and Fredo already left to take Quell and Scony to get patched up. Both of them were hit but it wasn't anything major. I'm glad dude didn't have a solid shot. We were on him soon as he tried to sneak up."

"My radar was alerted immediately. I agree, had we waited to see what he was on before pulling our weapons, shit could've been catastrophic. My gut wasn't wrong today. I felt this shit before it even happened."

"It's all good. Nobody died and the memorial did exactly what we needed it to do. Put shit in motion. Them muthafuckas set the tone so I hope they're ready for the aftermath."

We were walking slowly back to the funeral home and there were police everywhere. Several officers, I assumed, were taking statements from people around the parking lot. There was no way me and Honey could get to our vehicles because the exit was blocked by a police car. As I surveyed the scene, a female pointed in my direction. If there weren't so many pigs around, I would've shot that bitch in her pinky toe for drawing attention to me. The officer approached cautiously with his hand on his service weapon. I locked eyes with him until we were standing toe to toe.

"How are you?" The officer asked, sizing me up.

"I'm good. What can I help you with?"

"It was brought to my attention that you were involved in the shooting which took place here. Can you tell me what happened?"

"Whoever told you I was involved is a bold-faced lie. The only thing I'm guilty of is running when the bullets started flying. As far as what happened, I can't help you with that either because again, I was worried about my life and my life only."

Glancing down at his name plate, I remembered his name and badge number as he snarled at me. Why Officer Cox was upset with me was something I couldn't understand, but his body language said it all. When he took a step forward, I moved two steps back.

"I need to search you for weapons. Would you mind facing the wall and placing your hands against the building?"

"In fact, I do mind. I'm not complying with that because you don't have probable cause to search me based off hearsay. Since you want to be on bullshit and insult my intelligence, I can do one better. Cuz, get Bartholomew Joseph on the line. Make sure you let him know Officer Cox is a male who's trying to search a female. Last time I checked, that shit was against the law."

Amusingly, I observed the little bit of color Officer Cocksucker had left drain from his face. He backed away from me slowly but knew better than to say another word. The attorney Cheno had on his payroll wasn't to be fucked with. He always had CPD by the balls when his name was mentioned. See, Bart didn't play. He would sue the fuck out of the city at the drop of a dime and win. He didn't go back and forth with the police. He took that shit straight to the media so sweeping the incident under the rug wasn't an option.

"Aye, Officer Cox!" I yelled. He turned around slowly. "Would you tell yo' people to let me get my car out?"

"Sure. Sure, no problem."

I waved Honey along, leading the way to the lot.

"Is that attorney even real?" she asked out of curiosity.

"Didn't you see his reaction? Hell yeah, Bart is very real. Officer Cock didn't want to fuck around and find out. His ass is already aware of how Cheno's representation coming."

The officers parted like the Red Sea as me and Honey walked through the parking lot. Hitting the key fob to unlock my doors, I jumped in my whip once Honey backed out of the space. I stayed where I was until I found the song I wanted to listen to. With a wicked grin, the petty bitch in me turned up the volume, rolled down the window, grabbed a blunt and backed up slowly.

Fuck the police, coming straight from the underground.

A young nigga got it bad 'cause I'm brown

And not the other color, so police think they have the authority to kill a minority

Fuck that shit, 'cause I ain't the one.

If looks could kill, I'd be a dead muthafucka from the evil glares I received from the pigs. Bobbing my head to the beat,

I smiled and drove off. Glancing down briefly for a lighter, I was about to spark up until noticing an unmarked in my rearview. I should've known my actions would cause a reaction for them muthafuckas to harass me. Soon as I pulled away from the light, the red and blues forced me to the side of the road.

"Ain't this a bitch." I laughed.

Casually throwing the blunt along with my Glock in my secret compartment, I hit the button on my key fob to lock everything down. I reached into the glove department and retrieved my registration and insurance as the officer approached my vehicle. With the paperwork and my license in hand, I held it out the window.

"License and—"

I waved the papers before he could get out what he was trying to say. "What did you pull me over for?"

With shifty eyes he told a bold-faced lie. "You have a taillight out on the rear right, and I smell marijuana."

"Siri, call Bart Joseph," I said out loud. When the phone started ringing, I tapped my fingers on the steering wheel. "What you not gon' do is pull me over on bullshit. You got the right one today because how the hell you smell marijuana from inside your car that's behind me? Your colleagues should've told you all about why they allowed me to leave without incident."

Bart answered but was quiet throughout the exchange.

"Get out the car!" The officer demanded aggressively. When I didn't move, he proceeded to pull on the door handle. "Get yo' ass out before I drag you out, black bitch!"

"Officer, this is Attorney Bartholomew Joseph. Your job is to protect and serve, not bully and throw racial slurs. Miss Brown will *not* exit her vehicle. If anything happens to her, a hair out of place, I will have your badge! The department and your ass will wish you took the training course to do your job effectively. You will wish you never approached her with the bullshit. Your pension won't be enough to buy a

7

stick of gum when I'm through with you. Now, allow her to go about her day and you need to head directly to the precinct to tell your boss to call me ASAP! As a matter of fact, I'll contact him myself. What's your name and badge number?"

Quickly glancing at his information on the officer's uniform, I gave Bart what he needed to get shit in motion. "Officer St. Patrick. Badge number 2258."

For the second time within the matter of thirty minutes, I'd witnessed a cop fighting the urge to shit on himself. Without saying a word, Officer St. Patrick handed my paperwork back then walked backwards to his vehicle before peeling away. Bartholomew Joseph got his ass right together and I loved that shit.

"Breeze, whatever is going on, I need you to lay low. Stay out the way. Understood?"

"I hear you, Bart. Thanks for coming through."

"Aways. Get to your destination and remember what I said."

Bart hung up and I merge into traffic. Heading eastbound on 79th, I cruised through the street. As I approached an intersection, a woman on her phone walked out in front of my car, causing me to slam on my brakes.

"Bitch, what you gon' do, hit me?" She screamed.

"I should've! Get the fuck off yo' phone and watch where the fuck you walking! Ain't no muthafuckin' crosswalk in the middle of the damn block! Don't come for me when it was yo' fault you almost died."

"Kiss my ass!" She said continuing to cross the street. "Dike ass bitch almost hit me. I ain't gon' lie, if I was into women, her ass could get it 'cause she was fine as hell."

I heard what her dusty pussy ass said and couldn't do nothing but shake my head. Her birdbrain ass could never get a minute of my time in this thing called life. The driver behind me laid on their horn, prompting me to pull off. I hit Honey's contact on my phone and waited for her to pick up.

"You okay, cousin?" she asked the moment she answered.

"Yeah, meet me at Cheno's. I got pulled over by one of those stupid ass pigs soon as I pulled off. Talking 'bout my taillight was out and he smelled weed. Lying through his teeth. But I thank God for Bart because he got that muthafucka off me in a flash."

"Lawd, the universe is really trying to hang us. Hurry up and get to the suburbs. I'm going to stop home to shower and change since you aren't remotely close. I'll see you when I get there."

"Bet."

Meek Mills' *Dreams and Nightmares* blared through the speakers as soon as the call ended. Bart said lay low, but I didn't think I was going to be able to do that. Niggas was coming out the woodworks on our ass and there was a new player at every turn. We needed to find out who was on this nigga Cheese's team because the shit was a complete mystery at this point.

I arrived at Cheno's thirty-five minutes later. Using my key to gain access, I walked in like I lived there. My brother was pacing the floor with his AirPod in his ear. The sling on his arm reminded me of what he'd been through. The way he was yelling told me he was talking about what took place at the funeral home. My eyes went to the living room and there was a woman dressed in scrubs sitting on the black leather couch. Placing my keys in my pocket, I strolled over and took a seat on the loveseat across from her.

"Hello. I'm Breeze, and you are?"

"Amari. Mr. Brown said he needed someone to care for his wounds and I took him up on his offer."

"So, you're a nurse?" I asked with a raised eyebrow.

"A Nurse Practitioner, actually. Is that going to be a problem?"

"It won't be for me. I'm his sister. Cheno usually don't let nobody know where he lays his head. I'm surprised you are sitting comfortably while he's pacing with no shirt on, and it appears his bandages haven't been touched. I'm just saying."

"That's all I'm here to do. I'm a professional who is assisting a former patient. That's it, that's all."

I believed what Amari was saying but I knew Cheno. He may have reeled her in with the *I need you to take care of my aftercare.* In a matter of time, her legs were going to be resting on his shoulders or against her ears. Cheno was a pussy-chaser, and with Charlie leaving and entertaining another, he was free to do whomever he wanted. How it played out was another story. Cheno and Charlie loved each other but their toxicity was about to shine through.

Cheno was no longer in the room, and I took that as his way of not saying too much in front of his company. Instead of sitting and looking Amari in the face, I got up and went to the bar in the far corner of the room. I had to give it to my bro, though. Amari was a little cutie. She was thick in all the right places and her caramel-colored skin was flawless. She was beautiful and nobody could say any different. Pouring a double shot of Crown into a glass, I threw it back.

"You want something to drink?" I asked over my shoulder.

"Water, if you have it."

I retrieved a bottle of water from the mini fridge under the bar and walked it over to her. Amari took it and said thanks just as Cheno walked back into the room. The fire in his eyes was clear as day. I knew he was madder than a muthafucka knowing he couldn't voice his thoughts at that moment.

"Amari, you ready? I have some shit to take care of and I don't want you waiting around any longer than you have."

She nodded, taking a quick sip of her water before twisting the cap in place and stood so Cheno could lie on the couch. Amari had a body these hoes were paying big money for, and her shit was natural. I flamed up while watching her remove the bloodstained bandages. My brother's eyes were soaking up Amari's beauty while mine were fixated on her backside. His intentions were just as I thought. Cheno was going to fuck the shit out of her lil' thick ass.

10

Honey entered, breaking me from what should've been off limits to me. She sat next to me at the bar, placing her purse down with a look of inquisitiveness. "Who the fuck is that?" she whispered.

I pulled on the blunt, letting the smoke flow through my nostrils. "Your cousin's nurse." I smirked.

"Breeze, Cheno gon' take that woman down. You hear me? Charlie is going to beat the fuck out of him."

"Charlie ain't gon' do shit. You heard the shit for yourself. She already moved on. Cheno was asking me about the nigga yesterday at the hospital. That is not my business just like whatever he's doing ain't either. I know that's your girl, she will forever be my sister, but stay out of their shit. I already know this is about to get messy before they find their way back to each other. This time is different because Charlie has never entertained anyone outside of Cheno. No matter what he did behind her back."

Honey sneaked a peek at Cheno and he and Amari were all smiles as she cleaned his wound. His mouth was moving but we couldn't hear what was being said. When Amari playfully hit him on the chest, I shook my head.

"Got 'em." I chuckled turning around to mind my business.

Amari finished what she was doing and started cleaning up the small mess she made. When she had everything in hand, I pointed in the direction of the kitchen. She disappeared and I smirked at my brother as his orbs followed her ass the entire way.

"Don't ruin that woman's life, Cheno." Honey said. "You and Charlie may be going through some shit, but you and I both know it's not a done deal between y'all."

"Ain't nobody on that. I needed her to make sure a nigga don't get an infection around this bitch." Amari came back, wiping her hands on a paper towel. "Thanks, Mari," Cheno said, quickly diverting his attention to her.

"No problem. Anything else you need before I leave?"

"Nah, I'm good. I'll see you next time."

"Yeah, I'll call in a few days. You take care of yourself, Mr. Brown," she said, slinging her purse over her shoulder.

"Aye, call me Cheno. That Mr. Brown shit ain't gon' cut it."

"Cheno it is. It was nice meeting y'all. Enjoy the rest of your day."

The door closed behind Amari and I burst out in laughter.

Cheno's head jerked in my direction and the shit only made me laugh harder. "What's funny?"

"You. Talking about you ain't on that but you gave her ass a nickname and didn't even peep the shit."

"Her name is Amari and that's what I called her."

"Nigga, you said, 'Thanks, Mari,' while undressing her without using your hands," I said, lighting another blunt.

"What the fuck ever, man. What happened at the funeral home?" he asked, changing the subject. "Fredo told me from his point of view, but I want to hear it from y'all."

I ran the scene back to him and Cheno sat, listening quietly. Leaning forward with his good elbow on his knee, Cheno appeared to be in deep thought.

"I got a good look at the nigga, but I'd never seen him before."

"Shit is wild out here, Cheno. Everything is happening nonstop and it's a fucked-up situation for all of us. When I was released and heading back home, I didn't imagine fighting to survive the way I had to for years on the inside. I'm standing ten toes down with y'all, but the shit at the funeral home should've been orchestrated better. That shit was sloppy, and somebody could've died today. The manpower was there. That nigga was not supposed to been able to get that close; let alone get away with letting off shots. In order for us to get back at Cheese, yo' muthafuckin' people need to tighten up and be ready for this war we're fighting blindly." Honey was pissed off and it was evident in her voice.

"I agree. You have every right to be upset, Honey." Cheno retorted. "If I was there, shit would've gone down differently. Trust."

"Upset? I'm beyond that! My man could've died behind this shit. Not only do we have Cheese and his people to deal with, now there's another muthafucka that has beef with G and Scony."

"What you mean?" I questioned.

"When you ran after the mystery man, I checked on Quell to make sure he was good. In the midst of that, I heard Scony say something about a chapter not being closed. Whoever the nigga was that shot him and Quell had no association with Cheese. It's an old vendetta against them two muthafuckas."

"I'm going to find out what's with that when I talk to G and Scony. I don't want you to open the shop at least until we figure out who the fuck that nigga is, and everybody involved with Cheese. Y'all safety is what I'm worried about right now."

My phone rang and it was Taz. That was my excuse to leave because I was tired of hearing people tell me to sit the fuck down as if I was really going to follow their lead. I stood, drinking the last of my Crown, then I headed for the door. Cheno's voice stopped me in my tracks.

"Where you going?"

"To the crib. Taz just hit me up. It's time for me to spend time with my girl so I can get my mind off the shit I went through earlier. What better way to do that than tongue-deep."

"Man, you something else." He laughed. "Did yo' daddy show up at the memorial?"

I held my head low as I chuckled lowly. Turning to face my beloved brother, I thought about what I wanted to say. "No disrespect but, is our mother in the kitchen cooking?"

"Nuff said."

"Dawson only give a fuck about one thing and that's money. He'll be calling on bullshit soon. I got a feeling we gon' have to handle that nigga, too. With you *out of the picture*," I said using my fingers as air quotes, "he gon' find out the hard way that he has two sons."

"Aye, yo!" Cheno laughed. "Be easy on him. You know he loves yo' manly ass...Sike!"

I couldn't keep the seriousness going and started laughing myself. "If Dawson loves me then that means you love men, nigga."

The laughter faded at that point. Cheno hated when I threw gay shit at him. In no way was he homophobic. He just didn't play with that side of my world. "What I tell you about that shit, Breeze? Get fucked up." He warned. "Yo' daddy's intentions will come to light eventually. If push comes to shove, I'll whoop his ass so he can disappear again. Simple, right?"

"Dawson isn't a simple nigga. I'm gon' have to kill him. Especially when he finds out you're not dead and has to continue paying on that damn policy he thought was going to fatten his pockets. Mark my words."

Opening the door to leave, I thought about what happened with the police on the way to Cheno's house. The incident that took place would be better coming from me instead of Bart because my brother would swear I was trying to hide something from him if I didn't. Turning to face him, I closed the door and took a deep breath.

"Before I go, the pigs were fucking with me, and I had to get Bart on the phone in order for them to let me go. Not once, but twice. They were on good bullshit so, I wanted to give you a heads up that the law is bound to be on our ass for a minute. Some bitch told an officer I was involved in the shooting."

Cheno sat quietly, shaking his head slowly. "This is another reason we have to lay low," he said glancing in my direction. "I know you want revenge and I do too, but we have to think this shit through. None of us can afford to get jammed up right now. We're going to have to make these muthafuckas think shit sweet for the time being. Give or take a month. That will give me the opportunity to heal properly and get the dice rolling on how to finish these niggas off."

"I'm not trying to hear none of that, Cheno. I was already minding my business when Sketty came to the shop to take me out. I'm not going to sit back waiting for them to try their hand again."

"Sketty was a stupid nigga! He knew what time it was when he ran up. They sent him on a suicide mission and he killed himself. You know what the fuck to do and when to do it. Long as you stay ready, you don't have to get ready. Big bro taught you that shit out the gate." Cheno barked. "I'm not telling you to live your life in hiding. What I will say is this, make sure all five of your senses are activated at all times. I will holla at Bart about what he wants to do about the harassment."

Cheno was quiet for a moment so I figured I'd make my exit while I had the chance. Soon as my hand grasped the doorknob, Cheno opened his mouth, shooting me with the bullet I thought I would be able to dodge. "Where's Charlie? She didn't show up?"

Speaking on Charlie was something I didn't want to discuss. Honey was no help as she sat, picking her nails as if she wasn't trying to indulge in the conversation.

Waiting for my beloved cousin to answer the question, Cheno grilled both of us when neither one of us spoke up. "Well?"

I sighed, cutting my eyes at Honey because she left me to answer alone. "She showed up and stayed the entire service. Where is she now, I can't tell you."

"Charlie was upset because of all the women in attendance. Not to mention the bullshit that was posted on your social media page." Honey finally put her two cents in. "I don't blame her."

"Those bitches couldn't wait for a nigga to be written off the face of the earth. I saw that shit you talkin' about but half of them hoes I've never touched. Their narratives were just that…theirs. Every last one of them wanted to say they had something going on with me. Many have tried, few have succeeded. I can guarantee there was probably one or two who showed their ass on that page, but the real ones ain't said shit out of line."

I stood quietly, hearing my brother out. It didn't matter how he explained the philosophy of his life, Cheno shouldn't have any females outside of Charlie. If she was the woman he claimed as his, why give others false hope? That was a question I'd asked time and time again.

"We know she walked out on the relationship. She's dating someone else, and obviously moved on. What are you trying to do with Charlie?"

"Yeah, I want to hear your answer to that question too because the way you were grinning at Miss Mari lets me know you have plans to see her again. And not to change those damn bandages. One of us can change that shit for you, but carry on." Honey laughed.

Cheno laughed along with Honey, and I noticed it didn't reach his eyes. One thing I knew about my brother was that he really loved Charlie. Deep down Cheno knew he had fucked up what they had.

"On some real shit, Charlie ain't trying to leave me alone. I've already told her to do what makes her happy, but on temporary terms. When she don't find the happiness that she's looking for, Charlie will be back. I am her happy place."

"You're full of shit!" I laughed. "If you call getting caught with these bitches her happy place, you're the delusional one, brah. Charlie was miserable in that situationship. She's done, Cheno. There's no coming back from what you've done to her. Whoever has her attention better hold on to that shit. Gon' 'head and pursue Miss Amari because Charlie got a man right now," I sang in my best Chante' Moore voice.

"Yeah, okay. Watch what I tell you."

Cheno was out of his damn mind if he thought Charlie was doubling back to his community dick ass. She would be stupid to leave what she had going on to come back to my brother. The way she said dude wined and dined her then bought all that shit she didn't want to accept, and in turn left that shit outside her door. Yeah, he was a keeper, even though I didn't know who the nigga was. It didn't matter because he brought a smile to her face by just talking about his ass. I shook my head as I grabbed the doorknob. The drama was brewing right before our eyes. Cheno always kept his cool about most things. There was just something about his tone that was different.

"Leave Charlie alone, Cheno. Things might get ugly. Let it be."

"You're right, sis. Shit gon' get ugly," he said, leaving the room.

Honey gathered her purse, following me out of Cheno's home. I locked up and headed to my vehicle. The look on Honey's face told a story and it was filled with worry.

"Breeze, do you think Cheno would hurt Charlie?" she asked as her voice cracked.

"Nope. But that nigga is a different story. Be ready for the storm that's bound to touch down sooner than later. Cheno may have told Charlie to do her, but he didn't actually think she would go out and do it. There's something about a man not being able to deal with the same shit they dish out. My brother opened a can of worms that is going to be disastrous for both of them. I just hope and pray it doesn't lead him to a point of no return."

Honey stood, biting the skin from her bottom lip and that shit irked my soul.

I hit the unlock button on my key fob then opened the door. "I'll talk to you later. My baby is waiting. Don't let Charlie and Cheno drag you into their shit. They need to figure that shit out on their own."

"Okay. I love you, cousin."

"I love you more, Honey. Take yo' sensitive ass home and love on Quell." I laughed, getting into my whip.

As I backed out of the driveway, I knew for a fact Cheno was going to force Charlie back into his life by destroying the one she was in the process of building.

Chapter 2

Letty

Every day since the fight at the club, beating Honey's ass had been on my mind something heavy. The way she put hands on me and my sisters were something I wasn't expecting at all. Back in the day Honey was a fighter but she never came out on top when it was one-on-one. The bitch was throwing punches like Muhammed Ali and Laila combined. My ears still rang periodically out of nowhere. Sitting on the side of my bed, I was seething with anger just thinking about how I was going to get my lick back.

Cheese didn't make the situation any better. He ignored everything I remotely said about the bitch. No matter how many times he claimed to not give a damn about Honey, I knew better. Unbeknownst to him, I knew every time his sneaky ass was on social media. Cheese was the type of man who didn't spend his time online. So, why was his light always on late at night and his ass wasn't in bed with me? Instead, he was in his mancave probably talking to Honey.

The way he hurried to put his phone face down the moment I entered a room told me all I needed to know. He was hiding something. Proof was the only thing I didn't have to validate my suspicions. Cheese better pray to the good Lord I never obtained that shit. Both he and Honey would be begging for their lives after I was done with them.

Cheese hadn't been hanging out in the streets like he normally did. He'd go out to gather money and drop off work to his people, but was back in the house in a matter of a few hours. The shit he allowed his punk ass cousin to involve him in had Cheese in the house for days. Tank was wrong for what he'd done to Cheno, but Cheese was just as guilty because he didn't demand for Tank to do the right thing by giving the man his shit back. Instead, they were at war and people were dying behind it. Everything was good until Honey came back, bringing the demonic black cloud along with her.

As I sat, thinking about all the things which had transpired, Cheese entered the bedroom as if I wasn't even there. He bypassed me without a word as I followed his every move until he disappeared into the closet. His ass was about to leave the house. Not without telling me where the fuck he was going. The way he was moving secretively, and sneaky-like, I could smell his bullshit a mile away. Soon as he walked out holding clothes in his hand, my interrogation began.

"Where you off to?" I asked calmly.

"I'm going to the bike fest downtown."

The bike fest was an event where everybody and their mama came from all over to showcase their bikes for all to see. Every year it was held in a different location in the city. I hadn't heard anything about it until Cheese mentioned it and he didn't even think to inform me about it beforehand. There was music, food, and contests for the best bike. Sometimes they had some type of raunchy segment for the women to shake their ass for cash prizes. I was sure it would be no different at the one being held that day.

Cheese walked out of the room as he answered my question, causing me to jump off the bed to follow him. I saw him dip off into the spare bedroom where I knew he was about to iron his clothes. Standing in the doorway, I leaned against the doorframe with my arms folded over my chest. This negro thought he was about to ride out solo when we had been attending together for years. He had me fucked up.

"Why didn't you tell me?" I asked with an attitude.

"Letty, don't start that bullshit. You know what the fuck is going on in the streets, and the safest place for you is right here in this house. I can't take a chance on you getting hurt if something jumps off out there."

I cocked my head to the side because this nigga didn't look at me once while he attempted to force me to stay inside. That was an indication he was lying about his reason for not wanting me to attend. One thing for sho' and two for certain, he wasn't about to treat me like a little ass kid. I was too grown for any muthafucka to tell me what I could and could not do.

"Since when has any of that shit been a problem, Cheese? What happened to '*long as I'm with you, I'd always be protected*'? What's the real reason you're trying to leave me behind, huh? Is it that bitch Honey? You can tell me the truth. It's better than you standing there coming up with every excuse in the book for me to stay home."

Cheese's head turned quickly in my direction. "Why do you always bring that woman up when you're talking to me?"

"That lady has your undivided attention and I don't! Let's not forget how you treated me like a common hoe a few weeks ago." I snapped. "See, I've noticed the way you hide your phone, or hurry up and end a call the minute you hear me coming into a room. You're doing something you don't have no business doing, Cheese. The shit didn't start until you laid eyes on Honey's ass. If that's where the fuck you want to be, let me know. I'll gladly step aside while she slit your muthafuckin' throat for the part you played in killing her cousin."

Sitting the iron upright on the board, Cheese stalked over to where I stood with a deep grimace on his face. "Where the fuck you hear that shit from?"

When I didn't reply, he grabbed me by the front of the tank top I wore, scratching my chest with his nails in the process. I winced from the pain but never broke eye contact with him. Cheese was going out of his mind with the way he kept handling me. It seemed like all the respect he had for me no longer existed and he was ready to be done with the relationship we had. Jerking to free myself of his hold only caused him to pull me back into him.

"Who the fuck told you that?" he asked again through clenched teeth.

"I went to see Larisa to make sure she was good after burying Lord and she told me everything that happened. The problem is, you should've been the one to put me up on game. I've been out shopping, getting my hair and nails done, going to work, and could've been targeted for something I had nothing to do with. The only thing you've said is for me to be careful before allowing me to go about my day. But now you want me to stay at home. Yeah, okay." I sassed. "I bet you put word on the street that Honey bet not be touched."

The realization hit me like a ton of bricks when Cheese didn't deny that shit. The rage in me was building up slowly but surely as I waited for him to prove me wrong. He never did. Instead, he let my shirt go and went back to tending to his clothes.

"Larisa talks too fuckin' much. Stay away from her because I'm quite sure she's being haunted just like Tank's ass. While she's telling you I had a hand in that shit, which I didn't. Did she tell you she was the one who set the nigga up? I'm guilty because Tank is my cousin. I didn't know about what happened until it was over and done with."

"So, you had nothing to do with his murder?" I asked.

"Hell nawl! I'm standing ten toes down with my cousin because them muthafuckas ain't gon' touch him. I don't give a fuck what he did. You are another story though. I'm not about to put you in the line of fire. I'm gon' tell you again, stay the fuck away from Larisa! She's on some gung-ho shit and it's going to get her killed. Larisa ain't about that life but want to get payback for Lord. She's going to get herself killed and I don't want you nowhere near that."

Cheese was dancing around the main thing I wanted to know about and that was Honey. He spoke on everything except that bitch. It didn't matter because he answered my question when he didn't feel the need to talk about it. He gave me reason to watch his ass like a hawk and he was going to be my prey when the time was right. Two could play the game Cheese was trying to entertain Honey's wack ass with. I was going to make him think he had me in check for now. He was going to see me later. Believe that.

"Well, have a good time," I said, turning to leave him alone.

"Letty, I swear I only want what's best for you. Stop allowing your insecurities to think for you. I love you."

I walked away without responding because the words I wanted to say would have us tearing that muthafuckin' room up. When I got back to our bedroom, I closed the door and snatched my phone from the nightstand. Hitting the contact for Shaveen, I waited for her to pick up while watching the door in case Cheese decided to come in.

"What you want, Letty?"

"Damn, is that the way you answer the phone for your little sister?"

"Girl, you interrupting me from doing my damn hair. I'm trying to get ready to hit the bike fest. I know you gon' be there with Cheese so again, why are you on my phone?"

"You knew about the fest and didn't tell me?"

"Hell, since when do I gotta keep you updated on what's going on when yo' man knows all about the shit before its announced. Wait, he didn't tell you?"

"Nope. He just told me while ironing his clothes. The nigga talking about it's not safe for me to go this year but I know that's bullshit. All he told me was it was downtown. Where exactly is it being held because I'm going anyway."

"That's fucked up. It's going to be at Grant Park. Come pick me up. We can ride together."

"Okay, cool. I'll call Shalonda to see if she rolling too."

"Don't bother. She's still in her feelings about getting shot and the fact she had to lie to Aiden about what happened. Now, she's trying to save face for them bougie muthafuckas she calls in laws. Shalonda will learn she's blacker than black, not Caucasian."

"While her ass trying to keep up with the Ellsworth's, she better hope her name is in his will. Her family has never made her choose between us and them folks. She better wake up and smell the damn coffee before they have her ass in that house scrubbing the baseboards as punishment."

"Your ass stupid." Shaveen laughed. "Hurry up and get yourself together. We're about to have fun."

"I'm waiting for Cheese to leave before I start getting dressed. He's being sneaky and I will see firsthand what he is up to. I won't be too long. I'll call when I'm leaving the house."

"Do that. I'll be waiting."

Patiently waiting for Cheese to come back into the room to shower and dress, I was becoming antsy as hell because I was ready to get myself together. After damn near an hour, he finally found his way back into our bedroom fully dressed. The smell of his cologne filled my nostrils and the nigga smelled and looked good in his black shorts, red shirt, with red and black retro 11s. Cheese walked over to the dresser and placed his Cuban linked bracelet on his arm along with the matching chain. Again, he was silent as a lamb and I didn't like that shit at all.

"So, you really going to the fest without me?"

"Letty, I've already discussed why I didn't want you accompanying me out today. It's for your own good, baby."

"Is it for my own good, or are you planning to meet up with Honey?" I asked seriously.

Cheese turned toward me with fire in his eyes then shook his head while putting his diamond earring in his ear. "One thing you don't want to do is talk some shit into existence, Letty. I've told you time again Honey isn't even on my mind. Stop with the foolishness. You not doing nothing but driving yourself crazy with your accusations."

"Accusations? You've been tip toeing around me for months! If it ain't Honey, who is it then?"

"Why would I be cheating and you live right here with me, Letty?" Cheese asked irritably.

This muthafucka thought it was impossible for him to cheat because we resided in the same house. Who the fuck he thought I was? A dumb bitch? I chuckled as I allowed his stupidity to resonate in the air for a minute.

"Cheese, you have distanced yourself from me for months. The aura in this house has been stale and it feels like we are roommates who share space and food. Hell, you barely act like you want to fuck me. The way you jump on top of me and handle your business makes me feel you do it because I have the only pussy in this house. So again, if it ain't Honey, who is it?" I asked leaning back against the headboard then crossed my ankles.

"Man, you let some of the wildest shit come out of your mouth. Trust, if there was someone I was fucking, I damn sure wouldn't be in this muthafucka texting and talking to them around yo' nagging ass. Don't you think I'd be out with them, deep in something wet? You gotta use your head sometimes, Letty. The shit sounds dumb to me, so I know for sure it sounds insane to yo' ass. But this shit you doing right now is the reason I isolate myself from you. Don't nobody who is constantly being accused of shit wants to be around the person doing all the accusing. If you think I'm fuckin' off on you…leave," he said hunching his shoulders. Cheese snatched his keys from the dresser and adjusted his piece in the holster he had on his back. He then put on his biker jacket and stuffed his wallet in his back pocket as he walked to the door.

Soon as he stepped over the threshold, I called out to him. "So, you leaving without showing me love?" I asked, pausing his steps.

"When you grow the fuck up maybe we can get back to building what we started. Until then, find something to do that will mature your fuckin' mind because you're acting real childish right now. I'll be back later. Don't wait up."

With that he walked out without another word. My blood was boiling and Cheese must've forgot who the fuck I was. When I heard his bike rev up, I jumped out of the bed, heading straight to the closet. It was the beginning of September and the temperature had dropped to a cool setting. Being anemic was a downfall for me because I stayed cold once fall hit. What some called nice wasn't so much for me. Choosing a pair of blue jean jeggings with a long-sleeved pink t-shirt to match, I stood on my tippy toes to grab my pink and white Air Max from the top shelf. Once I was confident about what I wanted to wear, I threw the items on the bed and headed straight for the shower.

It took no time for me to cleanse myself, brush my teeth, and bump a few curls in my hair. Instead of applying a full face of makeup, I opted for a natural look for the day. After I moisturized my body and dressed, I was ready to hit the e-way to pick up Shaveen. Entering the closet again, I grabbed my white waist-length leather jacket and the pink Michael Kors purse I was going to carry. Transferring everything from my other purse, I picked up my keys and headed out while hitting my sister up. She answered on the first ring.

"I'm on my way," I said jumping in my whip.

"And I'll be outside when you pull up. Letty, whatever happened with you and Cheese, let that shit go and have a good time. Okay?"

"Fuck Cheese! He better hope I don't find another nigga to get under while he's playing fucked up games. I can show his ass how to be a muthafuckin' pimp."

"Don't turn the BMW into a hoe mobile, sis." Shaveen laughed. "You know I'm down with whatever. Just make sure you're ready to leave that nigga before you make a move."

"I know how this shit goes. You don't have to school me. I'm true to this, not new to this."

Connecting the call to the Bluetooth, me and my sister laughed and joked until I picked her up. It was time to head to the park to see what Cheese's slick ass thought he was doing behind my back. Giving myself a mental speech, I came to the conclusion that whatever I saw, I was not to address it in public. But Cheese better be ready to get his ass knocked out when he got back home.

Chapter 3

Honey

"You look good, Honey!" Spank complimented me as I dismounted my bike.

The black pants with money green camouflage print with the matching shirt went well with the customed leather jacket with the same style. Millie Mob was stitched in large letters across the back and along the right sleeve. Everyone in our crew had the same design but in different colors to match the bikes we owned.

"Thanks, boo. You're wearing the hell out of that black and white yourself," I said giving her a sisterly hug. Stepping back, I needed to know more about the bikers' fest before we got there. "Tell me what this fest is about."

Spank shook her head with a smile. "Niggas. Niggas. And more niggas!"

"Girl, you crazy. There has to be more to it than men. Coming from you I understand why the male species is your focal point, but tell me, why are you always talking about them and I have yet to see you with one?"

"See, that's where you're wrong. I do have one and his name is *Janifo*." Spanky smirked.

"Now, why would his parents name him Janifo?" I laughed. "What is the meaning behind it?"

"The name is all me, Honey. *JANIFO* is *just a nigga I fuck occasionally*. There's still room for other prospects."

The way I hollered one would've thought I was being harmed. My stomach hurt so bad in the process and I had tears running from my eyes. Wiping my face, I shook my head at her craziness and knew for a fact she was dead serious about what she'd said. Spanky was a bad chick who spoke her mind and didn't care what anyone thought. I liked that in her.

With everything going on, it took a lot of talking to her and Breeze not to go after Cheese and Tank for the past couple months. There was going to be a lot of people downtown and there was bound to be a problem if we were to run into any of them. We were set to have a good time and I didn't want to deal with any drama. Spanky and I were the first to arrive at the shop. The others were on their way.

"All bullshit aside, tell me about this fest."

"Oh, I forgot all about your original question. I was fixated on all the dicks I would have the privilege of choosing from. Anyway, the fest is basically a fashion show for motorcycles. Folks from all over come to Chicago to floss their rides. There is always a DJ, food vendors, drinks by the gallon, weed, and a slew of niggas and bitches. With this being your first time, you're definitely in for a treat."

The sound of an engine caused both of us to look in the direction it came from. Breeze and Taz had entered the lot. Blue was the right color for Breeze because she made that shit look good whenever she wore it. Taz had the orange on lock and the shit was exotic. As Taz walked toward us, Spanky took that opportunity to start some shit.

"Breeze has Taz this year. So, she won't have a pick of the litter."

The frown upon Taz's face was a clear indication she'd indeed heard what Spanky said. Breeze was walking slowly with her head in her phone, not paying attention to what was transpiring. The moment Taz stood in front of Spanky, I knew she was about to speak her mind.

29

"You damn right Breeze won't be scouting for them funky ass hoes. She has all she needs right here. Spank, don't start that petty ass shit today."

Breeze walked over with a look of confusion. Taz was nose to nose with Spank and she was legit mad. Breeze pulled her back by the arm. "What the hell happened in the short time we pulled up?" she asked.

"Spank is on her usual bullshit, talking about you gon' be on all the females at the fest."

"You serious right now, Taz? Spank says whatever comes to mind if she knows it's gonna bend a muthafucka out of shape. You should know this by now." Breeze chortled. "And every time, you fall for her antics. Baby, you are it for me."

Breeze kissed Taz deeply while squeezing her voluptuous ass. The two of them were so cute together but Taz had some insecurities she needed to work on before she ran Breeze into the arms of another. My cousin seemed to put her mind at ease by showing love in public. Patting Taz's butt a few times while whispering in her ear, Breeze stepped back and turned to Spank.

"Stop doing that shit, fam. You know what I put her through in the past. I don't need Taz thinking I'm doing shit behind her back."

"I was just fuckin' with her. Taz is too old to let shit like that bother her. If she was about her position, the shit would've been funny. I guess not, huh?"

"Spank!" I called out for her to leave the shit alone.

We still had to wait for the others to show up and I didn't want to do that by breaking up a fight. The way Breeze shot daggers at her told me I may have to do just that. To defuse the situation, I decided to pull Breeze away.

"Aye, cuz, come walk with me."

Moving slowly toward Quell's tattoo shop, Breeze fell into step beside me. The same butterflies I had the day of the memorial was in full effect in my stomach. It was the beginning of September, but the chill had nothing to do with the shiver that traveled down my spine.

"What's going on, Honey?"

"First, I want to apologize for Spanky…"

"That shit is already forgotten. Stop stalling and talk to me."

"Okay, I've been thinking about the fest. We didn't discuss if we see Cheese or his people. It is a huge chance they will be in attendance."

Breeze pulled a blunt from her pocket, putting fire to the end. The cherry formed as she took a deep puff. Blowing the smoke over her shoulder, Breeze coughed once before turning her attention back to what I'd said.

"They're definitely going to be there. Along with everybody and their mama. Nothing's going to happen, cuz. Stay ready, you won't have to get ready," she said, hitting the blunt again.

I caught her drift and believe me when I say a bitch was ready. Nodding, Breeze opened her jacket, revealing her piece, then laughed. At that moment the rest of the crew rode into the lot together. Charlie didn't come to play and neither did the others. When she took her helmet off my mouth damn near fell to the floor. Charlie's platinum blonde hair had spiked pink tips that matched her outfit to perfection. We were going to be the eye of attraction when we stepped on the scene at the fest. We walked back to the front of my shop, joining the others.

Breeze cleared her throat. "Aight, so y'all know niggas been quiet since they shot my brother. I need everybody to keep your head on the swivel. There have never been any serious incidents at the fest in the past outside of fighting, but it's a new muthafuckin' day and niggas ain't shit," Breeze said looking around at us all. "We can't allow anyone to catch us slippin' though. I shouldn't have to ask if y'all is carrying because that shit is automatic." She received nonverbal confirmation and that was all it took for her to

31

continue. "Cheno won't be in attendance but unfamiliar faces to Cheese will be blended all around us. So, don't wander off too far from the crew. We arrive together, we leave together. Nothing has changed. Let's move out and turn up," Breeze concluded, heading toward her bike.

"Hol' up!" Tiny said, stopping Breeze in her tracks. "If we see that bitch Letty..."

"Walk right past her irrelevant ass," I interjected. "We are going to have fun. Fuck the bullshit until we can't."

Tiny rolled her eyes at me before walking away. It wasn't a secret that everybody except Charlie and Breeze thought I was scary. Little did they know, I was far from it. Incarceration wasn't a playground of fun. Anytime I could avoid confrontation, I do the shit without thought because I know what I'm capable of doing. They saw firsthand how I threw hands, and the shit was mild because I held back. If I hadn't, Letty would've been carried away in a body bag. Just because I didn't welcome drama, didn't equate to me being afraid. Opening my mouth to cut her lil' ass up, Breeze hugged me.

"Fuck that. You don't have to explain nothing to no-muthafuckin'-body. We know what's up. Shake the shit off and let's roll."

***

The park was packed. Our group lucked up on a spot we could all park our bikes together. In spite of the weather, females were still damn near naked as if it was summertime to gain the attention of niggas. Spank was center stage right with them. Except, she was fully clothed turning heads. The wrapping skills I'd performed on our bikes brought the crowd our way and all I saw were dollar signs. Being the entrepreneurs we were, with every inquiry, someone left with a business card.

"Hello, Beautiful."

A deep baritone whispered in my ear. Automatically I became irritated because why was this person in my personal space? Instead of responding I moved forward, trying to get lost in the crowd. One thing I didn't need was a man other than Quell making me the center of his attention. The moment I felt a hand on my arm, I turned rapidly, ready to curse him out. The instant rage evaporated into the cool air soon as I looked up at the handsome man standing before me.

"Why are you running from me, Sweet Lady?" he asked with a smile.

My mouth opened and closed as if I was a puppet being controlled by its puppet master. The muscle in my mouth was inoperable and dry to the point it felt as if it was stuck in place. The ability to respond to the man just wasn't there. He knew it too as he stood in front of me showing all thirty-two of his teeth. His chocolate-colored skin was smooth as a baby's ass, and his eyes had me in a trance. The sun bounced off them, causing a hint of green to appear cat-like. It was a beautiful sight.

"I'm Elijah, but everybody calls me Eli. What's your name?"

Finally finding my voice, I swallowed hard. "Honey. My name is Honey."

"The name fits you perfectly. Are you from here?" Nodding, Eli licked his lips. "Well, I've been to Chicago on many occasions. I've never seen such a beauty like yourself."

"Elijah—"

"Eli. Call me Eli."

"Look, Eli, I'm flattered by what you said, but I'm seeing someone."

Just as those words left my mouth, a text came through on my phone. Reaching into my cross bag for the device, Eli was saying something, but I didn't hear a word as I read the message. It was from Quell. I didn't even know he was going to be out there.

Jaquellis: Tell that nigga to get the fuck outta yo' face, Honey. It don't take that long to tell his ass you are not on the market.

Me: I didn't need you to tell me what I had to do. It's already done. Where are you anyway?

Jarquellis: right behind you.

I turned slowly and sure enough, Quell was standing with a mug on his face. Eli was still trying to shoot his shot and I just walked away from his ass. If he knew like I did, he wouldn't follow me. Quell waited patiently for me and he looked good as hell, too. The morning sex we had played in my mind, causing my kitty to beat rapidly.

"Don't do it," Quell said lowly. "Ya boy is watching your every move."

"Who are you talking about?" I asked.

"Cheese. If you are going to get at him, he can't know shit about me. Act like I'm just admiring your bike, or another thirsty nigga trying to fuck." He smirked.

"You trying to fuck me, Quell?" I asked flirtatiously. "I think you're starting to love how I do that thing with my ass."

"Honey, stop playing with me." He adjusted his dick and it was sitting like a lump of coal. If Santa was to give me something for being naughty, I'd prefer that muthafucka right there. "On some serious shit, from what Breeze told me, all them niggas are out here. Cheese, too, so watch yourself."

Reaching in my cross bag, I acted as if I was looking for something. "Quell, are you sure you're going to be able to handle watching me interact with Cheese? I mean, you were ready to choke Eli out for trying to conjure up a conversation."

"That shit was different because the nigga don't know you from a can of paint. At least with that other fuck nigga, I know his ass gon' die in the process. I won't have to step in unless he oversteps boundaries. I'm gon' be cool. All I know is you bet not fuck that nigga."

Whatever I had to do in order to get close to Cheese would have to be kept to myself unless it's truly necessary to tell. I had to do what it took. Even if that meant fucking his ass. Losing what Quell and I had going on wasn't something I wanted to happen, but Cheese had to pay for what he did to Cheno. Quell's voice cut into my thoughts.

"We on the same page, right?"

Nodding, I placed a business card in his hand then walked the short distance to where the rest of the crew were. I felt the daggers Quell aimed at my back deep in the crevices of my spine. Glancing back at him wasn't going to happen. He'd have to speak on his jealousy when I got home. In the meantime, I was about to turn the fuck up.

As I approached our circle, Breeze leaned against her bike, exploring the perimeter around us. She handed me a flask filled with tequila as she blew smoke through her nose. Taking a sip, I nodded to the beat of Chris Brown's hit *Sensational* blaring through the speakers. Then, soon as I was about to whined my hips, it abruptly switched to Sexyy Red's ghetto ass and the hoes went wild.

Fuck my baby dad
Fuck my baby dad
Fuck my baby dad
I'ma fine ass bitch
I ain't in the house sad
Fuck my baby dad
Bow, bow, bow, bow, bow
That's that booty meat
Aye, aye, aye, aye, aye
That's them booty cheeks
Bow, bow, bow, bow, bow

I couldn't stand the way all those botched BBLs were throwing their fake ass around. Many of them were pretty in the face, small in the waist, and their arms and legs didn't match. They were out there looking like Chicken Little bobbleheads. I guess they didn't get the memo about the levels of surgery. But all the niggas saw was the ass. If they liked it, I loved it. To each its own.

All I could do was shake my head as I sipped my drink, watching the females twerking to the beat of what they called a bomb ass song. To me the shit was garbage, but who the hell was I to judge? If they looked up to the likes of Sexyy Red, more power to them. A little girl was out there with a group of adults, imitating what they were doing and it was a sad sight to watch.

"If that was my shorty, her mama's ass would be whooped."

Cheese's breath tickled the back of my neck, causing me to hesitate my movements for a moment. The evil expression on Breeze and Charlie's faces were another reason I stood still. The way my cousin's jaw clenched was a sign for me to lure his ass far away from her. Turning slowly, I took in Cheese's appearance and I could honestly say, he looked good. Too bad he fucked up any chance of being with me.

"Good thing it's not. Wait, you got a kid?" I asked.

"What if I said yeah?" he questioned, licking his lips as he lustfully scanned my body. "Would you still be willing to start over with a nigga?"

Hearing Cheese say that shit almost made me laugh in his face. In turn, I smiled widely because I had a role to play, and I had to stick to the script. He was so fixated on me that he didn't notice his broad in the background watching his every move. I did and decided to fuck with her the hard way. Cheese would have to deal with the aftermath when he stepped into the home he shared with the bitch. Letty standing where she was told me all I needed to know. He told her ass not to show up. Now, she couldn't do anything other than watch her man all in my face. Picking the conversation back up to answer his question, I ran my hand down the front of his shirt.

"La'Darrius, I was gone ten years. You better have an offspring out here somewhere because you ain't getting no younger. On top of that, if you do have a child, that's a problem for Letty. Not me."

Taking him by the hand, I led him in the direction of the food trucks. The smell of food had my stomach growling like there was no tomorrow. Plus, I didn't want to drink and get drunk as hell because I hadn't eaten. We passed Quell and I refused to look in his direction. Instead, I glanced up at Cheese and he was smiling at me.

"Nah, for real, I don't have any kids. There's only one woman I want to be the mother of my kids."

"Damn, you already have someone in mind. That's what's up. So, where would I fit into your life? I'm not step mama material."

Cheese stopped in his tracks, jerking my arm in the process because I was still walking. I turned to see what the problem was, and he had a deep frown upon his face. The way he glared was confusing. I only told him my truth.

"Honey, I handpicked the mother of my kids a long time ago. You are the woman I chose, so why would you even think you would be step anything?" he asked, pulling me into his arms. "I apologized for not being there for you during your bid. Seeing you locked away was something I couldn't handle. Staying away was hard for me because, had I made the drop like I was supposed to, you would have never been in the position to get pulled over."

Rolling my eyes as he spoke, I looked at everything but him. Cheese put his finger under my chin and turned my head back to him. To be honest, I didn't give two fucks why he turned his back on me. I took the charge and he promised to be there regardless. Instead, he laid down with my friend and was still shacking up with her ass 'til that day. There was no coming back from it, but Cheese didn't believe fat meat was greasy. He was going to find out what happened when Honey was crossed. I could tell Cheese thought I was the same person he groomed back in the day. The nigga was in for a rude awakening.

"We will never be what we were before, but I'm damn sure going to try my best to make sure to make life better for you. Honey, I owe you so much for the time you lost. I can't give you the time back, but I damn sure can put you back on your feet."

"Cheese, I don't want your money. I have my own business, and in due time I will be straight. The only thing I want is for you to cut ties with Letty. Starting over with you to see what we can become is something I truly want to do. We can't start making plans when that part of your life still exists. One thing I won't do is knowingly lie down with a nigga that has in-house pussy."

"I told you me and Letty is over…"

"Bullshit! If y'all was over you wouldn't hang up in the middle of a conversation, or stop texting suddenly when we are talking. Cheese, you still live in the house with her." I chuckled. "I'm far from stupid and I want you to stop acting like I'm a dummy. Close one door before you try to open another because I promise, I'm not the one you want to play games with. It's either you're in or you're out. There's no in-between."

With that, I stepped out of his grasp and headed to the Harold's Chicken food truck. There was nothing like a six-piece wing fried hard with lots of mild sauce and fries. Standing in the line, my phone vibrated. Taking my phone from my bag, I opened the message.

Quell: You look so damn sexy. No wonder that lame ass nigga can't keep his hands off you. I'm punishing that ass whenever you get home because I don't appreciate the way his ass keeps putting his hands on you.

Me: You need to cut that shit out. You know what the fuck this is. And don't threaten me with a good time, Mr. Chambers. You know I'm always down for all the nasty shit you want to do with me.

Quell: Nah, I'm going to take that shit to another level because I want you to remember who you belong to.

I didn't bother texting him back because his jealous ass was taking this shit too damn far. His words played in my head and I heard each one in his voice. My yoni was doing the salsa, the bitch was so happy. Quell was turning my ass out with the way he handled me in the bedroom. Cheese didn't stand a chance because I don't think my body would react to anyone other than that Texas nigga. Just thinking about what he was capable of had me craving a cigarette and I didn't even smoke.

"Who got you smiling all hard and shit?" Cheese's voice cut into my thoughts.

"Nunya. When you cut all ties with ya bitch, then you can question me about what I do outside of you. Until then, mind ya business."

Stepping up to order my food, I went into my bag to pay but Cheese beat me to the punch, adding his order as well. Thanking him, I moved to the music while checking out the scene. I had to do a double take because I could've sworn, I'd seen that bitch Danielle disappear in the crowd. It couldn't be because there was no way she was in Chicago. Danielle was from Detroit and had no business being anywhere near my city. Then again, Spanky did say people came from all over to attend the fest. Hopefully, it was just a female who looked like her. They always say, everybody has a twin in the world.

"Here you go," Cheese said, handing me the food he purchased. "Let's go over there and sit by the fountain. We can use this time to get to know one another for a little bit before I have to return you back to yo' people."

Nodding, I followed him with Danielle still on my mind.

Chapter 4

Tank

"Those bitches over there kickin' it hard," Short said, pacing. "We should go handle them for real. What the fuck are y'all waiting for? It's been weeks since Dro sent a message that they weren't safe."

"Nigga, look at what's going on here." I motioned around with my hand. "Do you not see all of these people? Not to mention, there are a zillion cops just waiting for some shit to pop off. It would be stupid to get active right now."

"If not now, then when?"

The goofy-ass nigga's trigga finger was itching but I needed him to calm that shit down. Short had been talking nonstop about getting back at Cheno's people since the day Sketty lost his life. They were best friends and Short was still hurt behind his boy's death. Sketty jumped the gun when he went after Cheno's sister by himself. Short was supposed to have gone with him but Sketty never called. No matter how many times we told him Sketty caused his own demise, he wouldn't listen.

"Whenever the fuck I tell you to move. Now is not the time."

Cheese walked up out of nowhere and I was glad he did. Short was two seconds from getting choked out because he was drawing unwanted attention to us. The way Cheese stood in front of Short with his nose flaring let me know shit was about to go left.

"You niggas been pussyfooting around too much for me. Since when do we wait around for something to happen in order for us to react? This shit should've been over a long time ago. Ain't nobody out here that's connected to Cheno but a bunch of females. How hard is it to silence them hoes?"

"Short, if you don't shut the fuck up and lower yo' muthafuckin' voice. This is not the place to discuss this shit! Drop it," Cheese snapped. "I hope when we do set out to handle business, yo' ass ready because the way I see things, your anger is going to get yo' wig split quick. I know you are still mourning Sketty, but the way you movin', you gon' end up in the same boat if you go after Cheno's sister on impulse."

Short didn't appear to be listening. He was staring a hole into the side of Cheno's sister's face. When he took a few steps in her direction, Sway grabbed him around the neck and walked him off in the opposite direction. Cheese watched them maneuver through the crowd until they were out of sight.

"That nigga is going to kill himself. Breeze is harder than some of these niggas on the street and Short is really underestimating her abilities at this point. Sketty was on the same shit and look where the fuck that got him."

"That's what I was trying to explain to him. Short ain't listening, man. Look, I'm just trying to chill out here. Trust, I've had my eyes open because there's no telling who's out here on that nigga Cheno's behalf. We know the ladies are out, but I haven't seen any of them southside muthafuckas. I'm surprised because they used to come out to events like this deep as fuck."

"Maybe it's because Cheno is no longer alive and breathing. It's a good thing they're not here though…"

"Yo, Letty is heading this way. She looks pissed," I said, cutting Cheese off.

Nodding in the direction Letty was approaching, Cheese turned with fire in his eyes. His jaw was clenched tight, and after a few seconds, he calmed himself down then shook his head. Cheese told me earlier Letty wasn't coming to the fest when I asked. She fooled the fuck out of him.

Letty and her sister Shaveen finally made it to where we were, and she wasted no time going in on my cousin. "So, like I thought, you didn't want me to come out because you knew that bitch would be here."

"Letty, what the fuck you talking about? I'm right here with my people."

"Yeah, now you are. Cheese, I saw you all in Honey's face, touching and hugging all on her. That's the reason you tried to make me stay home. What you gon' do is get that hoe beat the fuck up!"

"You've been in the ring with that girl twice and got yo' ass tagged. Sit this one out, Letty." I laughed, flaming up a blunt. "Honey might just put you out of your misery like the Russian did Apollo Creed in Rocky IV. I wouldn't want that to happen to you."

"Fuck you, Tank. Stay out of this!"

"I don't know why you mad at me. I'm just trying to save you from getting yo' ass embarrassed. Run up on that girl if you want to. Won't be no turning back."

Letty was huffing and puffing about what she was gon' do to Honey but she better sit her lil ass down somewhere. There was no way she could win in a fight or get Cheese's attention back. The moment Honey stepped back on Chicago soil and he found out, it was over for whatever she had with my cousin. There was no doubt that Cheese had love for Letty, but we all knew his ass was in love with Honey.

"I'm not mad at you. Just mind yo' business and stay out of mine. Can you do that?"

Holding my blunt up, I nodded and took a deep toke. Letty feisty ass was on one and I was gon' let her have that shit. She was going to break her own heart.

She rolled her eyes with her hands on her hip then put the target back on Cheese. "What was y'all talking about, huh?"

"None of your business. If you were at home where I told yo' ass to be, you wouldn't know I had a conversation with her. Now, would you?" Cheese asked.

"Hol' up…"

"Shaveen, this ain't got shit to do with you. Stay in yo' lane," Cheese said, cutting her off before she could even get started. "I've told you there's nothing going on with me and Honey. We have a past, so we can be cordial when we see each other. Honey wants nothing to do with me, okay. You have nothing to worry about when it comes to her, Letty. How many times do I have to tell you this?"

"Yeah, okay. She wants nothing to do with you, but I can tell you want more from her. I'm getting tired of arguing with you about the bitch, Cheese."

"Then don't! It's that damn simple! Yo' ass is worried about the next muthafucka when the girl ain't even worried about you. Tell me this. Who in their right mind would be willing to deal with someone that left them out to dry while doing a bid that wasn't theirs, when the muthafucka behind the shit left them high and dry?" Cheese didn't wait for Letty to answer. "No-damn-body. Stop worrying about shit that's not going on. Okay?"

Cheese opened his arms and Letty fell right in them. Her sister shook her head and I promise, I felt the same way she did. My cousin had just blown a lot of smoke up Letty's ass and she fell for it. A blind man could see the love that nigga had for Honey just by the way he spoke her name. Cheese soothed things over with his girl for now. They would be right back at square one soon enough. He was not giving up on getting Honey back into his life.

"Tank, be careful. I'm about to head out to spend some quality time."

Dapping my cousin up, I whispered in his ear, "You talked yo' way out of that shit smoothly. Tighten up because she's on yo' ass."

Letty appeared to be in a heated argument with her sister. They walked a short distance away so we couldn't hear what was being said. That gave Cheese the opportunity to speak on what Letty was complaining about.

"She's looking too hard, man. I didn't even know she was out here. She's right. I knew Honey would be here with Breeze. All I can say is, Honey agreed to meet up with me later, so I have to go home and put this muthafucka to sleep."

I laughed hard because I knew all along Cheese was up to no good. "How the fuck you gon' jump pussy like that, nigga?"

"I'm not. Honey ain't trying to go there with me. I just want to get to know the person she is today. In the process, I want to find out how she's feeling about what happened to Cheno. Maybe she will slip up and give me some vital information we can use against them."

"Use against them?" I quizzed. "I thought she was not to be touched."

"When I said them, I was not including Honey in that. Everybody else is free game though," Cheese said while watching Letty. "Tank, I have to tell you." He paused.

"Tell me what? You better spill it before the warden comes back."

"Shut up." He chortled. "I got Honey thinking I'm going to leave Letty for her. That's the real reason I won't be fuckin' her tonight. She refuses to sleep with me long as I'm with Letty."

"Man, you playing with fire. I'm gon' need you to decide what you want to do with yourself. We are at war with muthafuckas and you have to sleep with one eye open at the crib. That shit can't be what you call peace."

Before he could respond, Letty was back at his side. Shaveen was fighting her way through the crowd. Letty told Cheese she was ready to leave and her sister would bring her car back the next day. The look on my cousin's face said what he refused to say in public. The last time Letty allowed one of her sisters to drive her car, they wrecked that muthafucka and fought about paying for the damages. Cheese was pissed off and didn't buy Letty another car for damn near six months. He got tired of driving her ass around.

Once Cheese and Letty left, I sat back enjoying the music when Sway walked back up. Glancing around I tried my best to find Short and he was nowhere in sight. There was too much going on for him to be wandering around in the open by himself. Especially with the attitude he had before Sway led him away.

"Yo, where the fuck did Short go?"

"Man, ain't no hope for him. The nigga was crying and shit, talking about how Sketty was his brother and muthafuckas had to pay for that shit. I tried to talk some sense into him, but that shit went in one ear and out the other. So, I told him to take his ass home. The last thing we need is for his ass to start shooting out here and innocent people either get hurt or killed because of his stupidity."

"You did right," I said, taking a sip from my cup. "Have you seen the rest of the crew? Them niggas been missing in action since we touch down."

"Nawl. I'm sure they ass around here ass watching. It's cool. Let them have fun, because after today, we gotta make some shit shake. I understand where Short's coming from, Tank. We've been sitting around waiting for something to jump off when we should be the ones pulling the trigga. If they strike first, we will be burying somebody. The shit already took Lord out and damn near got me, too."

"I'll have something planned soon. My focus is on getting Cheese's head out of Honey's ass. Without him being all in, we could be up shit creek. To be honest, I'm afraid they're going to catch him slippin' and Honey is going to be the bait. I've tried telling him she is not going to forgive him for what he did to her. On top of that, there's no way she doesn't know we were behind Cheno getting murked. But my cousin is in love. I just hope he doesn't lose his life chasing something that would never be."

A group of females walked past us and one of them stood out to me. She was a beautiful redbone with a fat ass. Walking by she winked at me and that's all it took for me to reach out and halt her movements.

"Hey, pretty. What's up?" I asked, rubbing the inside of her wrist.

"You tell me." She smiled. Her accent wasn't one I was familiar with so I knew she wasn't from Chicago.

"Where you from?"

"Detroit. I came to see what ya city is about and to enjoy this bomb ass fest. It seems I found something else I may be able to enjoy, too," she said licking her lips.

Baby girl didn't appear to be the type to get down with a nigga she didn't know. The way she was eating a muthafucka up without contact told a different story. She was ready to get down with a nigga. Shid, she probably had plans to get down with as many muthafuckas as she could before she headed back to her city, but I was going to be the first in this muthafucka to hit that. Ain't no way I was letting her venture off to the next one.

"What's your name, beautiful?"

"Danielle. Yours?"

"I'm Tank. How long are you going to be here?"

"Until Sunday. Why, you trying to spend some time with me?" she asked flirtatiously.

"We can make that happen. You smoke?"

She shook her head yeah and I proceeded to roll up. One of her girls were all in Sway's face smiling like she hit the jackpot. Danielle made herself comfortable next to me while her friends groaned on the side.

"Danni, we not about to hang out here with two niggas. Y'all can stay here but we about to continue walking around." Danielle waved her off without saying anything to her. "Well, you know where the hotel is. I'll see you in the morning, slut."

By the way her homegirl said that shit, all they ass came here to find a nigga or three to lay up with. Danielle was in for a treat because I got all the dick she gon' need for the rest of the weekend. Hopefully, she was ready for the ride of her life.

***

Me and Danielle left the fest an hour after meeting because the weed and alcohol she consumed had her a little frisky. The way she was twerking on my dick told me she was going to be a great roll in the hay. They always said, the way a woman danced was how she fucked. I was anxious to feel how she threw that lil twat on my muscle. Sway wasn't trying to pass up on ol' girl he was with either. So, we got a room at the Best Western because it was the closest one to our location. Soon as we entered the room, Danielle washed her hands to eat the pizza and wings I bought from the food truck. The night was far from over with us because I made sure to get some drinks to go too.

"Damn, baby, slow down. The food ain't going nowhere. Here, drink this before you choke." I said handing her a bottled water.

"This chicken is so good. The pizza is on point too. Maybe I can come back to the Chi for food and dick next time. Wait, I have to see what you're working with first."

She laughed, I didn't. Speaking on my pipe was something I've never had to do and wasn't going to start with her ass. Danielle was going to be telling her girls I was from Missouri because that's just what the fuck I planned to do; show her ass what was up. As I walked into the bathroom I heard Danielle's phone ring. Leaving the door open to hear the conversation just in case the bitch tried to set a nigga up.

She had nothing to hide because she answered with the phone on speaker.

"Where you at, Danielle?" a female asked like she was her mother.

"Bitch, bye. You saw who I left with. I'm at a hotel not too far from the park. What's up, Peach?"

"Guess who I just saw?"

"I don't have time for guessing games. We're in Chicago, there's no telling who you could've seen out there. Just tell me." There was some back and forth going on in the background and it must've irritated the hell out of Danielle. "Tell them hoes to shut the fuck up! What are they trying to hide shit for, Peach? Peach!" she screamed into the phone. "Talk to me, got dammit!"

"Danni, they don't want me to tell you."

Washing my hands quickly, I exited the bathroom. Danielle's nose was flaring and she was mad as hell. I sat on the bed and picked up my phone like I wasn't paying attention to her conversation. She sighed loudly while wiping her hands on a napkin.

"Look, obviously you called to tell me who the fuck you saw. Now, spill that shit. Fuck what they talking about."

"I saw Honey."

The moment the name Honey filled the room, I looked up to see Danielle's reaction. Easing my Glock from behind my back, I held it close because in my mind the bitch was working with the other side. Just as I thought. It wasn't that easy to lay my black ass down and the muthafuckas failed miserably by sending a bitch to do their dirty work. Just as I was about to blow her shit wide open, Danielle saved her own life.

"Damn! I knew I should've stayed a little while longer. That hoe owes me a round or two of uninterrupted boxing. Hell, if I feel generous at the time, I may even stop her ass from breathing. Check this out, if you see her again, get that hoe's information like you want to keep in touch. She left long before we became come cool so she doesn't know your connection to me. I want that bitch head in her city."

"I'm not going to be able to get that information because her and her people just rode off on their bikes."

"Fuck! It's all good. Luck gon' be on my side before I leave this muthafucka. Chicago may be big, but it's not that damn big. Somebody gon' lead me to that hoe. Watch what I tell you. Anyway, I'm being rude right now. Text me when y'all get to the hotel. Oh yeah, Bianca is with me somewhere in this building."

"You two bitches always get the niggas! Suck enough dick for me."

I laughed lowly because shawty was pissed off. Putting my tool on the nightstand next to the bed, I got up and went back to the bathroom. My plan was to fuck for the rest of the night and in order for me to do that, I needed a little help. Taking the small baggie from my pocket, I sat on the toilet. Dumping a little bit of coke on the counter I used my finger to line it up. in one swift sniff I inhaled the substance squeezing my nose in the process. The remnants that were left behind was rubbed on my gums and I was feeling right. It was time to fuck Danielle into submission so she would do any and everything I asked of her. Including helping me take Honey and her people down.

Chapter 5

Cheno

Sitting back in the crib while everybody was out enjoying the last big event of the year was something I'd never done. The shit was necessary even though I felt ninety percent back to normal. It wouldn't have been wise for me to show up at the fest because gunplay would've been my focal point soon as I saw Cheese or anybody associated with his ass. Instead, I sent my folks out there to scope out whatever they could and sure enough, all those niggas were out there.

Fredo was driving while I rode gun as we headed to Markham. G hit me up and said he had somebody he wanted me to meet. Not asking any questions, we set out to check the shit out. He and Scony were two of the many muthafuckas that went to the fest. Some of them niggas were watching my sister like a hawk but that wasn't really needed. Quell told me that nigga Cheese was all over Honey and his ass was heated. At least he was going to be geared up from his madness to have my back in these streets.

"Aye, what the fuck we going out here for?" Fredo asked.

"I don't know. We'll find out once we get to the location."

All My Life by Lil Dirk played low and I bobbed my head while listening to the lyrics. My mama came to mind and all I thought about was leaving the life I lived behind. Money wasn't why I was still doing this shit because I had enough to wipe my ass with the bills like tissue. There was time for me figure out what my next move would be. Wasn't nothing shaking until I laid everybody down that wanted a nigga dead.

I pulled my phone from my pocket and decided to text Charlie to see what she was up to. It had been a few weeks since I'd seen or talked to her. Yeah, she was dating some lame nigga but that didn't have shit to do with me. Charlie would forever be my woman. With that thought in mind, I went against the grain and texted Mari instead.

Me: Hey. What you up to tonight?

The bubbles started moving the moment Amari received my text. That's the type of shit I liked, a woman who didn't hesitate to communicate promptly. Amari was a good girl and I really didn't want to taint her persona, but a nigga needed some pussy. Charlie was on one and I was cool with allowing her to do her until she couldn't.

Mari: Cheno. What a surprise. I'm doing an overnight at work. Are you okay?

Me: Yeah. I was just checking to see how you doing. Get back to work. I'll hit you up some time tomorrow.

Mari: That was sweet of you. I actually have a little time to chat with you. I'm in the cafeteria eating a salad. Nothing major.

Me: A salad? Woman, you better get some food. Over there eating like a damn rabbit.

Mari: Lol a salad is enough considering what time it is. I don't need anything heavy.

Fredo pulled up to the location G gave me and I was confused. Why would he want to meet at a warehouse? There were a few cars already parked outside and that shit had a nigga's guard all the way up. It was bad enough the muthafucka called me out here, then he didn't tell me others would be in attendance. Shit wasn't sitting well with me.

Me: Aye, I have some business to attend to. Enjoy your rabbit food and I'll hit you when I get to the crib. Is that cool?

Mari: Yeah, that's fine. It may take a little longer for me to respond depending on the time. Be careful out there, Cheno. Ttyl

The way Amari responded had a nigga feeling good inside. She was just a nurse that helped a nigga out in my time of need, but I felt like I've known her forever. If I didn't get anything out of meeting her, I was quite sure we would have a forever friendship.

"Charlie must've told you she was coming back to the crib. That's the only way you would be smiling from ear to ear." Fredo said, minding my business.

"Nah, that had nothing to do with Charlie's some-timey ass." Checking the clip in my Glock, I snapped it back in place and secured it in the holster. "Let's go see what's going on in this muthafucka. Maybe then you will stay the fuck out of my affairs with yo' nosy ass."

I got out the car with Fredo behind me. The door of the warehouse, opened causing me to draw my weapon.

Scony emerged with a smile. "Put that shit away, Cheno. We on yo' side, nigga."

"What the hell we doing here?"

"You damn sho' about to find out. Put it like this, Operation Get At Them Niggas are in full effect. Are you down for the cause?"

"Lead the way." I grinned with my tool still in hand.

Scony entered the building and soon as I stepped foot across the threshold, somebody hollering "help" echoed off the walls. Looking around, I could tell the warehouse wasn't a place to store any type of merchandise, it was a fuckin' torture chamber. There were chains hanging from the walls, chairs that looked like they were made to execute a muthafucka, a table with big ass nails sticking out of it, and a furnace in the corner. Not to mention all of the different types of knives hanging on the wall like they were art work.

"What is this place?" Fredo asked walking beside me.

"The Dungeon." Scony laughed. "It's where all the magic happens when niggas get out of line. It's the Devil's playground."

"Help me! Somebody, they trying to kill me!"

"That muthafucka gon' lose his voice before his life and I don't like that." Scony scoffed, picking up the pace. "We need his ass to run his mouth the same way he's hollering."

"Where's G? I know he ain't sitting there while all that's going on. I would've shot his ass."

"Cheno, this muthafucka is soundproof. G is in his office chillin'. That nigga in the red room by his damn self. But not for long."

Scony hit a button on his phone and G walked out, adjusting his tool on his hip. Punching in a series of numbers on the wall next to a red door, he pushed it open. I walked in and a nigga I'd never seen before was sitting in the middle of the room with his hands tied behind his back. Soon as I stepped fully into the room, dude's eyes almost popped out of his head. An evil grin spread across my face immediately. It felt like a spirit traveled through my body, morphing me into someone or something else.

"Lord...Lord killed you!"

"Nah, Lord *almost* killed me. See, when one sets out to do a job, they must make sure they succeed and the job is complete. Yo' boy didn't do that and here I am. I'll make sure I complete the mission I'm on, though." I spotted a chair in the corner and walked to grab it. When I got it, I set in it directly in front of the dude and sat down. Running my hand down my face, I rubbed my hands together. "So, um, what's yo' name, man?" I asked calmly.

"Why the fuck am I here?"

"You know why you're here. Y'all tried to kill me! Now, I'm trying to talk to you man to man but you making this shit hard. What is your muthafuckin' name?"

"How you coming to me man to man and I'm tied to a chair? If you gon' kill me, do that shit!"

Scony stormed over to the muthafucka and punched him in the mouth. "Who the fuck you talking to? I'm not this nigga. I wanted to kill yo' ass before I put yo' pussy ass in the trunk!"

I stood up and pushed Scony away from the muthafucka. I had to play the good guy in this situation or we wouldn't get shit out of his wannabe tough ass. So far, he was holding his own and he was right; how could he talk man to man being tied to a chair? "Untie him."

"What? Hell nawl!" Scony said glaring at me as if I was crazy.

"Untie him. I just want to talk to the nigga."

"Do it, Scony. This is Cheno's show. Let him run it."

Scony didn't like the shit but he did what he was told. Once the zip ties was off, Scony looked down and snarled. "Try anything and yo' ass gon' meet yo' maker, bitch."

"We gon' take this from the top. As you know, I'm Cheno. I can't talk to you without being able to address you as well. So, again, what's yo' name, man?"

"Jermaine. But I'm known as Short on the street. Look, Cheno. I didn't have nothing to do with you—"

"I didn't ask you shit other than yo' name. I'm gon' be the one to lead this shit the way I want it to go. Not you," I said, resting my elbows on my knees. "Short, how old are you?"

Scony scoffed and started pacing. He had the look of death in his eyes. I wanted to laugh so bad but I had to keep the serious expression on my face. I also had to stay in character so Short thought at least one of us was going to save his ass from getting toe tagged.

"Is there a problem, fam?"

"Hell yeah! You questioning this nigga like he's interviewing for a muthafuckin' job or something. This muthafucka was at every meeting when his people came up with the plan to kill yo' dumb ass and you sitting there playing nice. Beat his ass!"

"Can't we all just get along?" I joked. "There's too much violence going on today and I'm trying to turn a new leaf. I'd rather this young man spend a few years in jail instead of eternity in a grave."

"You out of yo' muthafuckin' mind. I'm not standing around, listening to you rationalize with this nigga. All that Louis Farrakhan shit you doing is a waste of fuckin' time. Holla at me when you ready to take the pacifier out of this nigga's mouth and replace it with my Glock!" Scony left, slamming the door behind him.

G stood back with his hands crossed over his chest, not saying a word. I turned back to Short and he had tears in his eyes. I guess my little speech gave him a glimmer of hope. To be honest, I didn't know where I was going with this shit, but I had to keep it up because it seemed to be working. For the time being.

"See, this is about me and you. I'm keeping them off yo' ass. To be frank with you, they wanted me to come in and shoot yo' ass up like ya boy did me. I'm not on that. I give you my word that you will only do about two-or three-years tops if you tell me what I need to know."

Short held his head down, looking at the floor. Clearing his throat, he started talking. "Tank and Sketty came up with the idea to rob yo' trap on their own. The rest of us didn't know shit about it until you started looking for Tank."

"How long have you known Sketty?"

"That was my brother. Me and Sketty went way back to grammar school. When he told me he was going to work for you, I was all for it. Obviously, he and Tank had their plan in motion from the start. Sketty was still on Cheese payroll, but he didn't know what was going on because Lord was the one who paid us. Cheese tried to stay out of the way unless it was something serious going down. Y'all didn't have to kill him, man. They forced him to go after your sister, Cheno. Sketty jumped the gun and went out by himself."

"Ain't shit I can do about that. I can stop you from dying. There's no way I can bring a muthafucka from the dead. If it was possible, my mama would be the first to get that treatment. Anyway, where the fuck is Cheese and Tank hiding out?"

"Hiding? Them niggas ain't hiding. They were just at the fest."

"You know what the fuck I'm talkin' about!" I had to calm myself down because I almost let the spirit out. "Their trap on 15th has been shut down. Where are they serving from?"

"I'm not telling you that," Short said looking me in the eye. "It's bad enough I've told you the shit I did. They got families. I'm not about to put innocent people in jeopardy."

"So, you telling me you ready to die then, huh?" I asked. "If I remember correctly, I stated if you told me everything I needed to know you would go to jail, right?" Short nodded. "Anything other than that, you die. Right now, you are reneging on the agreement. Where can I find Cheese and Tank?" I barked.

"Cheese shut 15th Street down but they are still working the trap on 18th and Karlov. Damn, I don't believe I'm snitchin' on my niggas." Short shook his head.

"They would do the same if they were in your shoes. Where them niggas live?" I said, getting right back to it.

"Cheese lives with his girl in Bolingbrook. 374 North Ashbury Lane. Tank still lives with his mama. You already know where that is because y'all shot her shit up."

"Is there anybody else I need to worry about other than them two muthafuckas?"

"Yeah, other than all the workers on 18th, there's Sway. He lives off Washtenaw and Warren. Man, please don't kill them babies. They don't have shit to do with none of this shit." Short pled.

"Do I look like the Grim Reaper to you? I'm not even gon' kill yo' ass and you pleading for me not to kill kids. Nigga, you gotta be stupid." I snapped standing to my feet.

56

"If the information you gave pans out, I'm gon' set shit up for you to get arrested for a small possession charge. Cool?"

Short nodded and I motioned for G and Fredo to follow me out. Soon as the door closed, G was in my shit. And Fredo wasn't far behind.

"What the fuck is you doing?" G snapped. "You got some lucrative information but that muthafucka ain't walking out of this building!"

"I agree with G and Scony. You trippin', Cheno."

"Fredo, you should know me better than that. Short ain't leaving this muthafucka. I just told him that shit. I'm going in there to beat the fuck out of him."

"No, you not. Save that energy for the big fish. We gon' let this muthafucka beat his own ass." G smirked. "The room is a gas chamber."

G walked over to the TV on the wall and grabbed a remote. Powering the television on, G hit a few buttons until the room he was looking for was on the screen. Short was walking around with his head in his hands. Increasing the volume, Short was mumbling to himself. We stood watching for a few minutes then Scony joined us.

"What's the play?" he asked.

G handed me a phone then the remote and pointed to a green button at the top. "Whenever you're ready, push that button to suffocate his ass."

With a deep scowl on my face, I studied Short as he continued to mumble. Then out of nowhere his voice rose a little bit and every word was heard.

"These muthafuckas gon' die for killing my brother. When I get settled in whatever jail I'm sent to, I'm putting Tank on game. I'll be out in no time, then we can get back to the money."

I laughed because his dumb ass really thought he would live another day. At this point, he was going to die trying. Pushing the button with my eyes still fixated on the screen, Short spun around in a circle as gas flooded out of the vents.

He dropped down to the floor in an attempt to stay clear of the gas. It didn't work. In a matter of minutes, the room was filled to capacity with the deadly vapes. Short could be heard coughing as if he couldn't catch his breath. He clawed at his throat, peeling away the skin.

G hit a button and the lights went out in the room. Then he flipped a switch, but I didn't know what effect that had on the situation. Once again, G hit another button and the room lit up green and I could see Short fighting to get his clothes off while holding his breath. The man was suffering in a matter of minutes worse than he ever had in life. His body shook uncontrollably, causing him to fall to his knees. When he threw up, I knew it was over for his ass. His once light skin turned purple right before my eyes. Short wasn't giving up and he thought he would be able to survive. There was no way out for him. The moment his eyes protruded from the sockets; I knew he was done.

"I can't watch this. Make sure y'all clean this shit up."

"Hell, we coming with you. That nigga gon' suffer for a few hours before he finally dies. I'll come back tomorrow and put his ass in the furnace." Scony laughed. "We should've saved that kill for that nigga Tank. The shit was epic and it was my idea to come up with that chamber."

Leaving the building, I went straight to the car and smiled. As I watched Short fighting the evils he couldn't see, I rooted for him to just give up. My mind was going full speed on ways to kill the rest of these muthafuckas so I could retire from the streets. Fredo got in the car and I shook my head to let him know I didn't want to hear anything about what had happened.

"Take me home, brah."

Chapter 6

Charlie

The fest was a fun time to be had. I hadn't enjoyed myself so much in a minute. Things became a little grim when Cheese came over grinning in Honey's face. The way I wanted to shoot his ass on the spot was hard to contain. Breeze was on the same time but swallowed that shit and let it go for the time being since we were in the presence of a lot of people who didn't have anything to do with the vendetta we had going on. Honey led him away once she saw our reaction to him being in our space. Quell wasn't too happy with seeing how his woman seemed to be enjoying Cheese's company. Hopefully, he would keep his cool until Honey completed her part of the mission. Otherwise, things could go bad.

I'd arrived home safely and all I wanted to do was sleep. Honey talked to us about opening the shop in a couple of days, so I needed to use the time I had left to relax before heading back to work. Walking through the Air BnB, I thought about how the house wasn't my own. First thing in the morning, finding a place of my own was going to be top priority to jump start my day.

I removed the biker jacket as I headed to the closet with a smile. We received a lot of compliments for them at the fest as well as plenty of new clientele. Customizations by Honey was about to be busier than usual. Good thing we had a few applications we could possibly consider for employment.

Hanging the jacket in the back of the closet, I stripped naked then threw the clothes in the hamper. I headed straight for the shower, turning the water on full blast. Soon as I attempted to step inside, my phone started ringing. I ignored it.

Fifteen minutes later I sat on the side of the bed, moisturizing my body. My phone chimed reminding me of the call I'd missed. Before retrieving the device, I wiped my hands on the towel. There was a missed call and a text from Caesar. Opening the message I smiled.

Caesar: Hopefully, you had a good time with your friends. Care for some company?

My yoni thumped with excitement because the sexual tension between me and Caesar couldn't be ignored a moment longer. We'd been going on dates and spending a lot of time together. In the beginning Caesar came off as a creep. I explained how material things weren't the key to win me over. I soon found out he was just a genuine gentleman who loved to show a woman how much she meant to him. That woman happened to be me. From the moment he feasted on my tender lips, I'd been curious about the sex ever since. A bitch had to go with the flow and pretend it wasn't on my mind. The gig was up because there was an itch I needed to have scratched.

Me: I'm always down for your company. Give me a few minutes. I just got out of the shower.

Caesar: No problem. Text me when you're ready.

Me: Okay.

My nerves were through the roof knowing what would transpire once Caesar walked across the threshold. For some reason only fifty percent of my nervousness had to do with the actions I looked forward to performing. The other fifty was Cheno. He was the only man I'd been intimate with in years. Learning Caesar's likes and dislikes in the bedroom was a task I was willing to take on. It was part of moving on and that was exactly what I planned to do. Fuck Cheno. I had to do what was best for me.

It took roughly ten minutes for me to shake the jitters off before I got the nerve to text Caesar. The chime of the doorbell was music to my ears. With only a long t-shirt covering my naked body, I made my way to the point of no return. Every step I took sent an electric like current to my lady parts. I was mesmerized the moment I laid eyes on Caesar. He looked good standing before me dressed in a black tank, grey sweatpants, and slides. I stood still like a bump on a log, damn near drooling from my mouth. His voice brought me back to reality, snapping me out of the lustful stupor I found myself in.

"Are you going to allow me to come in?" He smirked. "And where are your clothes?"

Caesar scanned my body with pure lust as he waited for me to welcome him inside. I anticipated him licking me from head to toe the same way his tongue glided over his lips. The shit was sexy.

I finally moved to the side so he could enter while pulling at my shirt. "To answer your question, I'm sure you know there's nothing open this time of night except twenty-four-hour restaurants and legs. I have high hopes of my legs joining the club," I said locking the door.

Soon as I turned around, Caesar swooped me in his arms, holding my cheeks in the palm of his hands. Burying his face in the side of my neck, a shiver traveled down my spine. I could feel the heat radiating from my love box. Caesar was activating one of many spots that would put me in the mood. He didn't have to try hard because my mind was set the moment he texted.

"Where's your bedroom?" he asked, massaging my cat with his fingers.

"Straight ahead. First door on the right." I moaned, tightening my arms around his neck.

Caesar followed my directions without missing a beat. Gently lying me on the bed he stood, admiring my slick inner folds. I gave him something to enjoy by placing my hand between my legs then strummed my pearl. It hardened to my touch, causing me to moan lowly.

Caesar swiped my hand away. "There's no need for you to play with her. You do enough of that when I'm not in your presence. Tonight, it's my job to make her fat ass cry. I got this covered."

In a swift movement, Caesar pulled his tank over his head before falling to his knees. He grabbed my legs, tugging me to the edge of the bed. Soon as his soft lips wrapped around my clit, the sweet secretions of my kitty made its escape. The last time Caesar ate my box was nothing compared to the assault he was putting on me this time around. Spreading my legs wide, I gave him full access to do whatever.

"Shit!" I moaned as I caressed the top of his head. "Fuck!"

For a full five minutes Caesar devoured my pussy with aggression and I loved every minute of it. *"I'll kill any muthafucka I see in yo' face, Charlie."* If it wasn't for Caesar choosing that precise moment to insert his tongue into my ass, I would've pushed him off. Instead, I encouraged him to go harder. The way he orally pleasured my sacred hole sent me into a euphoric bliss I longed for. Finding his way back to my bud, Caesar's mouth made me cum long and hard, wetting his chest in the process.

"You taste so good," he said, standing to his feet. Wiping my juices from his beard, Caesar pulled a gold wrapped condom from his pocket then dropped his pants to the floor. I was glad he came prepared because protection was the furthest thing on my mind when I agreed he could come over. Caesar stroked his manhood and it grew bigger before my eyes. Rolling the latex on, his eyes never left mine. We were at a point of no return when he tapped my thigh.

"Toot that ass up for me."

Doing as he requested, I got into the doggystyle position with anticipation. Arching my back, I felt Caesar rub his hand over my ass. I knew what was coming next. His mushroom head penetrated my hole and I gasped loudly.

"You ready for all this dick, Charlie? There's no turning back, so I hope you got that nigga out yo' system."

I responded to his question by pushing back on him to enter me fully. My walls clinched around his pipe like a python swallowing its prey. Caesar groaned out in pleasure and I smirked before rocking back and forth. My ass jiggled with every bounce and the shit felt good. The sound of our bodies connecting was the only sounds heard until I picked up speed.

"Damn, girl, throw that ass back," he muttered.

Working up a sweat I tried my best to make him tap out. Every time his balls hit my clit, I had the urge to cum. The feeling was sensational and I didn't want it to end. We had just started but the room was heating up like a sauna. Sweat coated my forehead and I could feel the beads gliding along my spine. Caesar gripped my hips and pounded into me hard. My turn was over at that point. He took the wheel and was back in control. The way the tip of his dick hit my g-spot had my mouth opened wide.

"Oh, shit! Yes, like that! Fuck me, Caesar. Fuck me!"

There was no holding back. I needed him to know he was doing the job he set out to do. The way Caesar was staking claim to my goodies had me on a natural high. Our bodies molded together perfectly, and like he said, there was no turning back. The only man I could think of was him. Nobody else mattered. I waited months to get sexed in the manner Caesar was delivering. He slowed down a little bit, going in and out of my kitty slowly.

"Damn, that shit sexy as hell. You coating this muthafucka up, bae. Turn over."

Changing positions so I was on my back, Caesar wasted no time spreading my legs wide as they would go, then eased

63

into my kitty. The way he stroked my folds, it was evident he was making love to my soul. Caesar rocked his hips from right to left, hitting spots I didn't know existed. The movement had my pussy squirting uncontrollably. He put his member back inside and repeated the act, getting the same results.

"Oh my God! What the fuck!" I screamed out in pure pleasure.

My legs wouldn't stop shaking and I couldn't stop cummin'. That had never happened to me before. I didn't know what type of spell Caesar had casted upon me, but he had me right where he wanted me...under his command. Soon as he entered me again, he fed me endless dick, causing me to cum with every stroke. Caesar finally focused on himself. The veins in his arms, neck, and the side of his head were bulging as if he had been struggling the entire time to hold his nut. My falsetto was on point as he fucked me hard. I felt myself about to cum one last time and, of course, we came together.

"I'm cummin'," I moaned.

"Me, too," Caesar groaned as he tried his best to stay inside of my tunnel while my juices spewed out around his dick.

Falling onto his side, he was breathing as if he had run a marathon. I wanted to get out of the wet spot. The only place I could escape to was the head of the bed because it was soaked from the middle to the foot, all on the left side. I didn't have the energy to change the sheets, which wouldn't have mattered because the mattress was wet as well.

"Do you always cum like that? I mean, so you squirt at any giving time?"

"Unfortunately, I do."

"I've never had a woman cum like that so many times in all my days of having sex. There's no way I'm letting you go. The only way we will be separated is if you do something foul to me. I don't think you are capable, so we won't have to worry about any of that."

"There you have it," I said getting up to shower.

"Where you going?"

"To wash away my sins. You want to join me?" Looking over my shoulder, I gave Caesar a wicked grin then switched my ass to the bathroom.

He jumped up, following like a hungry hound.

***

I was awakened by Caesar planting kisses all over my face. Our late-night tryst didn't end until about six in the morning, and tired was an understatement. There was no way I was getting up to do anything. That included talking to him. Instead, I rolled over and snuggled back under the sheet. My entire body was aching, but it only put a smile on my face because I remembered every bit of the cause. Me and Caesar fucked all over the house, including the shower and ended up in one of the other bedrooms to sleep.

"Hey, beautiful, I'm about to head out," Caesar said continuing to kiss me. "I scrubbed the bed in the master bedroom and sanitized the rest of the house. All you have to do is put sheets on the bed. I'll talk to you later."

"Mmmhmm." I said sleepily as I hugged the pillow.

He laughed, giving me another kiss then walked out. I was too tired to even get up and properly walk him out of the house. Hearing the door close, I snuggled back under the sheet, allowing sleep to take over. The ringing of my phone is the reason I woke up hours later, causing me to groan out loudly. Looking at my watch, Cheno's name appeared, and I quickly declined the call. He was the last person I wanted to talk to after the night I'd had. When I told him I was done, I meant every word.

Moving on from a relationship where I had to fight and argue with other bitches to one that had me smiling every minute of the day was something I looked forward to. The drama was behind me for the time being. Caesar was on the road to winning my heart, but I knew better. Everything was great in the beginning then it went downhill later. Taking things slow was my objective and I wasn't going to say it wouldn't go further just yet. There was a huge possibility.

The constant ringing of my phone prompted me to get up to start my day. I headed to the master bedroom to jump in the shower. Caesar had done an exceptional job cleaning the house and I was grateful because I didn't have the energy to do the shit myself. Entering the bedroom, I looked around and sniffed the air. There were no signs of what we'd done anywhere. Noticing a stack of bills on the nightstand next to my phone, I walked over and counted them. Shaking my head, I placed the two thousand dollars where Caesar left them, then headed to the bathroom.

After taking care of my hygiene, I threw on a black Nike sweatsuit before going into the hall to get sheets for the bed. It took no time to make the bed, then I got comfortable to find a permanent place to live. Buying a house in the city was a huge no for me. I looked on the outskirts of the city and the houses were beautiful. Being in the house with only the sound of the keyboard keys was driving me crazy. I picked up the remote, going to the *YouTube* app on my TV. Finding a True Crime channel, I found a playlist and let it keep me company.

The men nowadays were killing women left to right because they didn't want to be with them. Watching those cases had me in my feelings because Cheno kept calling my phone, giving me crazy vibes. Truth be told, I didn't know why he was acting the way he was. It was his fault we weren't together in the first place. Had he not been fuckin' around with every bitch in the city, he would still have me in his life. Don't nobody have time to play the option game with his ass. I guess he thought I would be the one who looked over the shit he was doing. My silly ass did that shit far too long but not anymore. Since I wasn't at his beck and call and he knew I was dating someone else, Cheno fucked around and found out that my life didn't end when he and I did. Now he couldn't take what he had been dishing out. My text alert sounded and it caused me to chuckle because I knew who had sent the message.

Cheno: You must be over there with yo' lil boyfriend. That's why you not answering yo' phone.

I could read the hostility in his words, and I was all for his shenanigans. He didn't understand he was getting a dose of the medicine he forced me to swallow for years. It was cool when he had me calling his phone all times of the night, but it was a problem when I did it. Cheno was about to understand, what's good for the goose was good for the gander.

Me: Actually, I'm not. He left a few hours ago. I didn't answer my phone because there is nothing for us to talk about.

Cheno: What the fuck you mean he left a couple hours ago? You gave my pussy away, Charlie?

Me: See, this is why I didn't answer the phone! I don't have to explain anything to you, Cheno. We are not together anymore. What I do with my life is no longer your concern.

Cheno: You gon' make me fuck you up! I specifically told yo' ass the shit you on is temporary. I also told yo' hot pussy ass not to fuck the nigga!

I knew going back and forth with him was dangerous, but I had to humble his ass. Cheno had me in his good graces and I wasn't enough. That was not my fault. It was all on him. Now he was in his feelings because I decided to entertain somebody other than him.

Me: Cheno, you sound ridiculous. How many times did I cry about you being out with other hoes? Too many to count on too many occasions. You are finding out firsthand how the fuck I felt when the shit was happening to me. The difference between me and you is, I'm single and you weren't. For the record, you can't tell me who to fuck!

Cheno: So, you fucked him?

I didn't even reply to his ignorant ass because I'd wasted enough time arguing with him. Placing the phone back on the bed, I went back to the task at hand. I looked through the house listings and filled out a few applications. Closing down the laptop, I walked to my dresser and grabbed a pair of socks to put on my feet. Once again, my phone chimed and I groaned in frustration. I opened the text mad as hell.

Cheno: Is that a yes? You fucked him?

Me: Yup. The same way you fucked all them busted ass bitches. Now leave me the fuck alone, Cheno!

Slipping my feet into my all-white sneakers, I texted Breeze to see what she was doing. When she responded for me to pull up at her crib, I snatched my keys, purse, and the money Caesar left for me, then headed out. Cheno and his bullshit were forgotten as I started my car, backing out of the driveway.

Chapter 7

Cheno

Charlie had me fucked all the way up. She got her a piece of dick and thought she could talk to me like I was a lil nigga. It was nice to know her ass thought I was joking when I told her not to give my shit away. Not to mention, what she had going on was on a temporary basis. Charlie failed to realize what I did in the street was something she couldn't do to get back at me. I fucked them hoes and still loved my girl. She, on the other hand, wouldn't be able to do that without adding her emotions to the mix. It's all good because she crossed that line already. She can stay her ass over there.

The sound of the doorbell brought me out of my thoughts as I poured a glass of Remy. When the banging started, I became irritated as hell. Snatching my Glock from its place under the bar, I made my way to the door. Without even asking who it was, I pulled the door open, taking aim.

"Woah, nigga! What the fuck is yo' problem?" Scony asked with his hands up in the air.

"I could ask you the same question while you beating my shit down like you the muthafuckin' police."

"Man, put that down so we can come in. I got some shit to run by you." G gritted.

Shaking my head, I stepped to the side so they could enter.

Scony walked in and stopped in front of me. He glanced down at my tool then back up at me. "Make that yo' last time uppin' that bullshit on me without using it."

"Nigga, now if I shoot you in the ass, you would reconsider talking crazy to me. Either come in, or get the fuck out. Yo' choice."

"Wait 'til I tell Pearl about this shit. You gon' get that ass toe up!"

The way he said he was going to tell made me bend over laughing. Scony sat on the sofa and crossed his arms over his chest and that only made me laugh harder. I made my way into the living room area and sat at the bar. Taking a sip from my glass, I picked up the blunt I pre-rolled and lit fire to it.

"You niggas childish as fuck," G said seriously as he stood to his feet. Walking over where I was, he proceeded to pour himself a drink. "Quan got back to me about that nigga Dro. He is Kelvin's brother and the muthafucka is out for revenge apparently. Quan sent a photo, too. Low and behold, he is the nigga who shot Scony and ya boy. His name is Caesar Brisco."

"So, hold on," Scony said, joining us at the bar. "Why did this muthafucka pop up now to avenge his brother's death? We killed that pussy nigga years ago." I offered Scony the blunt and he waved me off. "I didn't see you roll that shit. I'm good."

"Shid, more for me."

"According to Quan, Caesar been here for about five years. He's originally from Pittsburg and was raised by his grandmother. The nigga owns that new restaurant downtown called Brisco's but the only way anyone would know is if they dug deep like Quan did. He got a cracker named Oliver St. Claire portraying to be the owner."

"I gotta give it to him, that shit was smooth. Had he stayed in his tax bracket, his secret would've never been revealed. Now, his muthafuckin' head is on the choppin' block." Scony snarled. "Where is this nigga laying his head?"

"In Downers Grove. Cheno, I'm gon' need you to scope out the restaurant and his crib. Caesar, Dro, or whatever he goes by knows who we are. Plus, on the street, you're dead. It's perfect."

"I'm down to do whatever it takes, but y'all do know I have my own shit to tackle, right? I'm not trying to be out here dead forever."

"Trust me when I tell you, all this shit goes hand in hand. Dro works with Cheese and Tank. We gon' kill two birds with one stone and anybody else standing in the way. It's about to be a war in the city. Be ready. I'm going to send everything you need to your phone."

"These muthafuckas fucked with the wrong niggas. We about to take this shit back to 2017," Scony said raising his glass in the air. "Salute."

"Salute!" Me and G yelled together.

"I need you to get dressed, Cheno. We have to head over to Pearl's to make sure she's good. I need to make sure them niggas haven't found out about her."

Hearing him say Pearl may be in danger, I jumped up and went to change my clothes. It didn't take me long before I was back in my living room where both of them were still waiting. Going to the closet, I strapped my Sig in the right side of my holster and walked over to the bar to do the same with my Glock on the left.

"Pearl is straight because nobody knows her connection to me." I stated.

"Yeah, that may be true, but everybody knows her affiliation with me. The same way we found out about Dro; they could've done the same with her. What we're not going to do is assume she's safe."

G headed to the door as he talked and I was right on his heels. Pushing the garage opener on my fob, I walked inside soon as the door opened completely. My old school Chevy was my car choice for the day. It wasn't the time to be flashy. A nigga had to roll as if I was riding dirty. Mo3's *Broken Love* kept me company while I smoked. The track spoke on everything I was going through at the time. From losing the homie Free, to Charlie fuckin' off with another nigga, and muthafuckas snaking me…twice. Once by stealing from me, then trying to take my life.

Yo' patna dead, you know who did it. So why he still breathing?
Yo' bitch got caught texting a nigga
She said that ain't cheating
Nigga, you crazy if you fall for that
'Cause that hoe sneaky

I laughed to keep from crying because Charlie went further than that shit. She actually laid down, giving up the goods. It is what it is though. There were other pressing issues I had to deal with. Turning on Drexel, G parked in front of Pearl's crib; I had to pull further up the block. We met at the door and could hear her talking to someone inside. Using his key, G unlocked the door, rushing in.

"Granny, who the fuck is this, nigga?" Scony snapped.

My mind automatically went to the worse scenario when my eyes landed on Ease. Why he was at Pearl's house was the magic question because if I wasn't mistaken, I told his ass to forget this muthafucka even existed.

"This my lil baby, Ease. Since Cheno brought him by, he's been checking on me."

I stormed over to Ease and pulled him off the couch by the back of his shirt. He stumbled a bit before I slammed him against the wall. Scony stood with his arms crossed over his chest with an evil grin on his face. The way he was standing let me know he was waiting to see if he had to tap in.

"Cheno, turn that boy loose!" Pearl yelled from the couch.

"Nah, because I told his hardheaded ass never to come back over here! Niggas gunnin' for me and everybody affiliated. He may have led them muthafuckas to you."

Ease sucked his teeth and I tried to knock them bitches to the back of his throat. He may not care about what was going on, but I did. If anything happened to Pearl, his ass was going to get the same treatment. Times ten. In the meantime, I was good with giving him a small taste of what could soon be his trip to the hospital.

"G, get him off that baby!"

"He good. Sit down. Cheno ain't gon' hurt him too bad. You know how shit goes, granny. The nigga didn't listen, now he got to suffer the consequences. I'm with fam. If this muthafucka brings heat over here, that's his ass. This needs to happen."

Ease's mouth was leaking from the blows I delivered. He was balled up in a fetal position trying to protect his head at every turn. It took everything in me not to stomp his ass out. Scony finally pulled me away from him. I was fuming like a pit bull in a dog fight.

"That's enough, homie. I think he got the point."

I took all my frustrations out on Ease. To be honest, I didn't feel an ounce of remorse. Ease slowly gathered himself as he rose to his feet. He wiped his mouth with the sleeve of his shirt then glared in my direction. The nigga acted like he had a lot of shit to get off his chest.

"Speak yo' peace, Ease." I snarled. "I don't want to hear shit else about this after you leave. Unless…heat comes back to this house."

"Man, Cheno, you know I wouldn't put grandma Pearl in harm's way. Nobody followed me over here. Before you ask, I was watching my surroundings the entire way. I'm gon' eat that ass whoopin' because it comes with the territory."

Pearl was pissed and it was mainly towards me. She would get over it eventually. Pearl cursed all the way to the kitchen. Scony's dumb ass was fighting hard not to laugh and she caught him.

"Demarius, this is not a laughing matter. He could've really hurt that baby!"

"Come on, Pearl! With all due respect, this nigga grown as fuck, so stop callin' him a baby. You were out in them streets pistol-whippin' niggas for less back in the day. Don't lose yo' mind now."

The sound of dishes clackin' in the sink told all of us Pearl was angry as fuck. G walked toward the kitchen and a loud pop followed by shattered glass had us running to the kitchen. All except Scony. He ran out the front door with gun in hand. Pearl was lying on the floor and blood covered the front of her shirt. My heart stopped in my chest as my eyes locked in on her lifeless body.

"Help me get her to the car!" G yelled.

We sprang into action because calling for an ambulance would take too much time. Getting Pearl inside G's car, I jumped in the backseat with her. Tears ran down my face and once again I was praying to the man upstairs to save the only woman I had in my life to call mama. In that moment, anyone who knew better would know, when thug's cry, nobody was safe.

Chapter 8

Tank

Staying ten steps ahead of Cheno's crew, I'd been keeping my eye on them lame muthafuckas for days. The fest gave me a light opportunity to free my mind from the bullshit. In fact, I peeped the bitches at the park, but I didn't take action because Cheese would've died that day trying to protect Honey. The lil baddie Danielle been keeping me company until I decided to handle business. Shawty wanted to tag along but I told her no. She swallowed a nigga whole and I gave in to her pleas.

One hour prior

And Then What flowed through the system as me and Danielle sat back, observing Cheno's trap. The muthafuckas were still making loot hand over fist. The fiends were out in droves getting their medicine. I had the urge to run up in that bitch and rob their ass again. I held back because that wasn't why I was out there. Cheese goofy ass still had his money on hold by not opening his shit back up and that shit pissed me off. Seeing them niggas going hard through the beef had my blood boiling.

"And then what! When I see Honey, I'm beating her ass! And then what! We gon' see how she really is wit' them hands. And then what!"

"She gon' fuck you up!" I laughed.

Danielle rolled her eyes with an attitude. After learning her history with Honey, I knew the Detroit native stood no chance defeating her. Danielle would be a great distraction though. Maybe I was wrong. She may prove me wrong by blocking one of the checker pieces off the board. I was sure to jump start the bloodshed. One of the niggas walked out of the trap then jumped in his whip. Of course, an evil muthafucka like myself was on his ass.

"Who is that?" Danielle asked.

"Somebody that may lead me to my first hit. I hope you ready to show me you down."

"What you mean?"

"Open the glove compartment. You didn't think ridin' out meant you wasn't gon' put in work. Have you ever shot a gun before?"

Danielle retrieved the pistol, checked the magazine, then snapped a bullet in the chamber. The shit was sexy as fuck. I didn't say nothing when she didn't respond to my question. Her actions spoke for itself. The car stopped on the 75th block of south Drexel. Parking two cars back, I watched as the nigga went into a white house and I assumed it was his grandma crib because an elderly woman let him inside.

Patiently waiting for the dude to come back out, I placed my tool in my lap. The plan formulating in my mind was to have Danielle drop his ass soon as he emerged from the residence. Running the plan by her, she was ready. About thirty minutes later, two vehicles rolled up the block causing me to scope them out. The dark tint of my whip hid the fact that anyone was inside. Two older cats walked to the same house I was watching. Another muthafucka was walking down the sidewalk glancing around as he made his way toward the others. It wasn't until he got close enough for me to fully see him that I realized who the fuck it actually was.

"That muthafucka dead! How the fuck is this possible?"

I was madder than a muthafucka as I watched Cheno climb the steps without a care. Zooming in on the other two niggas, I recognized them as G and Scony. According to the stories I'd heard, those two weren't to be fucked with. That shit was about to become a myth because my name would ring bells once I eliminated one or both of them. Being associated with Cheno's devious ass added them to my hit list.

"He didn't look dead to me," Danielle's dumb ass said. "I'm confused."

"Of course, he didn't because the nigga ain't!" I shot back. "That's Honey's cousin. One of my soldiers gunned his ass down and he was presumed dead. His muthafuckin' people even had a memorial for him. From the looks of it, that nigga failed. If Lord wasn't already in the ground, I'd riddle his ass up myself!"

"What you wanna do?"

Thinking long and hard, I wanted to wait a few before I made a move. Danielle sat watching the house as I got lost in thought. My phone chimed taking my mind off what I had seen briefly. The text was from a hoe I'd been smashing for years, but I wasn't interested in what she had to say because a message I missed had my undivided attention. Short hadn't been heard from since he left the fest and I had been waiting for him to hit me up. I was glad he reached out because I was hoping like hell them niggas hadn't snatched him up. Opening the video, I pressed play. The scene before me was one I didn't recognize then Cheno's bitch ass appeared on the screen.

"Aye, Tank, what's up, foolie? Close ya mouth nigga, it's really me. See, when you come after a real muthafucka you gotta make sure they're truly dead. Ya boy didn't miss, but he didn't finish me off either. You and yo' people killed Free, shot at my niggas, and even went after my sister. And only killed one." He laughed shaking his head. *"I'm gon' give you a word of advice. If you want shit done right, you may need to do the shit yourself. Tank, this shit could've been squashed long ago but you wanted to make your mark as being a killa.*

Let me be the one to inform you. I'm going to be the nigga who hits yo' entire entourage and I've started with ya boy."

A scene appeared like a movie behind Cheno and the image almost made me sick. Short was in a room, clawing at his neck. It seemed like he was struggling to breathe because his face was a light shade of purple. I couldn't see what caused him to act that way, but it was a gruesome way for anyone to suffer. I had to turn my head away the moment Short fell to his knees. I couldn't watch a minute longer. When I was about to stop the video, Cheno laughed as if he heard a joke of the year. What I was witnessing wasn't funny at all. Danielle strained her neck to see what had my attention.

"What the hell is happening to him? He is fighting himself! Wait a minute, dude is dying. Look at the color of his skin, Tank. There has to be some type of poison in the air of that room."

Short started throwing up then the screen went black. Cheno cleared his throat with a smile. I couldn't believe I was still watching but I had a feeling the nigga had more to say.

"It don't pay to fuck with a muthafucka and his people, Tank. It was never about the money. It was all about principle. Now, it's about killing every muthafuckin' body involved because this shit is personal now. Each and every one of you bitch made niggas gon' wish y'all had stayed the fuck on the westside of the city. Oh yeah, you're the first person in the world that knows I'm alive. Get the word out, pussy. And get ready to use that lil shit you stole to bury yo' people. See you soon, bitch."

Tossing the phone into the cupholder, I opened the door to my ride. "Get in the driver seat and be ready to take off when I return."

"I thought you wanted me to put in work," Danielle said holding up the gun. "Why did you give me this?"

"You still gon' get to bust that shit. I need you to do what I just told you for now."

Paying close attention to what was going on around me, I crept into the gangway of the house. Luck was on my side because the old lady was in the kitchen. She appeared to be upset while washing dishes. I didn't want to kill her, but I definitely wanted to send a message to the niggas who were somewhere inside. She looked to her left and I took aim letting off a single shot. Making a dash back to my car.

"Go! Drive this muthafucka like yo' life depends on it!"

Danielle was ready to the point she had pulled up to the house making it easier for me to get away. Her daddy, or uncle or some man had to be the person to teach her how to drive because she was pushing my whip with precision. I gave her turn by turn directions even told her to run lights. Danielle did not disappoint. Against my better judgement, I guided her to my crib in hopes she kept the location to herself. I mean, she isn't even from Chicago. Who will she tell where I laid my head?

"Are we going to sit in this house for the rest of the day?"

Danielle asking me that stupid shit brought me back to present time. I looked at her as if she was crazy because I'd just popped an old muthafucka and she expected me to go out to parade her ass around the city. Danielle had me fucked up.

"I plan to sit my ass right here until I hear from my cousin."

"Well, I'm leaving tomorrow and I need to see what Chicago is about. I'm going to hit my girls up and catch an Uber back to the hotel. Hit me up if you want me to come back for another round. I can make that happen."

Sitting back on the couch, I stared at the wall thinking about what she'd just said. Danielle had the type of pussy to make a nigga crave the shit hours after hitting. I damn sure wanted her to come back and smash before she left to head back to Detroit. I just wasn't about to spend the money to get her to the hotel and back via Uber.

"How about you take one of my cars. Therefore, you would have a ride to move around without spending too much money with ride shares. Afterwards, you can come back and spend the rest of the night with me."

"That's alright with me. Where are the keys?" she asked sitting next to me to put her shoes on.

I got up rubbing my nose to retrieve my keys. Danielle was standing by the door with her bag in hand. We had gone to Target to get her some clothes since she didn't have any of her stuff with her at the hotel. The leggings were hugging her ass right and I wanted to dive back in her tunnel but it would have to wait until her return. Giving her the keys, Danielle tried to kiss me and I turned my head giving her my jaw instead.

"Oh, now you can't kiss a bitch, huh?" She chuckled. "You wasn't doing all that last night. Why change up now?"

"I didn't mean shit by that. It's a lot on my mind right now." Pulling her into me by her waist, I planted a quick kiss to her lips. "Enjoy the rest of your day and hurry back. Danielle, don't wreck my shit."

"Boy, I know how to drive. Long as I have GPS on my phone, the bitch will give me directions while I drive for me and all the crazy folks on the road. Trust me." she smirked walking out the door.

I watched as she climbed behind the wheel of my Suburban then sent her a text.

Me: If you get a chance, go check out Honey's shop so you will know one of the places she be. I don't know if she's there, but you will have a lo on her.

Danielle looked down and I knew she was checking her phone. She glanced up and nodded before backing out of the driveway while placing her device in the holder on the dash. I stepped inside then locked the door. With Danielle out of my sight, I could get high the way I wanted. Shit was about to get rough, and I had to be in a better mindset to deal with it. My nerves were rattled as I thought about the way Short lost his life. There was no way he survived what he went through. I felt bad for the homie because I wasn't there for him during his time of need.

Cheese hadn't hit me back and that was part of the reason my anxiety was going haywire. One would think if a muthafucka hit yo' jack about something important, a nigga would call in a matter of minutes. Not his ass because I hadn't heard from him. I had even given him my address to pull up on me. Still nothing. Waltzing into my bedroom, I went to my stash and pulled out a bag of dro, a wood, and three baggies of snow. My cocaine habit started years ago but my usage wasn't as frequent back then as it was in the present day. I kept my activities to myself and tried my hardest not to let the cat out of the bag.

Going back out to the front of my house, I went to the kitchen and poured a glass of White Hennesy on the rocks then grabbed a beer from the fridge. I hit the power button on the remote soon as I sat on the couch. After finding the Bears vs Green Bay game, I went to work rolling up a fat blunt. Sprinkling a little bit of snow over the weed, I sealed that muthafucka up tightly. My mouth watered for a hit so I prepared two lines and snorted that shit up like a vacuum. Throwing my head back, the remnants of the drug flowed down my throat and I felt an instant high. But the image of Short fighting for his life was still vividly playing in my mind. I lit the blunt and took a long pull then blew the smoke through my nose. That did the trick. Bobbing to a beat only I could hear, I smiled. The vibe I was on was lovely and I didn't want to come down for nothing.

Ding-Dong!

I could've sworn I heard something but couldn't put a finger on what it could be. The drugs had me higher than a kite and the weed added the finishing touch. When the sound didn't repeat itself, I went back to enjoying my alone time. That is until the loud knocks startled me.

"Who the fuck could be at my door? Don't nobody know I live here," I mumbled to myself. "Shhhh! Don't say shit, Isaac. If you stay quiet, they will go away."

Ding Dong! Ding Dong! Bam, Bam, Bam!

"Tank, I know you in there! Open this muthafuckin' door!" Cheese's voice bellowed through the door.

I couldn't get my bearings together so I could let him in. Trying to rise to my feet was a struggle and took longer than I expected. The banging continued and I burst into loud laughter. "Give me a minute!" I yelled with a slur. "I'm having a hard time getting up."

"Are you hurt, cuz?"

"Nah, just had too much to drink. Be patient with a nigga. Damn!" Finally getting to my feet, I stumbled and hit my knee on the corner of the table. "Muthafucka!" Limping to the door, I unlocked it, opened it a little, then made my way back to the couch.

Cheese entered and looked around slowly. Cautiously, he closed the door and joined me. He sat across from me scanning the items in front of me. When he zoomed in on the snow, I tried to snatch it up fast hoping he didn't actually see it.

"You on that shit, Tank?"

I picked my blunt up and put fire to it. The cherry blazed on the end as I inhaled deeply. Blowing the smoke out, I reached across the table so Cheese could hit it.

"Nigga, I'll slap the fuck outta you! What type of muthafucka you think I am? That shit laced like a wig and you expect me to smoke behind you! I can smell that shit in the air and it damn sho' don't have the aroma of pure weed." Cheese's voice thundered. "Now, again, how long have you been putting that shit up yo' nose?"

"Man, calm yo' ass down. You blowing my high."

"I wanna blow yo' muthafuckin' head off. That shit got you out here living reckless and now I know why. Cocaine is a hell of a drug that would have a nigga suckin' dick for bare minimum. You stole drugs from Cheno just to sit back and sniff the shit up. Yo' ass hustlin' backwards as fuck!"

Cheese was mad for the wrong reason. He shouldn't have been going hard about what I was doing on my own time. Instead, he needed to concentrate on the bullshit that was taking place around him. So, I did what anybody in my position would do. I deflected the subject away from me.

"I found Short."

Cheese sat up straight. "Where was he?"

Scrolling through my phone. I clicked on the video and handed it to him. "What you about to see is disturbing. At least it was for me. We got to end this shit, Cheese."

"Wait a minute! This nigga ain't dead?" Cheese asked pausing the video.

All I could do was shake my head no. Observing his reaction while he watched the rest, Cheese tossed the phone on the table and got up. At that moment, his device started ringing. He tapped away on it then put it back in his pocket before turning back to me.

"How the fuck is Cheno alive and breathing, Tank? Dro was at the memorial and confirmed they actually had a service for the nigga!"

"I don't know how the hell he survived! I did my part. You need to ask Lord. Oh, dead muthafuckas don't talk."

"Don't fuck around and find out, bitch! This is not the time. Short is nine times out of ten deader than the nigga in Weekend at Bernie's and you got jokes. That's why you shouldn't be snorting the bullshit in your pocket. Keep it up yo' ass gon' be next." Cheese growled. "How the fuck did they get at Short anyway?"

"I can't tell you that either. He left the fest after me and Sway stopped him from approaching Cheno's sister. His ass was wildin' out and was in his feelings about Sketty. You saw that shit! Yo' ass was standing right there!"

"I did see Short in rare form but he walked away with Sway. Y'all just let him leave by himself knowing the opps were more than likely watching y'all like Short was watching his sister."

I cocked my head to the side and looked at him crazy. Cheese needed to be put in his place because his ass could've kept an eye on Short too. If he thought blaming me for some shit we all should've been on the lookout for. He was out of his damn mind. I wasn't the only one in the wrong.

"*I* let him leave? Nigga, if you didn't have yo' head so far up Honey's ass you would've been able to talk some sense into the muthafucka yo'self. I'm not about to sit here while you lay all yo' burdens on me. I'm nobody's keeper and Short is grown as fuck. If he wanted to throw a tantrum because he couldn't kill a female with a thousand witnesses it was best for him to go do that shit by himself. Don't ever come at me like that, Cheese. Hell, you should've taken him with you after you saw how he was acting."

I was heated and didn't appreciate the way he was talking to me as if I was child. "This is why I do my dirt alone. It's too much of a hassle trying to keep up with everybody else's position."

"Tank, you should've kept what you were doing as a solo mission then. Your actions are what led us to the position we now stand. I'm tired of this shit." He said pulling his phone out of his pocket. "For the record, Honey don't have nothing to do with how I'm moving. Stay out of my business and worry about the problem at hand."

"Humph, I guess that's why you didn't notice Letty watching yo' every move yesterday, huh?" I laughed. "How did that work out for you when you got home?"

"I'll let you know when I get there," he chortled. "Again, mind yo' muthfuckin' business."

Cheese never looked up from his phone as he spoke to me. I had no clue what he was doing and really didn't care. Sniffing loudly is what brought his attention to me. He shook his head slowly judging me from afar. I was hooked on cocaine and that nigga was hooked on Honey. At least my addiction was killing me slowly. Honey was going to kill his ass quickly while he was in the pussy. Mark my words.

"Is there anything else you want to tell me before I get out of here?" Cheese asked.

Picking up my glass, I stalled a little because once I revealed that I may have killed an old lady, Cheese was going to go off. There was no way I could allow my cousin to roam the streets thinking the only threat was Cheno being alive. I had to let it be known that he now had G and Scony on our asses too. Clearing my throat, I threw the liquor back wincing from the burn in my chest.

Telling him about my adventure earlier, I watched his every move. Cheese's jaw clenched tightly as the story went along. My eyes lowered to his hands and I noticed his hands were clasped rigidly as he tried his best to contain his anger. Once I finished, Cheese spewed what was on his mind.

"At what point did you think it was okay to shoot somebody's grandma?" Cheese shouted. "Yo' ass didn't like the feeling when them muthafuckas shot up Verna's crib! That booga suga got yo' ass out here doing crackhead shit, Tank! Kids, old people, and women are off limits. Except in this instance, the bitches are fair game. But I stand by the kids and elderly. You crossed the line with this one. Did they see you is the question?"

"I don't believe so."

"That's something I need to know because G and Scony ain't shit to play with. Those niggas are legends around the entire muthafuckin' city!"

For the first time since I kicked off the beef, Cheese appeared to be nervous. He paced back and forth with his phone to his ear. My phone rang and he looked over at me. I answered knowing it was him calling me and the rest of the crew on a group call. When everyone was on the line, Cheese barked loudly.

"Meet me at the muthafuckin' warehouse on Kedzie. Not now, but right now!" Ending the call, Cheese stalked over to me grabbing my shirt. "If anybody else on this team dies, you going in the hole with them. You fucked up for real this time, nigga. Get yo' shit together and you better beat me to the warehouse or I'm beating yo' ass!"

Shoving me back onto the couch, Cheese stormed out of my crib slamming the door behind him. Slowly rising from where I was sitting, I headed to my room to get myself together. Danielle wasn't coming back too soon so I had plenty of time before she arrived. Cheese wasn't going to allow me to live my actions down. I may as well head out to face the music.

Chapter 9

Cheese

Tank's stupid ass was making things worse than it already was and I was sick of his shit. Seeing Cheno on that video made me feel as if I was about to shit on myself. The moment he saw that nigga in the flesh, Tank should've hit my line. Instead, the nigga took flight to shoot an old ass lady. My thoughts were, why didn't he wait the shit out and shoot one of them niggas? I couldn't expect a fuckin' junky to make sound decisions. That's why I needed to step up to the plate and end this shit once and for all. It was going to be a much harder task because Cheno had some heavy hittas on his side.

I weaved in and out of traffic while trying to shake all the thoughts in my head. One that was beating the fuck out of me was Honey. We chilled at the fest for a good while before she texted me when she was leaving. I had reserved a room at the W hotel when she agreed to spend the night with me. I hit her back giving her the address and she met me there without hesitation. Parking her bike in the parking lot, Honey hopped in the car with me then we went to 31st Street beach just to spend a little more time outside. Letty was blowing my line up for hours.

That wasn't the problem I had though. Honey and I talked for hours and not one time did she mention Cheno being alive. In fact, she shed a few tears behind his untimely death. Either she was distraught, or she learned how to act the part while being in prison. I was conflicted because the devil on my right shoulder told me not to trust her ass because Cheno was shot by one of my people. But the angel on my right told me she was clueless about the nigga being alive and had no idea I had anything to do with what happened. The angel was winning because I spent the entire night with Honey wrapped in my arms. If she wanted to kill me, she could've done that shit while I slept.

"I'm going with my first mind," I said out loud. "Honey don't suspect shit."

Traffic was light giving me nothing but open road to push my whip to the limit. I was trying to come up with so many ways to handle the situation but nothing made sense. All of the things I thought of was not anything a smart man would try to execute. I couldn't go in on impulse and needed a good source of action in order to come out on top. The sound of my engine purring was the only sound to keep me company until my phone rang. Glancing down at the dash I huffed in irritation as Letty's name appeared on the display. I'd been avoiding her calls since yesterday and I really didn't want to hear her complaints. To get the shit out of the way, I answered.

"Yeah," I said the moment the call connected.

"Is that how you address me now, Cheese?"

"Man, come on. What is it?"

"You didn't come home last night. That's what the fuck it is!" Letty yelled. "See, you think you slick. You thought coming home with me was going to ease my mind about what I saw at the fest. Cheese, you only pissed me off more when you left after fuckin' me when I went to sleep. Why you didn't tell me you were going out?"

"What you fail to realize is I'm not obligated to check in with you or nobody else for that matter. I pay my way in this thing called life and do as I please. So, again, what do you want?"

The laugh Letty let out on the other end of the line was one I knew all too well. It was how she began her bullshit rants. I had about ten minutes to hear her out before I left her ass in tears. Every question that was bound to come my way, I was going to answer truthfully. Somebody should've told her ass about asking shit she wasn't ready for.

"Were you with Honey all night? Don't lie either."

"Yup."

"Did you fuck her?"

"Nope."

"You a muthafuckin' lie, Cheese. Ain't no way you spent the whole night with a bitch and didn't fuck! You must think I'm boo-boo the fool!"

"I didn't fuck her but if I did, ain't shit you could do about it," I said calmly. "I tell you the truth and you come back telling me what I did. So, why ask if you already got it made up in your mind that I slept with her."

"What else is there to do all night, smart ass?"

"Letty, you know first-hand that it doesn't take all night to bust a nut. I can tell you this though, I did eat her pussy. Are you satisfied now?"

The line went silent, and I smirked because I didn't even do that much to Honey. Far as we got was to the stage of kissing. She said she wasn't taking it there with me long as I was with Letty and this was my chance to end the relationship. Yeah, I knew the way I was going about it was wrong, but Letty wasn't who I wanted to be with. Honey was. If that meant I had to deaden what I had going on with the woman I was with, so be it.

"Cheese, you told me you would never step out on me," she cried. "Honey comes back on the scene and it's fuck me! I guess you needed to go back to who makes you comfortable. She knows you better than you know yourself and I want you to be careful. I've told you this before, Honey don't want you. She wants something from you and that's blood. In case you have forgotten, somebody on your payroll killed her cousin."

"Letty, Honey has nothing to do with that. You have it all wrong. But I'm glad you understand where my heart is. I promise to pay for your living expenses and anything else you may need to move on with your life."

"You must've misconstrued what I said. At no point did I agree to move on with my life. What type of bitch do you think I am? For years I've been warming your bed and it won't end the way you've obviously planned. Thank you for telling me Honey has your heart. She can have that shit long as I still have a hold on the dick and your bank account."

"Since you didn't understand what I was telling you in the lamest terms, I'm going to try to do it without sparing your feelings. I'm done, Letty. I have no intentions of entertaining two women. I mean, the shit can be pulled off, but I swear on everything I love, you will get the short end of the stick. Minus the dick. The only thing I can promise is a place to lay your head. Don't expect me to be there often. An allowance will be in place for the next six months, food included. Just to keep shit one hunnid with you, the dick will definitely be off the table."

"You sound stupid as fuck! That sounds like by having me in your crib, it gives you the right to dictate what I can and cannot do long as I'm living in your house. The minute I entertain another nigga, that's when the fight gon' start. What's good for you, won't taste too good when I run that shit back. We both know this."

I had to laugh listening to her because what she said was far from the truth. The only reason I threw the option for her to stay in my spot was because I didn't want to put her out like that. I had another place she knew nothing about and it wouldn't put me in a bind to leave her there. Letty was losing the battle by forcing my hand to disappoint her.

"Sweetheart, I don't give a damn who you fuck. Don't bring no muthafucka to my crib. That's all I ask. You gon' need somebody to rod you out because it won't be me."

The sound of Letty wailing into the phone had me fighting the urge to hang up on her ass. My delivery was foul, but it needed to be said. The way I felt about Honey didn't come out the blue. Letty was around during the time me and Honey was together. She knew how deep my love for her ex-best friend was. Me on the other hand was not passing up the opportunity to be back with the love of my life. I pulled in front of the warehouse and killed the engine.

"Aye, look. I got some business to tend to. I'll call you when I'm done."

"You don't have to, Cheese. I think you said all you needed to say to me. Now, let me fill you in on what's on my mind." She paused. "There's a side of me you have never seen and I've tried to keep that demon at bay. This what you wanted though. I'm here to let you know, yo' bitch will never live comfortably while fuckin' with you. The life you think y'all gonna have will never prosper. I'm whooping her ass and yours too if it comes to that. Ain't no way I'm taking the disrespect lying down."

"Letty," I said cutting in.

"Aht, aht. You won't silence me. I let you talk, it's my turn. I've been around far too long, Cheese. I know all about what you do when you're not with me. That's something you shouldn't have included in this so-called relationship. I will have the Feds running all through your operation. Fuck wit' it! If you thought I was going to go away quietly, you thought wrong. I'm invested, nigga! I'm not trash that you can take out and place by the curb. You gotta jump me out of this relationship, bitch!"

Letty was being vindictive, and I wasn't about to entertain it any longer. I hung up before flaming up to ease my mind. Not only was I wired about the shit that awaited me inside the warehouse, now I had to worry about her ass sending the pigs at me. My crib was going to be my next stop after I put a plan in motion for Cheno. Entering the warehouse, everyone I'd called was in attendance; except Tank. I didn't expect him to actually beat me to the spot since he had to clean himself up and get dressed. He didn't have too much time to make his way though. Sway met me at the door. We dapped each other up.

"What's up? You sounded kind of frantic on the phone. Fill me in," Sway said stepping back.

I was prepared to give him the short version of what had taken place when the door opened and Tank entered. Scoffing at his ass, I walked deeper into the room glancing around. Dro, Meaty, Roc, Face, and Yellow Boy stood waiting to hear the reason they were summoned to the warehouse. Tank sat on a wooden crate in the corner away from the group. The nigga was still high as fuck and that pissed me off even more with him. It was my cue to get the meeting underway so he could get out of my eyesight.

"As everybody knows, we have been in a bind with the Cheno situation." Looking around, I acknowledged the nods letting me know they were listening. "There have been a series of events that has taken place in the past months. One being the fact Cheno was wet up and, in the aftermath, we lost Lord and Sketty in the process."

"Which is something to expect. We took two of theirs, and they came back and got at two of ours. It's the game we set out to play. Ain't no rules to this shit." Face stated.

"You are absolutely correct. That's why we are here today. The time has come for us to get the ball rolling and end this shit destructively. I will take full accountability for underestimating Cheno's people. One of ours was snatched up sometime yesterday. We not losing nobody else."

Face glancing around at the people in the room. He stared me down before opening his mouth. "Don't tell me them muthafuckas got Short." I nodded slowly confirming he was correct. "He was at the fest with us. How did they get to the homie?"

I almost shot daggers in Tanks direction, but I didn't want to victim blame. Instead, I told him I didn't know. Face walked around in a circle with his hands on top of his head. He and Short had a love hate relationship. The two argued about the littlest things which almost every time turned into them throwing blows. But they would hug the shit out then get back to the money. It was like sibling rivalry that never gone too far.

"Tank was sent a video message…"

There was no way I could explain what I saw in the footage because I was still struggling to get the image out of my mind. I walked over to the seventy-inch television that was mounted on the wall, then powered it on. Motioning for Tank to give me his phone. The muthafucka had the nerve to take his time and I fought the urge to drag him across the room. When he finally presented me with what I needed, I started the video and walked to the back of the warehouse. I couldn't stomach watching what happened to Short a second time. The video ended and I knew the precise moment when I heard my men going off.

"They tortured him! That was a fucked-up way for somebody to die!" Yellow Boy exclaimed.

"Fuck that! We need to discuss how Cheno is walking around filming a murder when he supposed to be dead!" Face rebutted.

Face's anger was valid. I felt the same way he did. His action was the same as mine when I first saw the video. That brought me to Dro. I stared at him long and hard until he stood tall defensively.

"You not about to blame this shit on me." Dro spoke up. "I came on to do a favor for Tank. Yeah, I went to the memorial, but the shit was over when I arrived. The niggas that killed my brother were the first muthafuckas I saw and I acted on it. Did I miss the target, I did. But it wasn't because of the niggas they had guarding the damn place; it was the bitches who came at my head."

"But did you see Cheno anywhere?" Tank asked.

I was bewildered by his question and wanted to punch him in his shit. "Cheno wasn't there! I know for a fact. Why would he show up if everybody who came out to mourn him thought he was dead? That was stupid on your part to ask. Remember what I said earlier. Leave that shit alone, it's messing with your thought process."

"Who are the people you were after, Dro?"

"G and Scony. I want them muthafuckas dead just like my brother. Best believe, I'm going to make it happen. In the meantime, I'm down for whatever y'all wanna do. If silencing Cheno puts me in the same vicinity as those pussies, call me the Terminator."

Walking back to the table, I picked up my phone after disconnecting Tank's from the projector. After syncing my device, one by one I put photos of Cheno and his people on the screen. I was leaving no rock unturned. Everybody in the room needed a visual of all involved. I'd also included any information I had on them.

"This as we all know is Cheno," I said pointing to his picture. "His trap is on 79th and Hoyne in the middle of the block. According to Tank, the trap is still in full effect, bringing in lots of money. Obviously, Cheno don't give a fuck about his workers, or he think they're safe. We're about to make him wish he would've closed shop."

"Shid, you need to follow that nigga's blueprint. Missing out on major money," Tank mumbled.

"Say that again so I can hear you clearly." I gritted. "If you hadn't brought this muthafuckin' heat to my establishment, we wouldn't be here today! Your best bet is to shut the fuck up and listen closely, so you won't fuck up this time around."

Tank stood up approaching me as if he wanted to thump. The nigga needed to realize I was the one who put him on his ass plenty of times in the past. I had been refraining from putting my hands on him but he was pushing all my buttons that day.

"Nah, let's state facts, Cheese. I didn't bring shit to you! If you hadn't approached Honey…"

"You would be a dead nigga! I don't know how many times I gotta tell you, she doesn't have shit to do with this!"

"Who is Honey?" Yellow Boy asked.

"The love of his life," Roc answered. "Honey was his chic back in the day before she went to prison. I heard she was out, but I haven't seen her. Y'all trying to rekindle that flame, fam?"

"Some—" Tank cut me off before I could respond.

"See, you leaving out valuable information, cuz. As a matter of fact, why Honey's picture not up there with the rest?"

"I told you she doesn't have shit to do with this bullshit! Leave her name out of it!"

"So, you not gon' tell them that Cheno is Honey's cousin?" Tank continued.

"Since when? Honey didn't have family other than her mama back in the day. That's the reason she came to live with you, right Cheese?" Roc quizzed.

"Didn't I tell yo' ass to keep her name out of yo' muthafuckin' mouth, nigga?"

Before Tank could respond I rocked his shit. The cocaine he inhaled had his muthafuckin' mind in disarray. It was time for me to show my cousin I wasn't to be played with. Tank knew my get down and he should've known I didn't do well with disrespect. Especially from family. When one crossed the line, they had to deal with what came with the shit they brought to the fight. Tank shook his head and swung wildly missing by a mile. Sway grabbed him from behind walking him away.

"We not doing this! You niggas trippin'!" He growled. "There's muthafuckas out there who need their ass beat and y'all choose to battle each other. That's not happening. We're family."

"Fuck you, Cheese! Honey is going to be the one to end yo' life! While you lovin' that bitch, she luring yo' dumb ass right into a trap. You got this though, cuz. I'm out of here because my opinion is not needed. I'll deal with Cheno on my own. Y'all stick with this nigga while he's holding information that can get you killed."

"Tank, you talking out the side of yo' neck right now. We need to stick together and ride this shit out. Once we've completed this mission, you're free to go your way. But for the time being, lets come up with a game plan to get at these muthafuckas." Sway lectured. "Go in the back and cool off. Leaving this building is not an option."

"Let his ass leave!"

"Cheese, pipe the fuck down! You ain't doing shit but escalating the problem further than it need to go."

The tension was thick and it was something I couldn't deny. It was wrong for me not to mention Honey's connection to Cheno. I felt the shit wasn't worth mentioning because Honey didn't have a damn thing to do with the beef we had with her cousin. Flaming up, I walked around the warehouse slowly before I exited the building. The fresh air did me good. Giving me a sense of relief. Tank opened a can of worms I knew would need to be addressed. Smoking half of the blunt, I stubbed it out on the side of the building mentally preparing myself to go back inside. My phone rang and I ignored it then went back to handle business so I could go home to deal with Letty. Soon as I stepped over the threshold, Roc was on my ass.

"I've never questioned yo' judgement, Cheese, but I'm with Tank on this one. Was his delivery malicious? Yes. He's right though. We need to know all parties involved in this shit. Honey can't be ignored. She's more than likely being used to set you up."

"I thought about it while outside. I will apologize to my cousin."

I was lying as I walked back to the television. Honey had nothing to do with what was going on and no one could convince me otherwise. My intentions were to make them think they were correct in the situation.

"I'm going to handle Honey myself. She is *not* to be touched in any shape form or fashion. I don't care who sees her. Leave her to me," I said clearing my throat. "Back to these pictures."

Going over every photo, giving information on each one, I pointed to the image of Cheno's bitch. When I turned to face the people in the room, there was something about the way Dro was staring daggers into the female's face. A touch of recognition was on full display. He knew her ass some type of way and I had to call him out on it.

"You know her, don't you?" I asked him straight up.

Dro nodded. "They warned you about yo' bitch, I may as well inform y'all that I'm also sleeping with the opp. Unknowingly, of course. Charlie never told me what her nigga's name was, but I know for a fact they are no longer in contact. As a matter of fact, when he died, she became happier about being out and about with me. So, Cheese, I can vouch about the women in Cheno's life knowing he's not dead. I bet he hasn't come out of hiding to them as of yet. I mean, Cheno even said on the video that Tank was the first to know he was still alive. Like you, I want to deal with Charlie on my own terms."

I heard what Dro said, but there was no way he was going to deal with Charlie. He wasn't me and I called the fuckin' shots. There was no room for anymore hiccups in my organization.

"Negative. I want you to bring her ass here and hit my line when you have the package. I'll give you a couple days for fun, but she will bring Cheno out to play. That nigga loves that bitch. No matter what they've been through. Charlie is the key to get this shit started. Cheno wants to play body for body. Let the games begin."

97

I could tell Dro wasn't down with putting Charlie's head on the chopping block, but that was how shit had to be. Somebody had to be sacrificed and it wasn't going to be Honey. We congregated a while longer putting things into motion. Tank eventually joined the party giving his input every so often. I could tell he was still hot about our exchange by the way he kept eyeballing me. He was cool long as he didn't voice whatever he was thinking out loud. About an hour later, I adjourned the meeting. We were hitting our first target the next night. Cheno's trap was going up in smoke.

With that part of the business taken care of, it was time to see if Letty still had all that bass in her voice when I got to the crib. I did a dash on the e-way and didn't give a damn about the law. When I pulled up, the threats Letty spewed from her mouth played over in my mind. With Tank on bullshit, Cheno being alive, and Short losing his life, my anger ignited once again. Taking deep breaths, I tried my best to calm down. That was short lived because Letty came her confrontational ass outside making a scene for the neighbors.

"I thought you weren't going to be here, Cheese. What made you come back? This my muthafuckin' house and I don't want you on my property!"

Snatching the keys from the ignition, I got out of my whip and stormed up the stairs two at a time. Letty called herself blocking the entryway so I couldn't come into my own spot. Attempting to push past her, Letty reached up and slapped the shit out of me. Her actions caused me to react. Wrapping my hand around her neck, her feet dangled above the ground. Never missing a stride, I stepped over the threshold closing and locking the door with my free hand.

"Let me go, Cheese," she croaked out.

"Fuck you! Yo' ass lucky I didn't slap you back," I said throwing her onto the couch.

Letty bounced off the cushions and onto the floor. She jumped up charging at me while swinging her arms. I stood there while she punched me in the chest with tears falling from her eyes. Usually when Letty cried, I would console her. That day, I didn't care if she cried until she was dehydrated. She was definitely showing her true colors when she didn't get her way. Letty wasn't used to me telling her no so I knew damn well she wasn't going to accept me telling her it was over. Letty had already said how she really felt earlier during the phone call. I was hoping like hell she expressed herself more.

"I hate you!" she wailed as she continued to throw punches. "You going to jail just like yo' bitch did back in the day. If I can't be with you, she can't either. Let them niggas behind them walls suck yo' dick for a few years. Maybe you would learn to appreciate a woman that loves the fuck out of you."

I laughed as she screamed out in a demonic rage. Letty was shocked I didn't feed into her bullshit and took the verbal banter to another level. She stepped back with an evil look in her eye and I just waited for whatever would come out of her mouth. No matter what it was wouldn't change the fact she had to go. Yeah, her ungrateful ass was getting out of my shit. I'd be a fool to allow her to stay after threatening to have me locked the fuck up.

"It's all good. You not even worth me crying over. There's other muthafuckas out there who would love to get between my legs. You not the only nigga with good dick," she smirked. "I know that for sure because I've been bouncing on a dick for a few months anyway. Since you didn't want to fuck me, somebody had to make this pussy cum."

My head whipped in her direction and she slowly made her way toward the stairs. Letty looked like she was staring at a ghost. She turned to run up the steps and I reached her before she could get to the top. Punching her in the back of the head, she fell forward hitting her head on the carpeted stair. I choked her ass from behind and squeezed with all my might. *I've been bouncing on a dick for a few months anyway. I'm going to tell the Feds about your organization. I heard you had something to do with her cousin getting killed.*

Letty's words sounded in my ears causing me to grasp her neck tighter. All the shit she said was violation shots and grounds for her snake ass to take her last breath. I was willing to still take care of her and even let her stay in my house. But the bitch decided to open her dick suckers to say the wrong shit to the right nigga. If she was actually fuckin' somebody else, the muthafucka could've made sure her goofy-ass was straight. There was always life after a breakup. Letty just wasn't going to live to see what it was about.

Letty's body went limp, piss ran down the leg of the jeans she wore, and a foul smell of feces filled the air. I let her go then stepped over her body to climb the rest of the steps to my bedroom. I'd killed the woman who I had grown to love and I didn't feel bad about it. Now, there was nothing standing in the way of me giving Honey the love and attention she deserved.

Chapter 10

Breeze

"We could've gone to the mall. Why do you want to shop on Michigan Avenue?"

Honey was about to get smacked for acting like a broke bitch. Ignoring her, I continued to drive throughout the congested downtown traffic. Honey tapped my shoulder like an irritating toddler. For a quick second I regretted calling her to accompany me to shop. The only reason she was with me was because Taz didn't want to get her ass out of bed. It was cool because I planned to buy my baby a few things anyway. Dealing with Honey and her nagging was something I was going to deaden before it had a chance to go any deeper.

"Cuz, I swear you aggy as fuck right now. To answer your question, there's a couple of stores that want my attention. Plus, I can afford to shop with the mayonnaise people. You can, too, just in case you didn't know." I laughed at her then stopped abruptly.

The truck ahead caught my attention. Actually, it was the license plate. *Tank16* was clear as day. My trigger finger started twitching. There weren't many Tanks in the city that I knew of, and Cheese's cousin came to mind. I'd been hoping and wishing I would see the nigga out and about. The day may have finally come. Forgetting about the reason I was downtown, tailing the truck became my prime focus.

My mouth watered for revenge after what happened to my brother.

"What's wrong?" Honey asked.

"You see that?" I asked pointing at the truck.

"I'm lost," she admitted.

The Range made a right turn. I did the same. In the process, I hit the button on my key fob, opening the secret compartment. As I reached inside for my bitch, Honey was digging in her purse. Stay ready so you won't have to get ready. My adrenaline was through the roof. Knowing I had the opportunity to split Tank's wig made my nipples hard.

"Read the license plate on the Range."

"I know you fuckin' lying! Today is our lucky day," Honey said excitedly. "Tank was my nigga back in the day, but he fucked up stealing then putting a hit out on Cheno. There's no love in street beef. He's about to get bodied by a couple of Street Princesses." Honey held her fist out for a pound and I looked at her like she had shit on her hand.

"Nah, you can own that prissy shit. I'm a muthafuckin' gangsta."

"Why you gotta act like you not a woman?" Honey rolled her eyes.

"Because I identify as a nigga! Act like you know and stop insulting my manhood." I laughed.

Honey waved me off. "What are we going to do to him?"

"Wait until he pulls over then go with the flow."

Following the truck for another five minutes, it entered a parking garage on Ontario Street. I got madder because Tank took me out of my way. He was going to feel my wrath for sure. It would be worth the time wasted in the end because I was definitely going to shop 'til I dropped to celebrate his demise. The truck pulled into an empty spot and I lucked up on one directly behind.

"We gotta make this quick and easy. You take the right, I got the left," I explained, screwing the silencer onto my tool.

"Let's get it," Honey said opening her door slowly.

There was no movement from the truck. Music could be heard coming from the interior. I crept lowly to the driver's door, gripping the handle firmly before snatching it open. The female's head whipped in my direction and the color drained from her face. Tears welled in her eyes as she stared into the barrel of my Glock.

"Don't fuckin' move." I snarled. I was pissed to see a couple of females and not Tank's pussy ass.

"I have five hundred dollars, this watch…"

"Shut yo' ass up! Ain't nobody trying to rob yo' ass! Where's Tank? That's all I want to know. It would be in your best interest not to lie."

"I left him at his house in…Oak Park. I can give you the address. Just let me go. I don't have nothing to do with whatever he has going on. To be honest, I just met the nigga at the fest yesterday."

Honey had her gun trained on the female in the passenger seat, but her focus was on the driver. The deadly glare she shot her way didn't go unnoticed to me. Honey collared ol' girl, manhandling her like a ragdoll. She walked around the back of the truck motioning me to switch places. I had no clue what was going on in Honey's head but it didn't take long to find out.

"Well, well, well. Look what we have here," Honey taunted with her gun trained on the bitch. "Danielle, what brings you to my city?"

Danielle did a double take then scowled at my cousin. There was a lot of malice between the two. It couldn't be denied there were unresolved issues which was going to get settled that day.

Danielle smirked, licking her lips. "Put the gun down. You ain't shit without it."

Honey nodded, stepping away from the truck. I kept my eye on Danielle in case she tried to be slick and took my cousin out. A talk would be had soon as this was over because Honey subjected herself to harm. There was a small delay in her movement, but eventually, Danielle exited the vehicle. Honey handed me her weapon before squaring up. I was still out of the loop about how Honey knew the bitch. I couldn't wait to hear the back story. In a flash, Danielle ran up and was knocked on her ass. She jumped to her feet like a Power Ranger.

"Bitch, I told you I was gon' get at yo ass, soon as I got out. They couldn't hold me for twelve since I gave them my best behavior. But here we are. Let's do this."

Danielle got off two good punches, staggering Honey a few steps back. The hits didn't faze her at all. I peeped what my cousin was doing and proudly watched the showdown. Honey allowed Danielle to assault her best she could then hit her with a quick uppercut landing a punch directly under the chin. Danielle fell backwards, hitting her head hard on the concrete bumper block. A one hitter quitter and the squabble was over. Danielle laid motionless on the ground.

"You fuckin' killed her!" Danielle's friend screamed, taking off running.

I ran after her and hit her ass in the back of the head with the butt of my pistol, knocking her ass out cold. I scooped her up in one motion then carried her back to the truck. As I opened the back door, the bitch started moaning. "I got some rope in my trunk. Get that shit, pronto!"

Doing as I asked, Honey came back within seconds. Tying ol' girl's legs and arms, I stretched her across the backseat. Danielle was still lying in the same position. Honey had either caused head trauma or actually killed the bitch. That was my least concern because we had to go. Running to my car, I pulled it beside Danielle's body and popped the trunk. After dumping the body inside, I went back to the truck and grabbed the other female then tossed her ass on top of her friend before slamming the trunk. Honey was already at the truck, getting all of their personal items. I took a towel from my backseat and wiped down everything in the truck before snatching the keys from the ignition.

"We gotta get the fuck outta here," I said jumping behind the wheel of my whip.

Honey jumped in beside me and I took off. My first instinct was to call Pearl so she could have the cameras wiped from the garage. I didn't need this shit coming back on us. I hit Pearl's contact; the phone rang but she didn't pick up. I tried a second time getting the same result. There was a gut feeling deep in my soul something wasn't right. Dialing up Cheno, he didn't answer the first time and my heart started beating wildly in my chest. Not wanting to think the worst, I took a couple breaths before trying my brother again.

He answered. "What's up, sis?"

"Have you talked to Granny Pearl? I called her twice and she didn't answer."

Cheno was quiet for a minute then asked, "What you need? Maybe I can help you out."

"I need her to get hold of her people to wipe some cameras for me."

Breaking down what transpired best I could over the phone, Cheno told me to hold on. I could hear him talking to someone in the background before he came back on the line. My phone chimed with a text but I ignored it until I finished talking to Cheno.

"I just sent you an address. Get there fast as you can without getting yo' ass pulled over by the pigs. In other words, drive like you got some sense, Breeze. Scony is going to meet you to take care of the problem. G is going to get his people to erase the footage. I love you, sis. I'll see you in a minute."

Heading to the expressway, me and Honey rode in silence. After a while I couldn't take being in the car without a word being spoken. I took the time it would take to arrive at our destination to pick her brain on her involvement with Danielle.

"Honey, how do you know Danielle?" I asked, taking my eyes off the road briefly.

"Danielle was in the halfway house with me in Seattle. We had so many altercations living in that raggedy muthafucka. I whooped her ass right before I came home, and she threatened to see me once she was free. Danielle is from Detroit. I never thought I'd see her again because she knew nothing about me nor where to find me. Coming face to face with her was pure coincidental. But I told her not to fuck with me. Now look what happened to her stupid ass."

"Damn. You did what you had to do, Honey. I don't want you to feel bad about killing her. She brought that on herself."

"Who said I felt bad? Danielle thought she was the big, bad wolf and I blew that bitch house down. She won't be able to fuck with nobody else. We followed that truck to get at Tank and I still caught a body. It's a win for me."

Honey chuckled causing me to glance her way. She sat back without a care and the shit made me see her in different light. There wasn't a doubt in my mind she didn't body a few bitches while locked up. Her hardened demeanor told a fraction of the story. The way Honey tried her best to be the negotiator for conflicts made me believe she was just fighting not to go back to that part of her life.

We rode the rest of the way listening to the radio. When I pulled up to the address Cheno sent to my phone, there was a Benz parked out front. Scony exited the vehicle then walked toward the building. He entered and a door rose immediately. Motioning for me to pull my car inside, Scony stepped to the side.

"Welcome to the Dungeon," he said as I got out of my whip. Scony hit a button to lower the door then walked to the rear of my car. "Pop the trunk so I can see what we got here."

I hit the trunk release button on my key fob then grabbed a blunt. After all the shit we went through, I didn't have the urge to smoke until that moment. Inhaling, I blew the gas out through my nose then hit it again.

"I thought you said one of these hoes were dead."

Me and Honey walked to the trunk to see what Scony was talking about. Sure enough, Danielle was lying motionless while looking up at us. Her friend was flopping around on top of her like a fish out of water, but Danielle didn't flinch at all.

"What did y'all do to me?" Danielle cried. "I can't feel anything from my neck down."

"You did this shit to yourself. That's the least of your worries though," Honey spat.

Scony left the room and when he returned, he pulled a steel table on wheels in our direction. Once he was back at the trunk of the car, he grabbed Danielle and tossed her on the table. The average person would've cried out in pain but not her. She wasn't lying about not being able to feel anything. Scony wasted no time getting the other female out of my whip. He placed her body atop Danielle's and pushed the table through the building. We passed many closed doors and I took everything in. We entered a room and it was set up like a crematorium. Opening the metal lid to the equipment, he pulled out a metal tray which extended a good length into the room.

Danielle's friend saw what was going on and started yelling. "You not about to put me in there! Untie me, bitch ass nigga!"

"Who gon' stop me," Scony asked sarcastically. "I was going to give you a chance to plead yo' case with the possibility of walking out of here, but yo' mouth wrote a check yo' ass can't cash."

Scony scooped her up in his arms and she tried to bite his chest. Instead of trying to stop her, he continued on with what he was doing. She started screaming for help repeatedly loud as she could. Scony laid her down on the tray then pushed it inside the machine. He turned his back to retrieve

Danielle. Her screams grew louder with every second that ticked away.

"Shut the fuck up!"

"Breeze, let her ass do all the hollering she wants. Nobody will hear her cries. It's the last thing she will ever hear herself do in this lifetime," Scony said bending down to pick Danielle up.

"I want to help with this one," Honey said stopping his movements.

Scony nodded as he moved to the end of the table to grasp Danielle's legs. Honey held her arms tightly, and at the count of three, both of them lifted her to a second machine and did the same as he had done with her friend.

Danielle opened her mouth as a lone tear cascaded out of her eye into her ear. "I'll see you in hell, bitch. Tank has plans to end your fuckin' life. I'll be waiting so we can finish this shit."

"Nah, you'll be waiting to get your ass beat. That's all I have for you. Until we meet again, keep the fire burning." Honey chuckled before pushing the tray inside.

Scony stood in wait as Honey stood beside the button that would start the process. Both women were begging and pleading not to be killed. Their cries weren't as loud since the doors were closed and locked, but could still be heard, nonetheless.

"Push the button so we can get the fuck out of here. The sound of them being burned alive is not going to be pleasant. Not to mention the smell of burning flesh will be embedded in your nostrils for weeks on end."

Both Scony and Honey pushed the buttons and the fire ignited with a slight click. Scony led us out of the room then closed the door behind him. No one said anything as we walked toward the front of the warehouse. Approaching my whip, I paused before getting inside.

"Thanks for looking out. I appreciate that. Tell G I owe him one."

"Tell him yo'self. I need you to trail me to the University of Chicago hospital. You will be filled in upon our arrival. For now, I have to lock up so we can be on our way."

"Why are we going to the hospital?" I asked.

"Again, you will be given all the details when we get there. You wasting time, Breeze," Scony replied calmly.

Taking what he said as my cue to leave the building, I got into my car and waited for Scony to raise the door. Once I backed out, I picked up Danielle's phone to search for Tank's location. Finding the information I needed, I used a small screwdriver to remove the Sim card from the device. Danielle had an older model iPhone and that was luck for me. I did a factory reset and put the phone in the armrest so I could throw it away at a later time. There was no way her disappearance would come back to me. The bitch was wiped from the face of the earth never to be heard from again.

***

"I wonder why we are meeting Cheno back in this hospital," Honey said as we walked slowly to the entrance. "Do you think he's having complications from being shot?"

"No. Cheno sounded fine when I talked to him. Something else is going on because he didn't mention even being here and Scony is being real hush about it."

We entered and the first person I saw was my brother. The look on his face told me something serious took place. His light skin had a tint of red to it and the worried lines couldn't be missed. G was pacing back and forth in front of the double doors leading to the back, and his wife was watching him like a hawk. It had been a minute since I'd seen Nova. I held off going to speak to her for the time being because I needed to holla at Cheno first.

"What's going on?" I asked, taking a seat next to him.

Running his hand down his face, Cheno's chin fell to his chin. When he looked up, I could see the hurt in his eyes.

109

The last time I saw my brother in that state, my mama was on her deathbed.

"Somebody shot Pearl. It's not looking good, Breeze. The doctor came out to give us an update about twenty minutes ago. They had to put her on life support. She may not make it."

"How the fuck did that happen?"

"As bad as I want to blame Ease, I can't."

"What do he have to do with granny getting shot? I'm confused." I asked adjusting myself in the chair.

"I met him over there during the time the trap was hit and specifically told him not to go back. When me, G, and Scony arrived, his ass was sitting on the couch like he lived there. I whooped that nigga's ass. Granny was upset and went into the kitchen. Next then we knew, she was on the floor with a gunshot to the chest."

I sat quietly taking in everything Cheno was saying but I couldn't get the fact of Pearl getting shot out of my mind. The doctor's said she may not make it and I wasn't trying to hear none of that shit. I sent a quick prayer up for Pearl. It wasn't her time to go. There was so much more life for her to live.

"I want to end Ease's life so bad," Cheno was saying.

"You can't blame Ease for what happened, bro. Somebody could've followed him or y'all. We would never know for sure. What I can say is this, it was Cheese and his fucked-up ass cousin who was behind the shit. Pearl just so happened to get caught in the crossfire. We have to stay focused on the problem because granny has to fight and we can't help her. However, we can go fuck some shit up with those muthafuckas."

"You're right. We killed one of Tank's people today and I sent him the footage. This shit is all my fault. I should've waited until I had the women in my life protected first."

"Cheno, you can't blame yourself, either. Pearl had all the protection she could've had at her home when this shit went down. It's a good thing too because she probably would have died if she was alone. Shake this off for the time being. Granny is strong."

I told him to shake it off to convince myself Pearl was going to walk out of the hospital to curse us out another day. Nova walked over hugging me tight. Standing to my feet, I moved toward the automatic doors and she followed. My nerves were getting the best of me and I needed to smoke to get myself under control.

"Breeze, what's going on?" Nova asked. "Grant won't tell me much of anything."

"Nova, there's a lot. You and I both know G is not going to give you the information you're hoping to hear. The less you know the better. How are the kids? I asked changing the subject.

"Don't do that, Bree. Fill me in!"

Shaking my head, I opened the door to my whip then sat down. Taking a blunt from the middle console and flamed up. "I won't tell you anything because there's reasons why your husband isn't revealing details to you. Once all this is over, I'm quite sure he will tell you everything you want to know. Until then, I think you will be safer not knowing." At that moment, Quell walked up on us. He glanced into my car then addressed me.

"Where's Honey?" he asked.

"She's inside. Is everything okay?"

"Nawl. I need to holla at her about this Cheese agreement. I think she should abort the mission and leave the get back to us. Shit is getting real and I can't sit back and allow something to happen to her."

"I understand where you're coming from with your concerns, but I don't think Honey is going to leave what she has started alone."

"We'll see about that," Quell said walking away in search of Honey.

Chapter 11

Honey

Seeing Danielle behind the wheel of Tank's truck brought my evil side to the surface. She talked a boatload of shit and had the audacity to say I was acting bad because of a gun. Handing that muthafucka off wasn't a thing for me. I'd cracked Danielle in her mouth and pushed her brain back too many times at the halfway house, so whooping her ass without interruptions were right up my alley. She got a couple hits in because I allowed her to get that shit off her chest. It didn't take long for me to chin check her ass sending her to the ground. What I didn't expect was the blow to kill her.

There was no remorse on my end. I put the bitch out of her misery. When we arrived at the Dungeon, I was surprised when Scony said the bitch was alive. Hearing Danielle say she couldn't feel anything from the neck down, let me know she was reaping what she had sown for years. Scony led us into a room that looked like a place to get rid of a body, I was excited in a way I'd never thought I could be. It was my pleasure to put her shit talking ass in that metal box. She was better off dead anyway. Life would've kicked her ass everyday she struggled to live with someone taking care of her. It would've been what I preferred, but at the same time she would have had the ability to send the law at me by running her mouth some more. I couldn't risk giving her the satisfaction.

I sat quietly as Cheno filled me in on what happened with Miss Pearl. He was telling me how he didn't want me to approach Cheese because he knew Cheno wasn't dead. My cousin was worried about me being killed behind his beef, but I wanted revenge. One thing I knew was Cheese wasn't going to hurt me. Turning my head toward the automatic doors the moment I heard them open; Quell stepped in. My man looked good in his black jogging suit and all black Nikes. The grim look he possessed took my focus off his appearance. He approached aggressively and I wasn't feeling it at all.

"What's up, Cheno? Honey, let me holla at you for a minute," he said walking back toward the doors. When he noticed I hadn't moved, he stopped in his tracks. "Not now, but right now, Honey."

"I know you ain't…"

"Just go see what he wants, Honey. Don't give these muthafuckas a show," Cheno said cutting me off.

Even though I didn't appreciate how he spoke to me, I got up and followed him out the building. Quell was pissed because he witnessed firsthand how Cheese was all under me at the fest. I asked him if he could handle it. He said yes. Now, he had a problem with it. Breeze watched as Quell led me across the parking lot to his vehicle. When he opened the driver door, I automatically went around to the passenger side and got in. Before he could get in good, I started going off.

"How dare you come at me the way you did! Who the fuck do you think you are, Quell?"

"First off all, lower yo' tone, ma," he said, running his hand down his face. "I'm not disrespecting you by far. If anything, I'm trying to protect you."

"Protect me from what?"

"Honey, I'm sure you're aware Cheno being alive has been revealed. Meaning, Cheese is aware. I want you to fall back on Cheese. Nothing good can come out of *you* going after him. Leave Cheese to us. It's not safe for you to be alone with him."

"Quell, I know Cheese better than he knows himself. I don't care what's going on between him and Cheno; he will not hurt me. I will play the role of not knowing Cheno is alive better than an Academy Award winner. Cheno too wants me to allow y'all to handle it, but I won't abort the mission. I've already agreed to meet up with Cheese later."

"Then cancel it! You made plans to meet with the muthafucka before Cheno sent the video to his cousin. Use yo' head, Honey! If you want to die, I'll make the shit happen. You are going on a suicide mission, and I won't give the okay. Shit is too hot for you to be out trying to sucker this nigga in. The gig is up! At this point, anybody can get it from both sides. It's time for you to listen to what I'm telling you."

Quell's tone had softened, and I could tell he was being compassionate as he could about the situation. Sitting back, I thought about what he and Cheno said and they were right. The love Cheese had for me could be pushed to the back burner since another one of his homies were murdered by the hands of Cheno. If they could shoot an elderly woman, there was no hope for what may be in store for me.

"Okay, Quell. I'll stop all communication with Cheese. Y'all better kill his ass viciously since I can't do what I wanted to him. He better hope Pearl pulls through. Is that all?" I asked.

"No, it's not all." He paused. "I'm not on no type of hater shit. Just to put it out there. I truly give a fuck what happens to you, Honey. My future is with you. I know you said a relationship is the last thing you want at this time, but that pussy says otherwise. It's me and you 'til the end. Are you willing to see where this could go?"

Quell and I had been tearing the bedroom up. We had no issues in the sex department. The both of us were using sexual pleasure as a way to keep our minds off what was really going on around us. I didn't know about being in a

114

relationship though. Things may not be the same once everything was over and done with. Hell, we didn't know how this would end. To make a commitment now would be crazy for either one of us.

"We will piggyback on this conversation at a later date. Can we please handle the business with Cheese and his crew, first?" I diverted the conversation to what I felt was more important.

Quell's expression indicated he wanted to say more but thought better of it. Instead, he nodded and opened the door to get out. He sat quietly before he spoke lowly. "Honey, I won't wait around forever. If this isn't what you want, be woman enough to tell me that my feelings are mine alone. I'm not the type of man who's going to chase, nor wait around for a female to choose me. I've already put it out there to you. Do whatever you feel is right. There's no pressure." With that, Quell got out of the car, leaving me sitting alone.

I had no doubt the feelings Quell confessed to me were real. Being a woman who was away from the outside world for a decade, I had a lot of making up to do on my own. Cheese may have fucked it up for everybody, to be honest. Settling down felt like a setup for disappointment. If I stayed alone, I couldn't be hurt by expectations. Quell expressed he wanted to be with me forever, but what would happen when he grew tired of being with the same woman? That was my fear. The door opening brought me out of my thoughts.

"You okay?" Breeze asked. "What happened?"

I nodded. "Yeah, I'm good. Quell and Cheno don't want me to go after Cheese. Both of them are worried about him doing something to me now that Cheno being alive is no longer a secret."

"I already know. They stated the same to me as well. In fact, they want me to talk to you about it because they think you're still going to reel Cheese in. By the look in your eyes, I agree with them."

Breeze had been more than my cousin since I touched down. She was more so my best friend. I'd never held my thoughts from her and didn't have plans to start. All of them were correct. I had no intentions of allowing Cheese to get away with the things he had done. Not only to Cheno, Free, and Miss Pearl, his ass had to pay for turning his back on me. I missed out on years of my life because of him. Cheese wouldn't be in the hate category with me had he been like he promised. He said fuck me, now it was fuck him.

"Breeze, I'm going to finish what I started. Cheese will die by my hands. Believe that. I will do as I said and leave the shit alone for a few days. In the meantime, I need your help."

Breeze sighed. "Honey, leave it alone. I think at this point, Cheese and his people are dangerous. I'm not saying you can't handle yourself, but you don't know the person he is today. You won't win this battle alone and I'm not going to help you kill yourself. Quell told me you said Cheese won't hurt you. I'm here to tell you, he will. It's either him or you and we both know he's not sacrificing himself. I won't be in the room when you try your hand with him."

"Are you going to help me or not?" I snapped.

"I don't give a fuck how mad you get! Listen to me, please. Stay away from Cheese."

"Since you not trying to hear me out, I'll tell you what I need you to do anyway. Find a way to get a sedative from Amari without Cheno finding out. However you get it is on you, but I need that syringe, pronto. I'm trusting you to keep this shit between us, Breeze. Don't disappoint me."

"Honey—"

"No, Breeze. I've told you what I expect. I'm done with it. Now, would you please take me home?"

"Honey, I have to stay to see what's going on with Pearl. Leaving right now is something I can't do."

"Drop me off at home and you can come back. I just want to go home so I can get my truck."

116

"What are you about to do, cousin?"

"Not what you may be thinking." I scoffed. "Today is the day I pay my mother a visit. She has a lot of explaining to do and there's no better time to confront it than the present."

"I will take you myself. You do not need to confront Vickie alone."

"Breeze, you are having a hard time listening. I don't want you to escort me to my mother's place of residence. She still resides in the same place I grew up. All I want you to do is take me to my vehicle. The first thing she will think is I'm trying to put on a show for you. Doing this alone is the best way to do this. I've put it on hold long enough."

"Would you promise to call if you need me?" Breeze all but begged.

"I promise. Now will you take me to my truck?"

"Yeah, come on. I'll shoot Cheno a message to contact me if there's a change with Pearl."

Exiting Quell's truck, I walked to Breeze's car quickly. What she had to do didn't concern me. My main objective was getting to my house fast as possible. Having a sit down with my mother would help ease some of the anger I had within me for the moment. Hopefully, she would act civilized and things wouldn't get too ugly.

I sat inside the Camero and snapped my seatbelt. Closing my eyes, I rested my head on the headrest to enjoy the ride. That was my way of saying I didn't want to talk about anything else and Breeze took heed in what I wanted. As I waited for her to pull out of the parking lot, Kevn Gates' *Big Gangsta* filled the void of silence for the ride. With her music of choice, I had to deal with all the thug shit that would play for the duration of the time.

Being shook out of my sleep was something I couldn't stand. "Whaaaaaat?"

"Wake yo' ass up, go in the house, and sleep that shit off. You too tired to go anywhere right now."

Glancing around I noticed we were parked in my driveway. Breeze was only informing me that we made it to our destination. I owed her a huge apology for snapping off on her.

"I'm sorry. I thought you were trying to wake me up to talk. I didn't realize we made it to the house already. As far as going to sleep, that's a negative. I've already told you what I was set out to do. I'll be in there long enough to take a shower then I'm right back out. Thanks for the ride. I'll talk to you later to tell you all about my visit."

Breeze popped the locks so I could get out. She waited patiently as I gathered my purse and phone before backing out. She drove off without a word. I didn't blame her at all. I wouldn't want to deal with myself another minute either if I was in her position. Unlocking the door to my home, I went inside and kicked my shoes off before heading straight to my bedroom. My phone was tossed on the bed, purse on the vanity, followed by my clothes hitting the floor. The next stop was the shower.

I went into the bathroom and flipped the light switch then headed across the room, turning on the water. The mirrors caught my image in the light, and I didn't like what stared back at me. My eyes had small bags under them, worried lines graced my forehead, my hair was disheveled, and the frown was the same as the one I possessed when I was locked up. It was a sad sight. My worries stemmed from what had to be done back at the Dungeon, the majority of it was the thought of going to visit my mother. I shook off the thoughts and took care of my skin before stepping under the steamy hot water.

As I lathered the loofah with Dove bodywash, the tears I tried hard to hold came flowing out, blending in with the water. My soul felt as if it was cleansing me of all the years I was forced to be strong because crying was a form of weakness behind that wall. For months I had to pretend to be a bad muthafucka until the shit became part of my reality.

Now, I was hard whenever the occasion rose. It was a matter of time before I turned into a deadly wolf.

Allowing the tears to flow freely, I finally got myself together in order to wash my body from head to toe several times then stepped out. Wrapped in a towel I went back into my bedroom and sat on the side of the bed. My mind drifted but before I could get lost in the past, my phone rang. I stretched to retrieve it and saw Cheese's name on the display. I wanted to ignore the call, but I couldn't.

"Hello."

"Honey, what's wrong?" Cheese asked with concern.

"Nothing. What's up?" Clearing my throat, I shook my head because I could hear the animosity towards him in my own voice and clearing that shit up was a must. "How are you?"

Cheese didn't say anything at first. "Um, I was calling to check on you since I hadn't heard from you today. You sure everything is good? It seems like something is on your mind. Wanna talk about it?"

"There is something on my mind but it's nothing for you to worry about. In fact, I'm going to visit my mother after all these years, and I just don't know what to expect. Once I get through this process, no matter what, I'll be okay. How's things with you?"

"Everything is good over here." Cheese responded. "I told Letty about us after she saw us at the fest. She was upset when I broke things off with her. Letty also confessed to dealing with a nigga behind my back. You don't know how relieved I was when she said that shit out of anger. It made it much easier for me to get her out of the house. I mean, I had to get the law involved, but the shit worked out in my favor. While she was packing, I walked in on her telling the muthafucka what took place and supposedly, he bought her a plane ticket to California."

I rubbed cocoa butter on my legs listening to Cheese tell me about the end of his relationship. Little did he know, I

119

didn't give a fuck what happened between him and that bitch. The only reason I told him to leave Letty was so he would think he had a chance with me. Cheese's days were numbered.

"Letty isn't going to leave the lifestyle you provided that easily. She'll be back. Trust. Long as she stays away from me, she will be safe," I expressed walking to my closet.

Choosing a pair of denim jeans and a Meesha's Pen Spit Fire t-shirt, I grinned as Cheese spoke to me from his heart. It was funny because he had ten years to lie. I would have never known he was doing so back then. Now, I could see through his bullshit like a one-way mirror in an interrogation room. At that point, I had turned into a snake in the grass gearing up to attack. The voices in my head started pleading for me not to react on my deadly thoughts and just leave it alone. Thus far it wasn't clicking.

"Honey, did you hear me?"

"Um, no. I was pulling a shirt over my head," I lied. "Repeat what you said."

"I asked if you would be willing to spend the night at my place tonight."

"So Letty can walk in and kill me in my sleep. I don't think so, La'Darrius. You tried it though."

Cheese huffed loudly into the phone. He was the last one to be irritated by anything I had to say. I didn't believe Letty left Chicago and he already wanted me to come to the home they shared. He had me fucked up. Gathering his thoughts, Cheese tried his hand once again.

"There's so much we need to make up for. Time has passed us by throughout the years and I want to show you how much I regret not being there during your trying times."

This muthafucka impressed the hell out of me with his French skills. Cheese threw the "we" word around as if it was valid in the situation. *We* didn't need to do shit. He was making my decision so much easier and harder on himself the more he talked. My trying times were fine without him.

The city will be fine without him as well once I made his ass disappear.

"I hear what you're saying. I would love to spend time with you but I won't say yes or no about tonight. It depends on the outcome of the visit to my mom's. My mood may not be the best and I wouldn't want to bring my sour mood your way." I paused. "Since we are starting over, I want to be able to ride your dick with you in mind, not the bullshit I have going on in my life."

"Is that right?"

If I remembered correctly, Cheese was sitting back with a smile plastered on his face while licking his lips, running his hand over his beard, and stroking his dick. He was just that freaky. Old habits never died.

"Girl, you got my shit on brick," he chortled proving me right. "Well, get yo' mind right and go easy on yo' bitch ass mama. Don't forget I owe her one from years ago. The ticket will never expire. Baby—"

Soon as he called me baby I cringed and hung up. Throwing the phone on the bed, I continued to dress. The conversation with Cheese was long forgotten as I grabbed everything I would need to leave the house. The shoes I planned to wear was downstairs by the door. After retrieving my phone, I turned off the light then left the room. Putting on my shoes and getting my waist length leather from the hall closet, I took a deep breath then exited the house as I prepared myself for what was about to take place with my mama.

Mama's Song by Carrie Underwood came on as I cruised on the expressway. Listening to the lyrics, I wished there was a moment I wanted my mama to worry about my wellbeing. She didn't even attempt to find me after putting me out in the middle of winter. Nor did she make one trip to the County after I was booked. So, worrying about me was the last thing she wanted to do because she didn't give a damn.

As I pulled into a space in front of the house I was raised, my anxiety level rose. Images of James watching my every move any time I stepped out of my room played before me as if I was back in the moment. My mama accusing me of seducing his perverted ass rang in my ears. My hands started shaking, heart was beating fifty beats a minute, and sweat beaded on my forehead. I reached for the gear shift. My inner child almost caused me to peel away. The bitch who had been through hell and back wasn't having that shit.

I pushed the button to kill the engine, then jumped out before I could change my mind about going forward. Halfway up the walkway, the door opened and the devil's daughter stood with her horns standing at attention. The scowl on her face told me she was ready for a battle even though I came in peace.

"Why are you at my fuckin' house?" She barked. "When you left, I never went looking for you, never put out a report, or none of that shit. That alone should've told you I didn't want you coming back here."

"Ma—"

"I'm not ma, mama, mommy, or mom. My name is Victoria Love. Put some respect on my name!"

The way she snapped hurt my feelings but I didn't dare let it show. Victoria was mad but if she thought I wasn't, she was going to fuck around and find out. My mama said a mouthful. I heard her loud and clear. The way she fumbled with the pocket of her robe made me a little uneasy. When Victoria realized I was focused on her hand, she eased it out slowly.

"Ma… I mean, Victoria. I don't recall leaving the place I called home. I remember like it was yesterday and you put me out in the cold. That's neither here nor there though. I didn't come here to fight with you. I want to sit down and have a heart to heart. That's all. Being that you never liked the neighbors in your business, can we go inside?"

Victoria backed up toward the door slowly never taking her eyes off me. She looked me up and down with her nose turned up before ushering me inside. Peeking outside briefly, Victoria came inside and slammed the door with force. Something else must've pissed her off more than she already was. It didn't take long to find out.

"Bitch, you came here to throw your money in my face? How the hell are you driving that expensive ass truck and you just got out of prison? I guess being locked away like a dog taught you nothing, huh?"

"Bitch?" I said staring at her like the crazy muthafucka she appeared to be. "You're assuming I was guilty of the charges against me. Well, I'm here to inform you, I wasn't. The apple doesn't fall far from the tree because I was in there behind a man. One I had so much loyalty for, I did a bid for him. Stupid, right?" I smirked. "For your information, prison taught me more than you ever have. It's not my fault you never did much of anything for me. Your *man* more of a child to you that you forgot you actually had one."

I was mad as hell and there was nobody around to stop me from hurting her feelings. It was free game and Victoria was going to feel the wrath of all I had stored inside. She wanted to fight, then it was time to rumble. She opened the door to get all the venom I was about to spit on her. I was putting it all on the table and hopefully, she would be woman enough to admit she failed me.

"There were plenty of days I was in this bitch while you were at work. James would lock the refrigerator so I couldn't eat. Any time I tried to tell you about the hell I was going through, your pick me ass dismissed it. Let's not forget when he was touching me!"

"Honey—"

"No! I stood listening while you tried your best to belittle me with lies. Now, I'm about to make you see what it feels like to hear your truth. I'm giving it to you straight with no chaser and you will give me the same courtesy by standing there with your fuckin' mouth closed."

I closed my eyes for a couple seconds. What I was about to say had my chest tightening because I had to relive the shit. It was something I had to do in order to finally put the past behind me. Whether Victoria had empathy for me or not, it would be the last day she would be in my presence. I had no plans of ever coming back to attempt reconciling with her. She didn't want to be my mother, cool. I honestly didn't want to be known as her daughter another day.

"James had been watching me from the moment I started developing into a young woman. He would watch me from the doorway of my room minutes after you left the house. I would wake up and your man would be standing in the doorway watching me sleep. On more than one occasion, he ate my pussy while I slept. Those were the times you would find me at Letty's house because I had to fight to keep him off me. James knew you wouldn't believe me and he was right.

The flashbacks were hitting me left and right all while I was locked away in an eight by ten cell! I wanted your man. Humph. That muthafucka wanted me! Then got mad every time I fought his ass off. Lucky is what I called myself because he never got the opportunity to actually sample the goods. If he had, his sick ass probably would've killed you in order to hold me captive in peace. All I want to know is, why didn't you believe me?" I asked.

Victoria stood open mouthed as I told her the things James had done. She could act surprised all she wanted. Her musty ass knew what the fuck I'd revealed had already been told years prior. My egg donor should've had the same reaction and more back then. The bitch was guilty as Diddy without the drugs and the parties.

"Stop acting like this is all new to you! I told you what he was doing to me and you called me a liar!" I yelled.

Anger replaced the shocked expression on her face. Victoria started walking up on me as if she was set out to do harm. I held my hands out to stop her. She smacked them down. The respect I had for her being my mother dwindled rapidly. At that point I saw her as a bitch on the street. If it came to it, I would react accordingly.

"How dare you stand in my house and disrespect me! James was my man. May God rest his soul. He did none of the things you are accusing him of. He was the only man who stepped up to be a father to your ungrateful ass because your deadbeat daddy was never there. So, for you to lie on him is a damn shame, Honey."

I laughed because dear mama was defending the piece of shit harder than before. Shaking my head, I stepped back to put some distance between us. Victoria had spit foam forming in the corners of her mouth looking like a vicious pitbull.

"Is it really a lie, Vicky? A lie changes every time It's told. Everything I've said about James is accurate and pretty much the same. You want me to be a liar to make me look bad instead of yourself. You ain't shit, just like your man wasn't shit. May that nigga rest in piss! To think that nasty muthafucka was any better than my daddy lets me know you lost your marbles a long time ago. My sperm donor wasn't shit but it didn't affect me because I never knew him! Your precious James did all I said he did and that's the reason he's no longer breathing."

"What did you say?"

At that moment, my phone rang and I ignored that shit. Whoever it was had to wait because Victoria had the look of death in her eyes after the revelation of what actually happened to James was revealed. I wanted her to try something so I could reunite her with that pussy-ass muthafucka. For the meantime staying focused was high on my hierarchy because her hand was back in the left pocket of her robe. Reaching into my purse, I glanced at my phone before silencing it again. Breeze was blowing up my shit and it irked my nerves. It wasn't the time for a casual convo and she knew where I was and what I had to do. The phone rang again. I placed one of my earbuds in my ear then answered the call.

"Yeah."

"Honey, I'm sitting across the street from your mama's house. I know you didn't want me to accompany you over here but I had a bad feeling about you being alone. I'm glad I followed my first mind to come watch your back from afar."

"If you think I'm about to forget what you just said, you out of your fuckin' mind! Get off the got damn phone and repeat that shit!"

Victoria's shouting took my attention away from what Breeze was saying. The way my words rattled her ass made me feel good inside.

"Don't hang up!" Breeze said sternly. "Hear me and hear me good. I don't know what's going on in there but y'all got company outside the door. Cheno and Quell should be here any minute to pick up the trash."

The door opened and in walked Larisa. She walked in slowly with a sly smile on her face. Closing the door behind her, Larisa hugged my mama as if they were well acquainted with one another. Their affiliation wasn't important to me because I didn't give a damn about the connection at all. What I was giddy about was finally laying eyes on the bitch who set my cousin up to be killed.

"Well, what do we have here?" Larisa sang. "You finally decided to come see Vicky after all this time. You have your nerve."

"You worried about the wrong shit, bitch." I sneered pulling my gun aiming it directly at Larisa. "If I'd known coming here would put me in the same space as you, I would've been here with bells on. You know how to hide well. How's life without Lord?"

126

Victoria swiftly brought her hand out of the mysterious pocket and as I thought, she was armed as well. Her shaky hand scared me more than the weapon itself because it was an indication that she was not comfortable shooting it. The door crept open and Breeze appeared behind both Victoria and Larisa. Avoiding the shift in my eyes, I did my best not to bring attention to the doorway.

"You thought you were the only one with a gun, Honey," Victoria laughed. "I brought you in this world, and I can take your tarnished ass out. You fucked up telling me you had James killed. That was the wrong move."

"And you pulling that muthafucka with delayed reaction was yours," Breeze said digging the barrel of her gun in the back of Victoria's head.

Victoria didn't flinch and I watched as her trigger finger moved slightly. There was no way I was about to stand there and let her get the shot off to end my life. Faster than Quick Draw McGraw, I hit her ass in the chest with a single shot. Honor thy father and thy mother my ass. Shit has been going well for me without the bitch all these years and I would continue to live a long and prosperous life thereafter. I watched as my mother took her last breath and didn't drop a tear behind it.

Breeze turned to Larisa with a menacing stare. Fear was written all over the hoe's face and at that moment Larisa knew she had fucked up. She couldn't take her eyes off Victoria's lifeless body as she backed away slowly. Her movements halted when the door opened once again and Cheno showed himself. Larisa was petrified. Pissed pooled around her feet and the tears ran down her face like water.

"Ch-Ch-Cheno," she stuttered.

"You missed me, huh?" He asked closing the door. "We'll catch up in a minute. Honey, go open the back door for the cleanup crew. I knew we were going to need their services."

Cheno looked down at Victoria's body and shook his head. "Damn, I didn't think you would actually take the heartless bitch out the first time around, Cuz," he chortled.

"I didn't intend to but I had to stay ready so I didn't have to get ready. The shit paid off."

Walking to let Cheno's people in, I opened the door and Quell gathered me in his arms. The workers walked around us continuing inside. My emotions were all over the place and at that point, I couldn't be strong another minute. Killing my mama was the hardest thing I'd ever had to do. Hell, spending ten years in the pen didn't have shit on what I had just gone through in less than an hour.

"Are you okay?"

I couldn't do anything other than shake my head no. My voice was caught in my throat making it impossible for me to speak. Instead, I sobbed in his chest. All the hurt bottled up came flowing out freely. I felt like a punk but it was overdue. With everything I had been through since I came home, I was ready to live my best life and enjoy it to the fullest.

"Baby, I got you. It's almost over. I promise. Where is your mama?" Quell asked wiping the tears away.

"She's lying on the floor in the living room. I didn't have a choice. She was going to kill me."

The tears ran nonstop with the realization of what I had done. Victoria wasn't the best mama one could have but I didn't want to be the one to take her off the face of the earth. What I really wished on her life was for that bitch named Karma to whoop her ass to the point she would take herself out.

"You did what you had to do. It was either you or her. You made the right decision because I wouldn't be shit without you. It's me and you against the world, Honey. Life as you knew it won't matter once I'm finished showing you what living is all about. Get out of here so I can clean up your mess."

Quell kissed me passionately before guiding me back inside. Victoria's body was covered with a sheet and Cheno's workers were picking her up to take her who knew where. Preventing them from leaving, I had one last request.

"Would y'all take her somewhere she will be found? Make sure you get the bullet fragments out. I want to be able to at least give her a proper funeral."

"I got you, ma," one of the guys said after getting confirmation from Cheno.

Larisa was standing like a scared nun in a strip club. I didn't know what they were going to do with her and frankly I didn't give a fuck. As I walked across the room, the bitch had the nerve to suck her teeth. So, I punched her in her shit and hoped like hell she swallowed them. With her hand over her mouth, I stood in front of her.

"Bitch, I hope you die slow. If it was up to me, I would spend an entire day dissecting yo' ass like a science project. I'm gon' let Cheno deal with you though. I'm quite sure his torture is going to be one hundred percent worse. You fucked with the wrong one at the right time. Good luck with that."

I left my mother's house and the memories it held. Soon as I received the call about Victoria's passing, it would be the last time I stepped foot in that muthafucka. On one hand I was hurt, but on the other I could smile because my shoulders were no longer carrying the burden of hurt from my mother not protecting me from evil.

Chapter 12

Cheno

I watched as Honey and Breeze left the house with a little pity. Having to kill your own mother would force anybody to have a mental breakdown. My cousin was no different and I was going to keep a watchful eye on her to make sure she was good. I didn't know what I was going to do to Larisa at this point. However, the bitch had to go. Her voice brought me out of my thoughts and I wanted to choke the fuck out of her.

"Cheno, I'm sorry for what happened to you. I didn't know they were going to shoot you."

My head whipped into her direction causing her to snap her mouth closed. I got a good look at her two front teeth. Honey did a number on her because they were tilted at an odd angle. She didn't have to worry about cosmetic surgery. I would make sure she was gummy than a muthafucka once I finished with her. Honey had put an idea of torture in my head and I was going to run with that shit.

"You knew exactly what them niggas was gon' do. That's why you helped set the shit up. I lost my woman behind yo' conniving ass, almost lost my life, and now you want to stand in my face and lie as if it was gon' help you. Nah, ma. You should've been satisfied with wrapping yo' lips around my dick instead of flapping them bitches by giving a muthafucka a play by play on how to get at me."

"Cheno—"

"Say my name one more fuckin' time and I will snatch yo' tongue out and shove it up yo' ass!" I sneered grabbing her by the throat. "We gon' walk out of this muthafucka and you gon' act like I'm taking yo' funky ass to ride this dick. Is that understood?" She bobbed her head up and down because I'd cut off her ability to speak.

"When I let you go, give me yo' muthafuckin keys. You won't be needing them after today. I want yo' phone too."

Larisa handed over her belongings. I looked down to pay attention to her movements and noticed she had liquid at her feet. Scrunching up my nose, I took a step back.

"Tell me that's not piss on that floor."

"It wasn't done on purpose. You scared the piss out of me when you walked through the door. How else was I supposed to react? I was told you died and even thought about going to your memorial."

"You wasn't going to do no shit like that. The wolves would've eaten you alive. My peeps stand ten toes down behind me. Why do you think you're in my presence now?"

I laughed loudly as I handed her the keys to her car. The confusion on her face let me know she was waiting for me to tell her she could leave. That wasn't happening.

"I thought you were going to do something with my car. Why did you give me the keys back?" She sassed. "Let me find out you put on a show like you were going to hurt me."

"Don't flatter yo'self. You gon' drive us to our next destination in your ride because yo' pissy ass won't be fuckin' up my seats. Sorry to disappoint yo' bird brain ass."

Shit was no longer comical and my words wiped the smile right off her cocky lips. Larisa was going to get hurt. It just wasn't going to be in the manner she was accustomed to when fuckin' with me. She stomped toward the door and I yanked her back by the sleek ponytail she wore.

"Oww!" She yelped.

"Did I tell you to move? I didn't think so. You will drive as if you are trying to pass Drivers Ed. If you bring any attention to your vehicle, I will kill you then and there. Do you understand?" Larisa nodded yes, but that wasn't good enough for me. I needed her to verbally respond.

"I can't hear you!"

"Yes, I understand," she said with a roll of her eyes. "Why won't you just shoot me now?"

"That's too easy. Your time to depart this life will come soon. Be patient, bitch," I said right before I hit Quell on his jack.

"Yo! We were just about to pull out of the alley."

"Hold up. There's been a change of plans. I need one of you niggas to drive my whip. This bitch pissed on herself and she can't get in my shit like that. So, we taking her car."

"Aye, go ahead and do that. Hit brah up when it's done." Quell had to be talking to my workers. He then started talking low to his niggas. "Come around front and y'all follow behind Cheno's car." He came back on the line. "Okay, brah, I'm on my way in."

Quell came through the back with a towel in his gloved hand. He wiped down the knobs and anything else that may have been touched after he locked up. He used another rag to clean up the puddle Larisa made then put it in a plastic bag. We left out of the house together and scoured the area to make sure no one was watching. Quell jumped in my car, and me and Larisa got in hers. Giving her directions to get on the expressway, I hit G's line.

"What up, Cheno?"

"How's Pearl?" I asked.

"Ain't no changes. She's still breathing and that's all that matters to me. We just have to take it day by day. Did you take care of the problem yet?"

"Fifty percent. There was an unexpected oil spill we had to cleaned up. I'll fill you in on the maintenance later. I need you to hit Quan to erase the chalkboard on Eberhart."

"I'm on it. Scony is waiting for you to pull up. Feel free to check all the rooms. It will help you figure out what type of fun you're willing to have. Make an example so it is known anybody can get it. Don't hold back."

"Fa sho. I'll hit you later, nigga."

Ending the call, I sat as I kept one eye on her ass. Larisa was mumbling the same thing repeatedly and I had no clue what she was saying until the word Amen came out of her mouth a little louder. The shit was kind of funny because the only time I'd ever heard her say anything about the man upstairs was when my dick was penetrating her soul. Larisa was in the same boat I was in when I begged God to spare my life. The difference between she and myself was the fact I told the truth. I specifically told the Lord I was going to fuck the city up before I made my promise to Him. Larisa on the other hand just thought she was going to get a pass. There was no helping her.

"Get off at 147th," I said to Larisa.

"Where are we going?"

"Just drive the fuckin' car. It doesn't matter where we're going. This is my show. You're only along for the ride. I mean, the drive."

Larisa looked over at me then signaled to change lanes. The exit was up ahead and this hoe was on some other shit. I watched the road as I slipped my Glock from the holster under my jacket.

"I will run this damn car into a wall. Hell, I'm going to die anyway."

Larisa wasn't about to test me. When I didn't say anything in response to her threat, she pushed the gas and raced across the lanes. Drivers screeched on their brakes and laid on their horns. I placed the gun against Larisa's head forcing her to apply the brakes safely. She got off at 147th and was stopped at the stoplight.

"See, I had no plans of ending your life, Larisa. You pushing me right about now though. Why would you do that bullshit?"

I lowered my weapon and placed it in my lap while I waited for her to answer. The words I chose made me sound like a bitch ass nigga. I didn't give a fuck because I was doing what I had to do if I wanted to get to the Dungeon alive. When a person had nothing to lose, anything could happen in a blink of an eye. Larisa was that person.

"Why would you tell me you'd kill me?" She asked. I nodded toward the light and instructed her to make a left turn. Driving forward, Larisa continued. "Cheno, you know I wouldn't purposely put you in harm's way. Lord used me when he found out I was sneaking around with you. Me and him haven't been together in damn near a year."

"Make a right at the light. Then make a left at the stop sign."

What I wasn't interested in doing was entertaining Larisa and her lies. If she was used, the messages she sent while I was on my way to persuade her not to press charges, wouldn't have even come off so maliciously. The bitch was knee deep in the scheme and she couldn't tell me different. Lord was her nigga and Larisa proved that shit the way she was posting on social media about getting revenge. It was water under the bridge. What I was going to do to her had nothing to do with me. It had a lot to do with Cheese's empire burning to the ground.

"Pull next to the black car."

"What is this?"

Larisa was paranoid once again. She looked around but there wasn't anything for her to see. The Dungeon was tucked away from the main road. Quell pulled my whip right next to Larisa and his truck followed. I would bet money Larisa had pissed on herself for the second time within the hour. Reaching for the handle, Larisa grabbed my arm.

"Answer me, Cheno. What is this?"

I scratched the side of my head before looking her in the eyes. "It's your final destination. Now, get yo' ass out. Don't try to run because you won't get far," I said grabbing the keys from the ignition.

By the time I got around to the driver side of the car, Larisa had locked the doors. She was slower than I thought. The keys to that muthafucka were in my hand. Where did she think she was going? Better yet, how did she believe I couldn't unlock the doors. Giving her the opportunity to get out on her own, Larisa didn't budge. I hit the button and snatched the door open then yoked her pissy ass out of the vehicle. Scony came out of the building and I walked toward him. Quell wasn't too far behind.

"What took you so long?" Scony asked.

"We had a mess to clean up. Honey ended up shooting her mama right through the heart. It's been wild, man."

"You dealing with her today? If not, I have just the room to hold her ass in."

"Nah, this shit took longer than expected and I have to head out to do surveillance on that nigga Dro. I'm not trying to drag this shit on another day. Hell, I need to get me some pussy too."

"That's what got yo' ass in this bind, nigga. Come on because I'm rolling out with you. That nigga tried to kill me and I want to see how the fuck he's moving."

"Shid, let me tell my people to gon' back to my crib. I'm going too. The muthafucka took a shot at me too."

Scony laughed as we entered the Dungeon. "Yo' ass walked away with a flesh wound. Through and through, nigga."

"It don't matter. The shit could've been detrimental."

Quell went back outside while Scony led me deeper into the building. He stopped at a closet and brought out a white jumpsuit. He walked to the end of the hall and opened the door to a bathroom. I pushed Larisa forward but it seemed as if her feet were planted on the cement floor. Taking hold of her forearm, I damn near had to drag her to the bathroom. She started hollering as if she was getting her ass beat.

"Somebody help me! I have been kidnapped and their going to kill me!"

I started laughing because the bitch was crying like Andy when Chucky came to that mental hospital to Ade due Dambballa his ass. Pushing her into the bathroom, Scony threw the jumpsuit at her before walking off. Larisa continued screaming at the top of her lungs and I watched her until I couldn't take it anymore.

"Shut the fuck up! You're wasting her breath and energy because nobody can save you. I don't care how much you scream; you won't be heard. Put on the dry clothes and hurry up. I have shit to do."

I closed the door and went to find Scony. Walking briskly through the dark hall, I came upon an all-white room. The walls, ceiling, and the floor included. Scony stood in the middle with his back to the entrance. He turned seeing me there and went to the corner. He took a white pad laying it in the center of the room along with a white bucket.

"Why are you making shit comfortable for her? She can lay on the floor until I get back."

"Cheno, this is the perfect room for your side chick," Scony smirked. "See, this here is the white room. Have you ever heard of White torture?"

I shook my head no.

"It's something muthafuckas in the middle eastern countries do as a form of psychological torture. You put someone in the room with all white everything then feed them nothing but white food and drinks; such as white rice in a white bowl, and milk in a white cup. You won't have to worry about that because we not feeding the hoe."

I laughed because he wasn't wrong. I was intrigued by what he was telling me and wanted to hear more. The shit didn't sound like torture to me though. As if he was reading my mind, Scony went on with the details.

"You keep them in this state for days, even weeks. This may sound harmless but depriving a muthafucka of color can drive their ass insane. They would eventually start hallucinating. Seeing and hearing shit that's not really there then start harming themselves. It's the perfect way to make a muthafucka self-destruct and take their own life."

"Yeah, I want her in this room," I said as the sound of a door opening caught my attention.

Larisa walked out of the bathroom with the jumpsuit on with her shoes. I motioned for her to hurry so she could see her temporary home. I walked into the room and before she could step a foot inside, Scony pushed her back.

"You gotta take off those shoes," he said handing her a pair of white socks.

She glared at him then hauled ass toward the door. Soon as Larisa touched the knob, a bolt of electricity had her doing the Harlem Shake until she fell to the floor. Standing over her, a nigga was scared to touch her out of fear of being shocked myself.

"Nigga, bring her here. That lil shit was equivalent to somebody getting tased. Wit yo' scary ass." Scony laughed.

I picked Larisa up in my arms and took her back to the white room. Scony took off her shoes and threw them in the furnace on the other side of the warehouse. Putting the socks on her feet, I left her to sleep so I could leave. Scony came back and locked the door then handed me the key."

"I'll send you the code to the building so when you want to come check on her you can. I won't be available at all times. Now, let's go see what this nigga is all about."

***

G sent the information on Caesar Aka Dro. His restaurant was downtown and he had a crib in Downers Grove. The nigga was very well off but been using his time to look for two niggas that wasn't hard to find. I wasn't knocking him for wanting to get back for what happened to his brother, but this street shit wasn't for a corporate muthafucka. Caesar was rubbing elbows with the white folks to keep his name under wraps and linking up with the hood niggas to do dirty shit.

Before we headed out, Scony had me and Quell follow him to his crib. We left our vehicles in his driveway then jumped in a silver Benz truck. I didn't understand why he wanted to do a stakeout in such a lavish whip, but I soon found out once we entered the suburban neighborhood. When Scony turned on the street, I knew we were going to fail the mission. Every damn house had a driveway and there was not one car parked on the street. The car was going to scream *I'm watching somebody* because it stood out from the rest of the scene.

"This ain't gon' work," I said looking out the window. "Either the law gon' ride down on us, or Dro gon' figure out we found his spot. One of the two. We have to come up with another plan."

"Sit back and relax. I know you don't think research wasn't done beforehand, did you? Quan scoped out the block via satellite and we will not be detected," Scony said rolling down the street. "The nigga stays in that two story house right there."

He pointed toward the house and rode right past it. He bent the block and went through a small dirt road until he was in front of a detached garage. Hitting a button on the visor, the door rose slowly. Scony pulled the car inside, parked, hit the button again, then got out. Me and Quell did the same then followed his lead. Exiting the garage through a small doorway, Scony walked across the lawn and up the steps of a home.

"Who shit is this?" Quell asked as Scony unlocked the door and stepped inside.

"I rented this bitch for a week. It was listed as an Airbnb so I snagged it. It will be our hideout until we bring this nigga to his knees. For now, we will sit and watch his every move."

After all I'd been through, there was no way I was sitting watching a muthafucka from a window. Tired was an understatement and I was going my ass in one of the rooms to catch a little shut eye. If Dro showed his face, somebody would let me know about it.

"Aye, I'm going to lay down for a minute."

"Aight," Scony said as he sat back in the chair he was sitting in.

I went into the first room I came upon and laid across the foot of the bed. It didn't take long for sleep to take over my body. Amira was doing her thang with the mouthpiece and my toes were balled up in my shoes. The feeling of euphoric bliss was tingling my ball sack and I knew my kids was racing to the finish line. My breathing became erratic just as I was shaken awake.

"Nigga, get yo' ass up and come see this shit!" Quell's voice rang in my ear.

The nigga almost got punched for fuckin' up the nut I was about to receive. Looking around, the room was pitch black so I'd been asleep for a good while. Drool covered the side of my face causing me to wipe it away immediately before sitting up on the side of the bed.

"You not gon' like this but I need you to be cool. We don't want to blow our cover," he said leaving me behind.

As I stretched and yawned, I got up and went back into the living room where I had left both him and Scony however hours earlier. They were staring out the window so I joined them to see what was so important that they needed me to wake up. At first, I didn't know what the fuck I was looking at until I spotted the whip I purchased for Charlie a year prior.

"The fuck she doing out this way?" I asked more to myself for loud enough for them to hear.

"She just went into that nigga's crib, yo," Scony replied. "Did you know she was fuckin' around with the opps?"

Charlie going against me was never a thought in my mind. She had every right to move on with her life after making it clear she was done with me. But to do the shit with a nigga who was in cahoots with the muthafuckas that tried to end my life was the ultimate betrayal. I had Larisa locked in a room probably ready to gauge her eyes out of the sockets for the role she played in the bullshit. While the bitch I had laid up in my bed for years may have had a hand in the shit too. Charlie's been sleeping with the enemy the entire time.

"Hell nawl!" I said heading for the door.

"Where the fuck you going?" Scony asked. "You can't go barging to that nigga's crib because you in yo' feelings. That's not how we gon' do this shit."

"In my feelings?" I cocked my head to the side. "I'm not in my feelings. Charlie was my bitch until I fucked around one too many times. I owned that shit, allowed her to do her, and haven't tried to get her back. Have I thought about the nigga she's fuckin' on? Yep. I also had plans to bring her ass back where she belonged. Until now.

The bitch knows everything that's going on and all who's involved. There is no way her stank ass don't know that nigga is out to kill me and my people to end this muthafuckin' war! I'm going over there to blow her fuckin' head off and his too! Kill two birds with one bullet sounds about right to me. Now, get the fuck out of my way!"

I was mad as hell because I've asked Charlie on several occasions about the nigga she was fuckin' with and she was closed mouthed about his identity. With a name like Dro, the muthafucka probably had a slew of women at his beck and call just like I did. She was just repeating the cycle with a twist. She was in the middle of a deadly game she wasn't ready to suit up for. Going against me for somebody she didn't know shit about, was dumb as fuck. I wasn't going to school her because she wouldn't need the lesson once I got finished with her.

Scony could stop me for the moment, but he wouldn't be there at all times and she was going to see me. I went back to the window fuming with rage. The door opened and Charlie stepped out in a beautiful black dress. The split traveled up her thick thigh. If the wind blew too hard, her pussy would've been exposed. Knowing her, she didn't have on any draws either. The pink stilettos on her feet matched the color of her hair perfectly. When I saw her hair for the first time at the block party, I loved it. I despised the shit then as I stared daggers at her.

Dro escorted her to a black Maybach GLS 600. Opening the door, he held on to her hand as she got in then he leaned inside briefly. After closing the door, the nigga looked around while running his hand down the front of his black suit jacket. He made his way to the driver door then stepped inside.

"I'm not sitting here while this nigga goes out without a care in the world. Scony, you should've been meeting him at the whip for shooting yo' ass!" I sneered.

"I got this," Scony said pulling out his phone. "He can go wherever he wants. I got his ass on my radar."

Scony held his phone up just as Dro pulled away slowly. This nigga had a tracking device on the vehicle. The red dot moved and my focus was glued to it. The only thing that took my attention away was my phone ringing. Removing the device, I saw Ease's name on the screen. I declined the call. I had nothing to say to his ass. When it rang again, a shiver went up my spine.

"What's the emergency?" I asked when the call connected.

"Get to the trap! Everybody is dead! They killed Mike," Ease sobbed.

"Where the fuck you at and why ain't you dead too?" I barked.

"I'm driving myself to the hospital. I got hit in the side. I don't know if I'm gon' make it, Cheno!" Ease started coughing. "It was Cheese and Tank. They came through with a few of their niggas. They didn't take shit either. The trap is a free for all and is wide open. Whoever wants to come up can do so right now." Ease started coughing uncontrollably. It sounded like he had more to say but he couldn't get the words out.

"Ease, stop talking. Get to the hospital, my nigga!" There was a loud crash. The sound of glass shattering filled my ears. "Ease! Ease!" I screamed.

"What happened?" Scony asked with his keys in hand.

"We gotta get to the Nine. Them muthafuckas hit my spot and killed everybody," I said running for the door. "Ease was shot and I think he crashed out while on the phone with me. You still want to wait? These niggas just drew a lot of blood. The wait is over!"

I was on demon time. My whole crew was washed away in one sweep. Charlie was going to get dealt with once I returned the favor of spilling blood on them niggas side. This time I'm gon' hit 'em where it was bound to hurt. For life.

Chapter 13

Breeze

"Damn, Breeze. Eat that pussy, ma."

Taz had both hands tangled in my hair as I ate her from the rooter to the tooter. I had been neglecting my girl while keeping my eye on the streets. A happy wife led to a happy life and I was going to take care of home regardless. Sucking on her clit was like eating a Charms sucker. Hell, I was trying to get to the center of the Tootsie Pop.

Humming into her center, the vibration of my tongue matched the way Taz's legs were shaking. I inserted three fingers into her snatch and found her G-spot immediately. Her sticky essence covered my tongue and I slurped it up. Taste like candy played in my mind. That shit spoke to me because that was exactly what my tastebuds were experiencing in that moment.

"I'm cumming!"

"Let that shit out and don't hold back," I mumbled in between licks.

I wrapped my lips around her nub tightly. The way her muscles gripped my fingers turned me on. It was a matter of time 'til she made it rain on my face. Taz was a squirter and she'd never knew she had the ability to do that shit until she got with a real pussy monster. Removing my fingers, I went face deep into her shit as I pulled her further into my mouth.

"Oh shit!" she moaned as her nectar coated the lower part of my face.

Taz thought this was the last round but I had more where that came from. Her kitty glistened like a glazed donut causing me to salivate like a dog. Standing to my feet, I grabbed my girl by both hands so she could stand up on the bed.

"I've had enough, baby. I'm tired."

"I'll tell you when you've had enough. I'm still thirsty. Now, stand the fuck up and put my pussy in my face."

Licking the cum from her thighs, Taz shivered as she stood before me. I loved the way she came for me because I aimed to please. Looking up at her from my position, I smiled.

"I saw this shit on Twitter and I wanted to try it out. You bet not fall. I don't give a fuck what happens. And you better cum any time you feel the need. Do. Not. Hold. Back! I want it all. Do you hear me?"

"Yes, baby. I hear you."

I licked her clit a couple times before I went to town. Taz held her ground for the first two minutes then I snatched her muthafuckin' soul. With my hands behind my back, I sucked on her pussy with precision. Bringing my hand to my center, her moans had me rubbing my own nub to the music she created.

"Uh, uh, uh, uh! Shit! Uhhhhhh!" Taz screeched. "Ohhhhh Goddddd!"

I heard every cuss word known to man in the seven minutes I allowed my woman to wet me up. The back of my head was sore from Taz pulling my hair at all angles. I didn't mind because I was getting everything, I wanted out of her and that was her juices raining down on me. Giving her yoni one last kiss, Taz collapsed like falling blocks.

"I think you should stay off Twitter, bae. The shit you just did made me feel good, but it was insane. The glimmer in your eye tells me you will be trying to eat my box like that daily and I won't be able to handle it. I'm not built for the freaky deaky shit you go looking for on the internet."

Taz was serious than a heart attack and it was funny. My response was licking the flavor of her from my lips. She laid on her side with her legs closed tightly together. It was her way of telling me the kitchen was off limits. While massaging her exposed cheek, my phone rang. I groaned loudly because I wanted to taste Taz again before she drifted off to sleep. The relief on her face told me she was glad whoever was calling saved her from another tongue lashing. I picked up my phone and hit the button to answer.

"Honey, what's going on?"

"Aye, I have a question for you," she said with a long pause.

"I'm listening," I said just as another call was coming through. I took the phone from my ear to see who it was and declined that shit.

"Do you know the nigga Charlie's been seeing is the same nigga that shot Quell and Scony?"

Honey must've had her information wrong because there was no way Charlie was entertaining a muthafucka who ran with the same circle as Cheese. Despite all Cheno had done during their relationship, it didn't warrant Charlie to switch sides on him. I was all for her moving on with her life, but not with the very son of a bitch that was against us. When it came to my brother, I didn't give a fuck who it was, I would shoot their ass dead. Including Charlie's ass too.

"Nah. Tell me you're lying."

"Quell called to tell me he would be home soon but he had to go check out something with Cheno. Before he got off the phone, the question was opposed to me. My response was almost identical to yours and I asked, why did he ask? Apparently, they were staking out the residence of the Dro dude and saw Charlie going into his house."

I took in what Honey said and still didn't want to believe it. I knew Charlie was staying in a house in Downers Grove and she said something about the nigga next door being the man she was seeing. I wondered if that was the same person

Cheno saw her with. Shaking my head, I dreaded asking Honey what I needed to know.

"Did this take place in Downers Grove?" I finally asked.

"Quell didn't say where it happened, but he did say her car was parked next door. Something happened because I could hear Cheno hollering in the background. Quell ended the call right when he was saying something about everybody being dead."

"I'm gon' call you back. As a matter of fact, come to my crib. Now!"

I hung up on Honey and dialed my brother's phone immediately after. Cheno answered on the first ring. There was a lot of crying and loud talking going on wherever he was and it didn't sit well with me. When Cheno finally spoke, my heart started beating at a normal rate.

"Yeah, sis."

"What happened?"

"Them muthafuckas killed everybody at the trap. The police all through my shit but I'm not worried about them finding anything because G got here to lock all the illegal shit up before they arrived. It's a good thing the pigs take their time answering to calls in the hood."

"Damn, bro. I'm sorry," I sympathized with his loss because those niggas were like family. "Please tell me Lil Mike wasn't there."

"Mike gone. Ease gone. Fredo gone." Cheno said Fredo's name with a lot of emotion behind it. That was like his brother and Fredo had his back through thick and thin. "I sent him over here to make sure everything was running smoothly. He should've been with me. All these muthafuckin' cops out here looking at me like I pulled the muthafuckin' trigga."

"Calm down, bro. We gon' get back at them niggas."

"Speaking of get back. I'm killing yo' muthafuckin' friend. You better tell me you didn't know about her sleeping with that nigga."

146

"Cheno, I know you're mad and all, but don't you ever insinuate that I'm a snake ass bitch. All I know about the nigga Charlie's been seeing is that he lives next door to the Airbnb she is living in. Other than that, I don't know shit." I snapped. "Honey called me asking if I knew and I told her the same thing. Charlie left the memorial when the nigga came through shooting. Maybe if she had stayed, we could've seen her reaction. She didn't."

"That's neither here nor there. The niggas were able to touch my people and they had to get their information from somewhere. Knowing she is getting dicked down by one of them, there you have it. My ex-bitch is a muthafuckin mole. I wouldn't put it past her slimy ass if they came to run up in my crib next."

"We not gon' even think like that, Cheno. Charlie ain't that type of female and you know it. Think about this for a minute. Did it ever occur to you that she may not even know the nigga is part of Cheese crew?"

"Oh, she knows. Charlie haven't been around in Lord knows how long. That tells me that she is a shiesty ass bitch."

"No. Charlie hasn't been around *you*. Nothing has change between her and the rest of us. To be brutally honest with you, bro, I wouldn't want to be in your presence after what you did either. I'm going to call Charlie and tell her to come over here soon as she can."

The line went quiet and all I could hear was Cheno breathing like a Kimono dragon.

"I'm on my way. If she shows up before I get there, do not let that hoe leave."

Throwing the phone on the bed, I walked to the bathroom so I could clean up before Honey arrived. As I stepped into the shower, Taz entered in all her naked glory. She joined me and started massaging my shoulders. My mind was all over the place and the thoughts were driving me crazy.

"Wanna talk about it?"

"No. You heard the little bit I said on my end. The less you know, the better. I want you to stay far away from the bullshit going on in the streets. Honey is on her way over."

I lathered my wash cloth and washed my body a couple times before getting out leaving Taz in the shower. I washed my face, brushed my teeth, then went to find something to put on. My phone was ringing and I peeked at the device to see who was calling. Dawson's name was on the screen but I made no movement to answer. He should've known when I declined the call earlier nothing would change the second time around.

Pulling a sports bra and black tank over my body, I stepped into a pair of basketball shorts. I put a pair of black ankle socks on my feet before going downstairs to roll up while waiting on Honey to arrive. I sat on the couch with my head resting on the back of it, Taz walked up on me with my phone in her hand.

"Your father has called three times since you've been down here."

"He's not my father. The nigga ain't did shit for me in forever and don't deserve that title from me," I said taking the phone from her hand. "Thanks."

The doorbell rang and Taz walked away to answer it. Honey walked in giving her a hug then came into the living room where I was. She sat next to me taking the blunt from my hand. Her actions were shocking because Honey didn't smoke.

"I know you not letting this shit stress you out."

"Killing my mama was stressful enough for me. I never thought I would have to do something like that to someone I once loved. It's a damn shame she never took the time to get to know me as her daughter. All Victoria saw me as was a hoe who she believed was after her man."

"Honey, you can't dwell on the what ifs. You didn't deserve none of the shit you've been through. I want you to concentrate on the woman you have become. I'm not talking

148

about the killer in you either. That shit is hereditary," I laughed. "For real, I see a bright future ahead for you. Quell, marriage, lots of kids, and just pure happiness. It will become your reality very soon."

"I was with you until the lots of kids part. I'm still fighting the urge to be in a relationship and you talking about me procreating. I think not." She chuckled. "Did you talk to Cheno?"

Nodding, I looked up at Taz. She rolled her eyes before going back upstairs. I was standing on the fact of my girl staying out of this street shit. If she was ever questioned, there would be nothing she could tell. I filled Honey in on what me and Cheno discussed. She was on the same page as me.

"Charlie isn't knowingly fuckin' with dude. It is a good chance they sent him to court her as get back." The look of uncertainty was displayed on her face after what she said. "Nah. Something ain't right. Charlie started seeing him way before Cheno was shot. There's no way she knew Dro was affiliated with Cheese. If anything, he for sure knew her connection to him. We need to call her, Breeze."

Honey's philosophy was on point. Charlie's life was probably in danger. Especially since Cheno killed one of their crew members. That was probably why the trap was hit. It was an eye for an eye and the blood shed wasn't going to stop there. Pearl was still fighting for her life because of one of them. G and Scony wasn't going to allow that to go. I picked up my phone to call Charlie. The phone rang until the voicemail picked up. Three calls later and she still didn't answer.

"She's not answering," I informed her.

Honey tried from her phone getting the same result. A bad feeling came over me and I suddenly needed a drink to calm my nerves. As I poured a glass of apple Crown, I went back to my phone to see where Charlie was. On the find my phone app, her phone pinged at a residence in Downers Grove. She must've left it at the house for whatever reason. Remembering I had something to give Honey, I walked to the kitchen and opened the refrigerator before going back to the living room.

"Aye, this is off subject but here before I forget. I bumped into Amira at the hospital while visiting Pearl. She gave me this and it's a deadly dose."

"You told her not to tell Cheno about this, right?"

"I didn't have to. The ten stacks I gave her better be more than enough to keep the information to herself. What I did tell her was if she told anybody about it, I would kill her whole family. The bitch was so scared she made a promise to leave Cheno alone. I told her that would get her killed too. As a matter of fact, I told her she better give my brother some pussy."

"No, you didn't, Breeze!" Honey yelled wide eyed.

"I sure did." My phone rang in my hand and I hoped it was Charlie. It was Dawson.

"What do you want?" I asked not hiding my attitude.

"Open the muthafuckin' door, Brianna."

"Open what door?"

I knew damn well he wasn't at my house. Dawson shouldn't even know how to get in touch with me let alone show up at my crib. The only way that was possible was if Nikki ran her mouth to Keyshae's bitch ass by telling her where I laid my head. It was either that or she told her talking ass mama. Either way, it was going to be on them hoes if their uncle ended up toe tagged.

"I'm at your house. Now, open the door so we can talk."

Hanging up on his ass, I ran to the closet and grabbed my nine. The nigga had some nerve showing up at my shit uninvited. There was nothing Dawson had to say to me but he was gon' learn how to talk with respect when addressing me. With my tool in hand, I stormed toward the door as Dawson started banging on it like a madman. I snatched the door open coming face to face with the man I hadn't seen since I was seventeen years old.

Dawson looked down at my hand then back at my face. "Why you got to act lie such a thug? In case you have forgotten, you were born a girl."

"What the fuck you want?" I asked. "Before you answer that, I'm beating the fuck out of one or both of your nieces and yo' old decrepit ass sister too. Just to put that out there. One of them hoes gave you the drop on me and I don't appreciate that shit."

"I'm your father. I should know where you live so I can check on you."

I laughed in his face. "Since when do you care about me? It's too late for you to be a father, Dawson. In case you didn't know, I'm the daddy now." I smirked. "Look, I'm tired of going back and forth with you. I don't need a father in my life. I've done just fine without one. It would be in your best interest not to show up here again after tonight. You are not wanted nor will you ever be invited. I don't want to build a relationship with you. Did I lay everything on the table for you?"

Dawson squinted at me then fixed his fuckin' face as I bounced my gun against my leg waiting to hear what he had to say.

"Can I come inside so we can talk?"

"Hell no. Anything you have to say can be discussed right here. I'm not going to stand here all night so; I'd advise you to get to talking."

"Since you don't give a damn about these white folks being in your business then we will air this shit out right here. Why didn't you tell me my son wasn't dead?"

"One because you don't have a son for me to talk to you about. Two, you were only concerned about *my brother* because of the money you thought you would receive after his death was confirmed. That's the reason you were never going to get the death certificate even if he was really gone.

Finally, you should've had this same energy when we were growing up. Maybe you wouldn't be going through the song and dance to be in the know about our lives."

Dawson stepped into my personal space as if he was about to hit me. My hand came up and the barrel of my gun rested on the tip of his nose. If he blinked wrong, I was going to shoot his ass point blank.

"You got a lot of mouth but have to point a gun in my face. What happened to the man you're supposed to be?" He growled through clenched teeth. "I'm about to whoop your ass like I should've done a long time ago."

"Then where the fuck you gon' live?" Cheno asked from behind Dawson.

Without waiting for a response, Cheno clenched the back of his shirt in his hand before dragging Dawson inside of my house. I saw the moment Cheno pulled up but didn't say a word. I was glad Cheno heard the threat for himself because it wouldn't have had the same effect coming from me. I closed the door then locked it once Quell stepped inside. Cheno damn near threw Dawson across the room.

"Cheno. I'm so happy you're alive!" Dawson lied.

"Nigga, please. I heard how you only called to ask about a fuckin' death certificate. Not one time did you ask what happened to me. All you wanted was money. Is that all I am to you? If so, here you go, muthafucka!"

Cheno tossed a wad of bills at Dawson's feet. He bent down and started picking the money up. The sight before me was sickening and it was obvious Cheno felt the same way. With one swift kick, he hit Dawson in the chin sending him to the floor on his back. Cheno released all of his frustrations on his sperm donor. The beatdown was something that was bound to happen and I had a front row seat to the fight.

"Muthafucka, you shouldn't have showed your face here! The way you walked out on my mama and us," Cheno stopped talking to beat his ass some more. "You knew not to come back trying to throw that daddy shit around! We don't need you, nigga! Yo' ass need us!"

Dawson was balled up on the floor. Cheno stopped punching him and started stomping him in the head. My brother was beyond angry. He was furious. Enraged. Exasperated that Dawson showed up threatening to put his hands on me. Every time his foot made contact with his dome; Cheno expressed that.

"My sister ain't never been touched by a nigga. Physically, sexually, or emotionally. I'm the only muthafuckin man she loves and that's because she knows I got her back, her front, and both sides. Yo' bitch ass threatened the wrong one at the right time. Had you come over yesterday, your fate may have been different. Too bad you chose today," he said kicking Dawson one more time then stepped back. "Kill this muthafucka!"

Honey got up and ran upstairs. I kind of understood why she did. It was because she had just done the same thing with her own mama. My outcome was not going to be anything like hers. Unlike Honey, I wasn't trying to rationalize with Dawson. Shooting him was going to be solely for my mother. I owed her that much. Aiming my gun, Dawson looked up at me with fear in his eyes.

"Brianna, please don't do this. I'm sorry for walking out on you. I apologize for not being there when Janice passed away. She was the love of my life—"

I let off one shot into his lying ass mouth. Ending his life rapidly. For a minute the muthafucka had me feeling a little bit of pity for him but when he said that bullshit about loving my mama, I knew it was cap and he was just trying to talk his way out of death. For good measures, I did what I promised him I would and shot him between his eyes. Cheno stepped over Dawson's body in order to get to me.

"I'm cool, bro. Get this muthafucka out of my house," I said going upstairs to check on my cousin and my girl.

Chapter 14

Charlie

I felt so beautiful sitting in the seat of the luxury vehicle beside the man who not only looked good enough to eat, but smelled exquisite as well. Caesar was laying it on thick the way he was showering me with so much attention. He told me I was all the woman he needed and I believed him too. When he called saying he wanted to take me on a date I'd never forget, I was all in. Caesar didn't just say get ready. The man made sure I had a dress, shoes, a purse, and accessories to match. Everything was delivered to the house along with flowers, champagne, and chocolates.

There was no way I could go out in the dress he bought without a fresh hairdo. I decided to take a closer look at the purse and it was filled with one-hundred-dollar bills. Caesar went all out to make sure I paid for nothing. It was useless to argue with him about being a provider to me because he wasn't trying to hear none of that. Caesar did what he wanted, when he wanted.

Once I was dressed and ready for our night together, I walked next door. What did I do that for? Of course, I should've known there would be a debate about why it was his duty to pick me up from my door. I agreed and vowed not to do it again. When we were settled in the car, Caesar held my hand while caressing the back of it with his thumb. "Into you" by Tamia played as we cruised the expressway.

We neared the exit toward his restaurant. I could feel Caesar glance at me and I turned with a smile. He winked before giving the road his undivided attention. The gesture alone had me blushing like a schoolgirl. It had been a while since someone had me feeling the way I was in that moment. Caesar bypassed his establishment then parked in the back. I was confused because he had never brought me to this area. Usually, he would park in the front and we would go inside. Caesar killed the engine and got out of the vehicle. Watching as he rounded the front of the car then opened my door. Helping me out, he hit the alarm before leading me across the way to an underground garage.

"Where are we going?" I asked.

"You didn't think I would take you to an all-black event without a chauffeur, did you?" Caesar smiled. "It's nothing but the best for you, beautiful."

As we entered the garage, a black and gray Rolls Royce Phantom Extended Series II was parked off to the side. I didn't think that would be the vehicle we would be riding in. Glancing around for a limousine or something of the sort, Caesar guided me to the very car I doubted would be one associated with him. My mouth dropped the moment the driver opened the door for us.

"This is beautiful," I said getting inside the expensive vehicle. "I've never been in a Rolls Royce before."

"Stick with me and I will scratch all your firsts off the list. All you have to do is tell me what they are. I'll make it happen with no problem."

Caesar was saying all the right things and I should've been used to it. There was something different about the way he said it that time around. His tone kind of fell flat and he didn't sound sure of what he said. Shaking off my feelings because I didn't want to messed up our date, I sat back admiring the interior of the car.

The windows were tinted, it was very roomie in the rear cabin. There was a dark partition to seclude us from the driver. If I wanted to suck the skin off Caesar's dick, I could do it in private. Maybe one day we would be able to scratch that off my list. Smiling from ear to ear, the ride was smooth and relaxing. Caesar opened the armrest to reveal a cooler-like compartment removing a chilled bottle of Champagne along with glasses.

He popped the cork and poured our drinks. I ran my hand along the door and noticed a system. Selecting some music that was mellow to help with the mood, I chose "By Your Side" by Sade. Soon as her voice started crooning, the lights dimmed. The only lighting was the small specks of lights which gave off the illusion of stars above our heads. Caesar handed me the glass of champagne then kissed me on the lips. He rocked to the beat as I sang with Sade.

You think I'd leave your side, baby
You know me better than that
Think I'd leave you down
When you're down on your knees
I wouldn't do that

I'd gulped down the champagne in three swallows and I didn't intend for that to happen. Caesar held up the bottle. I nodded for him to refill my glass. I felt a slight buzz and should have declined but one more wouldn't hurt. Drinking the second glass slower did not help at all. Before I knew it, I was out like a light.

My head was pounding as I came to. I was no longer in the Phantom. Attempting to palm my head, I couldn't because my arms were restrained. Panic set in because my first thought was, Cheese had finally caught up with me. I opened my eyes and closed them immediately after. White lights danced in front of me and my body didn't feel like my own. Willing myself to see what predicament I was in; I finally forced my eyes open. My worse fear was confirmed. I was confined to a chair.

Looking around, I for damn sure wasn't in a lavished ballroom for a party. My mind went back to the car ride. Did

Caesar drug me? Shaking my head no, I couldn't allow myself to pan that man out to be a villain. He had gone deep in his pockets to keep a smile on my face. There was no reason he would dress me to the nines just to bring me to this dirty ass place and tie me to a chair. I fought not to cry.

There were no windows so I had no clue how long I'd been out. I tried my best to listen closely for any sounds of movement or any conversations going on anywhere in the building. I heard a few voices in close proximities but I couldn't make out what was being said. As I thought about it, how the hell did my stupid ass agree to leave my phone behind?

My neck and back hurt badly. The tingling sensation in my hands and feet let me know the circulation was very poor in my limbs. Moving my fingers slightly drew attention because a gush of cold water was thrown in my face. I sputtered loudly then my head was snatched back.

"You're finally woke, huh?" A big burly nigga said smiling down at me. "Welcome to the party. You are beautiful by the way."

"Where am I? I asked in a shaky tone. "And where is Caesar?"

"One question at a time, ma," he laughed. "You are at my house. I'm the Boogey Man."

"This ain't yo' house! Where the fuck am I?" I screamed.

"Damn, you sexy when you're mad. But on some serious shit, you are where I want you to be. It really don't matter where you are. If you tell me what I want to know, you may live to write about your trials and tribulations. Deal?"

I didn't know this muthafucka from Adam and he wanted me to answer questions I may or may be able to assist him with. I was fucked. A tear rolled down my cheek.

"No need to cry, baby girl. This could be easy as you make it, or hard as fuck. It's your choice."

"Okay, I'll try my best to answer your questions, but you have to answer the only one I have for you."

"Ohhh, the nigga you were with. Right." He turned his head then whistled loudly. "Aye, Dro! Come in here, my nigga. She wants to know where Caesar at. I think you should be the one to fill her in on that."

Dro was a name I heard before and he was in fact affiliated with Cheese and his cousin, Tank. If my legs weren't bound to the chair, my knees would've been knocking together. I was frightened like a muthafucka because there was no way I was getting out of there alive. Not to mention, the way the dude summoned Dro, he thought the shit was a joke and Caesar was most likely dead already. When the door opened my fright turned into pure rage.

"Hello, my love. You're looking for me?"

"You son of a bitch! You drugged me, Caesar," I cried. "What did I do to make you do me like this?"

"I'm not who you will be answering to. I'm just here to find out the truth," he retorted.

"What fuckin' truth? Anything you asked, I told you. Enlighten me on what you're referring to!"

Caesar stopped addressing me and allowed the Boogey Man to take over. I couldn't believe he lured me to Cheno's enemies. I should've stood my ground and left him alone when he was persistent about me taking the gifts he showered me with on the very first date. It was too good to be true and I knew it from the start. Shaking my head, I cried silently without taking my eyes off Caesar. Tuning everything going on around me out, I missed the question which was asked. The Boogey Man hit me in the back of my head bringing my attention back to him.

"That nigga ain't shit to you! I'm your only ticket out of here. Now, where the fuck is Cheno?"

I knew Cheno wasn't dead, but he wasn't going to get that information out of me. If playing dumb was what I needed to do, then I was about to transform into Loyd from the movie Dumb and Dumber to get through the shit. There was no way I was turning on someone who saved me from myself. We may not be together, but I will forever consider him my family.

"Cheno is dead. Everybody knows that."

"You can stop telling that lie. I've seen the nigga with my own eyes alive and well," he said stooping down to my level. "Wanna try that shit again?"

"I don't know what to tell you. The last time I heard, Cheno was killed by…"

"Me, bitch!"

The muthafucka who was now foaming at the mouth was Tank. Something was off about him but I wasn't trying to push his buttons. I hoped like hell he didn't beat the fuck out of me.

"If you killed him then you know he's dead, correct?"

"See, now you pissing me off. My nigga did the deed and obviously, he didn't complete the job. Cheno is not dead and you know this because that's yo' nigga!"

Shaking my head no, "You're wrong. Me and Cheno broke up before he was killed. I learned about his death from his sister. After attending his memorial, I stayed away because I wanted no parts of getting revenge. I met Caesar and have been spending my time with him. If Cheno is alive, I don't know shit about it!"

Tank punched me on the side of my face damn near giving me whiplash. The hit had so much force behind it, my teeth chattered. Caesar stepped in just as Tank delivered another blow to my mouth.

"Aye, let her sit here for a while and maybe she will tell you what you wanna know. Beating her ass will only cause her to shut down."

"Dro, you won't be able to save this bitch. When I come back, I'm killing her ass whether I get my hands on Cheno or not. She will not leave this muthafucka alive. Her pussy got you acting soft, my nigga. Tighten up because you will be the muthafucka to pull the trigga."

Tank walked out in a huff. My face was swelling as the seconds ticked away. Caesar, Dro, or whatever the fuck his name was walked over to me slowly. He placed his hand on my chin and turned my head toward him. Jerking, I looked away.

"I'll be back to get you, love. "I believe you and I'm sorry for even bringing you here."

"Caesar, don't worry about me. You picked a side and I wasn't on it. Good luck out there in the streets of Chicago because *if* Cheno is alive, you muthafuckas won't be for long."

I sat stoically as he took the walk of shame. Caesar kept looking over his shoulder until he disappeared out of sight. At first, I was afraid, then the shock took over, but once everything was said and done, a bitch was irate as hell. Screaming to the top of my lungs, I released everything I held inside while preparing for them niggas to show up again.

Chapter 15

Honey

Quell made sure I got home safe and even tucked me into bed after everything was cleaned up at Breeze's house. When Dawson showed up, I knew things wasn't going to end well. My cousin hated him with a passion and she had every right to feel the way she did. For someone to come around in hopes of their child being dead for monetary value, was sick. Dawson and Victoria should hook up in hell because both of them were right where they belonged.

Breeze wasn't bent out of shape after pulling the trigger. In fact, she smoked a blunt while thumping the ash on his face. She even poured out a little Crown for the homies too. The way she celebrated Dawson's demise was borderline psychotic. I felt bad for her cousins because they were going to feel her wrath for thinking it was okay for them to give out her address. Whichever one did it, crossed the line big time. Breeze wasn't going to kill them, but once she finished with them, they were going to wish they were dead.

"You okay, baby?" Quell asked as he snuggled behind me in the bed.

"I'm fine. I just need to sleep."

"I have some shit I have to take care of with the crew. Get some sleep and I'll be back soon as I can."

"Quell, be careful. There's too much going on and I want you to make it back to me in one piece," I said turning to face him.

"And I will. That's a promise."

Kissing me tenderly on the lips, Quell got up to put on his shoes. As he was getting ready to leave, I had to tell him about Charlie. Something wasn't right and Cheo needed to find her if he wanted to or not.

"Aye, would you please tell Cheno…never mind. Hand me my phone off the dresser please."

Quell, did what I asked then kissed me once again. I called Cheno and waited for him to answer. I opted to voice my concerns with him myself so he wouldn't be able to shrug the shit off like it was nothing. In my heart, I felt Charlie was in trouble. Quell didn't leave like I thought he would. Instead, he stood waiting for me to get off the phone.

"Yo!" Cheno barked in the phone.

"Cheno, listen to me. I know you think Charlie is a snake but I think you may be jumping the gun."

"Honey, with all due respect, fuck Charlene! That bitch wanted to be away from me and went to work with the muthafuckas that tried to kill me, now she was gonna be the one getting killed with the nigga's dick in her mouth!"

I sat up when he said that bullshit and I was livid. Cheno had the nerve to be mad about Charlie being with someone else after all the pussy his dick had sampled while he laid beside her. At least she ended shit with his ass before entertaining another nigga.

"See, if you knew her like you claimed, yo' ass would know that Charlie would never knowingly wrong you. She is nothing like that hoe, Larisa or any other bitch you were secretly seeing behind her back. Charlie is in trouble, Cheno! Both Breeze and I called her phone repeatedly without getting an answer."

"That's because the bitch is somewhere getting fucked!" He seethed.

"Then explain why she left her phone at the house. You can't and neither can I! Charlie would never go anywhere without her phone. All I'm asking is for you to try your best to find her."

"I hate to be the one to burst yo' bubble, dear cousin, but I saw the bitch get in the car with Dro and she was all smiles. Ask Quell, he witnessed that shit too. Soon as I catch up with that nigga, she'll be back…in a muthafuckin' body bag. Tell Quell I'm ready to roll."

He ended the call and tears welled in my eyes. Cheno never talked down on Charlie before. At least not in the manner he'd just done. I didn't care what he said, my friend did not go against the grain. Quell sat on the side of the bed and wiped my tears away. I was mad as hell because I didn't know the first place to start looking for Charlie. But I was going to figure out something.

"Look, Cheno is upset right now. You have to put yourself in his shoes, Honey. The nigga she is with is the enemy. All Cheno sees is her feeding them niggas information. Everything about this shit is kind of suspect. Cheno can find out where Charlie is long as she's with Dro. He may act like he doesn't give a fuck about her, but he really does. We gon' see what's up. I promise to keep you posted. Clear your mind and get some sleep."

I got out of bed as I followed him downstairs to lock the door behind him. After making sure my home was secured, my next stop was the kitchen. I was hungry as fuck. Opening the refrigerator, my sights fell on a whole order of barbeque turkey tips and fries. I forgot all about the food after Breeze asked me to come over. Separating the tips from the fries, I threw that shit into the air fryer to heat up. As I waited, the package Breeze gave me came to mind. An evil grin appeared on my face when I thought about Cheese.

Quell eased my mind a little bit. Knowing Cheno had eyes on Charlie wasn't enough for me because it didn't mean he was going to make sure she was good. The nigga was talking about killing her for Christ's sake! If I thought Charlie was being grimy, I would help him kill her ass slowly, but I didn't. Charlie loved that idiot. He was the reason she walked away but of course; he was going to use everything in his power to make her out to be the bad guy.

Me: Hey, what you over there doing?

I found myself texting Cheese as the air fryer ding alerting me that my food was ready. I did the hungry dance while transferring the tips to a plate. The aroma in the kitchen was divine. My mouth watered and my stomach growled in anticipation of devouring the leftover meal. Grabbing a bottled water from the fridge, I walked my plate to the table and took a seat. The chime of my phone let me know Cheese had responded. He had to wait until I ate a few of the tips first. Wiping my hands on a paper towel, I checked the text.

Cheese: I just got home. I'm exhausted.

Me: Oh, well get some rest. I won't bother you since you're tired.

The bubbles danced around as Cheese responded. Playing on the fact of him saying he was tired, I almost knew he was going to come back with some shit like, "I'm not too tired for you." Cheese was so predictable. Especially when a woman like me paid attention to him for years. The tips woke up my tastebuds and I was in food heaven.

Cheese: I'm not too tired for you. A bother is something you would never be. What's on your mind?

I laughed so hard when I read his response I almost choked. Cheese was not using the head on his shoulders at this point. He was using his third leg that rested on his thigh as leverage. Quell was going to hate me for what I was about to do but I would have to deal with that later. Throwing a line that was sure to bait the big fish was imperative for me to do in the moment. I was going to use it to reel him in so I could holla *got 'em* in the end. It was dangerous, but somebody had to do it. Why not me?

Me: After dealing with my mama, I just wanted to take my mind off it all. Would you be able to get a room for the night?

Eating with a smirk on my face, it would be a matter of seconds for Cheese to respond. Just as I thought, he did exactly as I suspected. Finishing my food, I threw everything in the garbage before reading his response.

Cheese: Done. I knew you were going to need a quick getaway after that shit. I was ten steps ahead of you, ma.

Cheese sent a screenshot of the reservations at the Marriot Marquis Chicago on 21st and Prairie. I went upstairs to pack a small overnight bag; for show because I had no plans of staying the night. After gathering everything, I went into the bathroom and brushed my teeth then took a quick shower. Throwing on a simple Fenty Savage lounge set, I headed out.

Me: I'm on my way.

Cheese: I'll be waiting. Room number 2301.

Backing out of my driveway, I listened to Inayah's "Hot Sauce" as I thought about how I was going to handle this nigga. From what I gathered from Breeze and Quell, it wasn't a secret that Cheno's death was a lie. Cheese was aware of the information and I may be walking into a trap for sure. When I thought about how I was going to go about things with Cheese, I meant, was I prepared to carry on sexually with him. My worries had nothing to do with him doing anything to me because Cheese felt he owed me for the time I served on his behalf. See, I had the upper hand. I was too close to the situation but Cheese wasn't on high alert when it came to me, and that was going to be his downfall.

Traffic was light since it was well past ten o'clock at night. Hopping off the expressway at Pershing, I made a pitstop at Rothschild's to get a bottle. Cheese was a Remy type of guy who drank his liquor straight, so I purchased a fifth with a bottle of apple juice for myself. Taking the street to the hotel, I arrived in less than ten minutes.

Me: I'm here.

Cheese: Come on up. I'm waiting.

I sat in the car for a few minutes. Shaking off the jitters, I made the decision to tell Breeze what I was up to. She was bound to cuss me out but it was too late for me to turn back. I made the call and waited for my cousin to answer.

"Honey, did you get some sleep?"

"Not at all. That's not why I'm calling though. Don't be mad at me. I'm about to take care of Cheese. Please—"

"Where you at? I'm coming to you," Breeze yelled.

"No, cuz, I got to do this. I'll hit you when the job is done. Do not call nobody! I got this."

"Honey, if you don't bring yo' ass back, I'm gon' find you and kill you myself! You are so dumb! I knew I shouldn't have given you that shit!"

"Breeze, I gotta go. I love you."

I hung up before she responded because I didn't need to hear her say she loved me too. It was a given and I already knew she did. Grabbing the bags, I got out of my truck and hit the alarm. Bypassing the desk, I headed straight for the elevator. The hotel was nice but I wasn't there to admire the structure. I pressed the button and the doors opened immediately. Hitting the button for the twenty-third floor, I watched as each number lit up. I noticed there wasn't a number thirteen on the panel. This was not the first time I wondered about that but it was a random thought in the moment.

Finally, the doors parted and I followed the plats on the wall which led me to the room Cheese was in. While standing outside the door, I took a deep breath and knocked. It wasn't long before he opened the door with a smile. Motioning me inside, I gave him a side hug before going further into the unit. Cheese had the curtains opened and the view was astonishing. The Chicago Skyline was beautiful from the angle of the suite and I'd never experienced it in that form before. I was mesmerized and was thrown off from the reason I was actually there.

"It's beautiful, isn't it?" Cheese asked from behind.

"Yes, it is. I've missed out on experiencing a lot in the past ten years. My city is foreign to me. I should get out more," I chuckled.

Putting my bag on a nearby chair, I stepped out of my shoes. Holding the bag from the liquor out toward him, I smiled.

"I thought we should have this since we have so much to catch up on."

Taking the contents out, Cheese shook his head. "You remembered what I like to drink, huh?"

"Of course, I do. We use to have bottles of it in the cabinets like condiments. How could I forget?"

We both laughed as he put the bottle on the dresser, the apple juice in the mini fridge, then he grabbed the ice bucket. Running his tongue over his lips, Cheese looked me up and down before turning toward the door. When he left, I quickly grabbed my phone and shot Breeze a quick text.

Me: I made it to my destination. So far, so good.
Breeze: Be careful Honey. Don't underestimate that man.
Me: I won't. My eyes are wide open.

Turning my phone off, I put it in my bag then retrieved the small vial from the inside pocket. I stared at it for a minute before securing it in the middle of the bun of my hair. Soon as it was hidden, Cheese was coming back into the unit with ice in hand. I purposely faced the view so it appeared as if I was zoned out.

"You can make us drinks while I take a quick shower. Or you can join me."

"I took care of my hygiene before I left home. Have fun in there." I chuckled.

"Aye, I had to shoot my shot."

"And you missed. Bye, La'Darrius." I waved him off. "I won't put ice in your drink. You can handle that when you come back."

"Bet."

Cheese chose the right time to take a shower. The sedative I have will take thirty minutes to take effect and we were going to talk for about that long anyway. Soon as I heard the water come on in the bathroom, I peeked around the corner to make sure he was actually under the water. After confirming Cheese was indeed in the shower, I went to work. Emptying the vial into one of the hotel glasses, I waited until the water turned off before I opened the bottle. At the precise moment that Cheese exited the bathroom, I poured the Remy into the glass as he watched. Doing the same for myself, I added apple juice.

"You can put a couple cubes in there. I'm confident that you're not trying to poison me." I mugged his ass causing him to apologize. "My fault. I'm sorry for saying that."

"On some real shit. Why would you say something like that?" I asked.

Cheese picked up the glass I prepared for him, took me by the hand, and led me to the bed. He took two hefty swallows of the Remy. With the sedative and the alcohol, Cheese may feel real relaxed sooner than I contemplated. Especially if he kept drinking the way he was. I sipped my drink as I waited for him to say what was on his mind.

"Honey, I know I've told you many times how sorry I am for not having your back the way I should have when you were locked up. You are probably tired of hearing it but I really do apologize."

"That part of my life is over. I've already started my life moving forward. La'Darrius, you good."

"Am I? Sometimes, I feel as if you say what you think I want to hear. Look how long it took to even get you to spend time with me."

"*You* were the reason I didn't want to meet up. Why would I help you sneak around on your woman? The only reason I'm here tonight is because I'm trusting you and Letty are really done."

Cheese got up and went to pour himself another glass of alcohol. He threw back a double shot then poured some more. I looked on with surprise because I wondered why he drinking like that.

"You may want to slow down, La'Darrius," I said faking concern for his health but really wanted to know what had him in that state.

"My mind is heavy and there is so much I want to say and there's a few questions I want to ask too."

"How about you come sit down and let's talk about it. If your questions are geared toward me, I'm here to put whatever concerns you have to rest. Nothing is off limit."

Cheese stood staring at the floor and I walked over and hugged him from behind. He downed the contents in the glass then reached for the bottle again. Instead of watching him drown in his sorrows, I placed my hand over his to stop him. Cheese shook his head no and poured more liquor then closed the bottle.

Never looking at me, I felt something wet hit my arm which was still around Cheese's waist. He sniffled and I realized he was lowkey crying. Releasing my hold, I walked around to stand before him. Cheese turned his head away avoiding me seeing his entire face.

"Cheese talk to me. What's going on?"

"Honey, please don't look at me as a monster. I wanted to be with you and only you. Letty was preventing me from doing so. We argued about the night we spent together after the fest and she threatened to send the Feds after me. She didn't go to California with someone else, Honey. I killed her."

I stepped back in shock. The last thing I expected Cheese to say was he killed Letty. If anything, I was waiting for him to question me about Cheno being alive. He pulled me back into him and buried his chin on top of my head.

"Don't be scared of me. I would never hurt you, Honey," he slurred.

The alcohol was kicking in, or maybe it was the sedative I slipped in his drink. Not wanted him to fall out on the floor, I led Cheese back to the bed where we both sat quietly. He took a couple of sips of the drink before looking at the glass strangely.

"As I was saying, I won't hurt you. I love you so much and I've missed you." He paused. "The other day I had a meeting with Tank, Dro, Sway, Face, Meaty, Roc, and Yello Boy."

I ran the names over in my head because he had given important information I had to pass on to Cheno. Those were the last of Cheese's crew and no one was to be left alive in order to end this shit once and for all. I watched as Cheese blinked several times then rubbed his eyes. He looked at me then leaned over planting a kiss on my cheek.

"Honey, my people tried to convince me that you were only giving me the time of day because of what happened to Cheno. I never brought up the fact of knowing what happened to him and neither did you. Did you know Cheno was alive this entire time? Tell me the truth, Honey."

The glass fell out of Cheese's hand and his breathing labored. I knew the medicine was doing what it was supposed to do at that point. He fell back on the bed and I pretended to be alarmed by going to his aid. I ran to the bathroom, wet a face towel in cold water, then rushed back to his side.

"La'Darrius, what did you do?" I asked wiping his face.

"Nothing. I didn't do nothing." His eyes rolled in his head as he struggled to keep them open.

Amira told Breeze the sedative was only going to make him sleep for a period of time. I only used it to lay Cheese down so he wouldn't be a threat to my little ass. I kept up the charade until Cheese was out cold. Smacking him in the face told me the time started at that point. Going around the room, I collected the glasses and the liquor bottle. Then I went into the same compartment of my bag that I stored the vial, and removed a fentanyl filled syringe.

As I looked at Cheese lying back on the bed, I closed my eyes hoping God would forgive me for what I had done and again for what I was about to do. Cheese came after my family so he had to pay the ultimate price with his life. Walking slowly back to the bed, I sat beside him and lifted his arm. I chuckled because I used to joke with him back in the day about how he would be the perfect person to practice drawing blood on. Cheese had veins that stood out and would be hard to miss. Oh, how right I was.

Inserting the needle into a vein in his arm, tears rolled down my face. I hurried up and wiped them with the shoulder of my shirt before they could fall. Once the syringe was empty, I threw it in my bag and grabbed everything I had touched, adding it to my bag. Going into the bathroom, I snatched a towel from under the sink and wiped down the room. Using the same cloth to open the door, I peeked out before making my way to the elevator. Soon as it came, I pressed for the third floor. Soon as the doors opened, I scrambled to find the stairway.

Taking the stairs to the ground level, I went out a side door then walked around the building to my truck. I was shaking badly and had to sit for a few minutes to calm down. Pushing the button to start the engine, I carefully looked through my bag for my phone. I hit Breeze's contact soon as the device powered on.

"You good, Honey? Where you at?" Breeze asked.

"I'm on my way home. He's sleeping."

"Are you sure he's sleep?"

"Probably not all the way but he will be in a matter of minutes. I'm about to text you something. Just tell Cuz these are the ones that's left. I'll call you when I get home."

"Okay. Send it."

Breeze: Tank, Sway, Yello Boy, Roc, Meaty, Face, and Dro.

Backing out of the parking space, I cried all the way home. Killing Cheese was the last thing I had to do in the situation. The rest was up to everyone else. Taking lives did something to my soul. All I wanted to do was pray for forgiveness and hope like hell nobody close to me lost their lives.

Chapter 16

Cheno

I was on a mission to destroy these niggas lives. Cheese and his bitch ass crew fucked up when they killed my nigga, Fredo. I'm not saying the others didn't mean shit to me because they did, but that one was my ace. I rolled around on 15th and it was deserted. I remember somebody saying there was another spot them niggas had set up but I couldn't recall the location. It didn't matter because I was about to force Cheese and Tank to come see me.

Quell was riding shotgun in the car with me. His people were tailing as I drove to pay Tank's bitch ass mama a visit. Since they wanted to shoot old people, I was about to remind them they had one of them on their side too. Pearl was still hanging in there by the grace of God but it was lights out for Verna's old ass. She was lucky the first time around because I wasn't trying to kill her then. Now, I didn't give a fuck. Her son involved her in is bullshit when he kept coming for me.

Charlie was on my mind after Quell told me what Honey said to him. I relayed the shit to Scony and G so they were out staking out the car Dro and Charlie was in earlier. One of them would hit my line when they found out what was going on. We were about three blocks away from Tank's mama house and I had to make sure Wolf knew what the play was.

"Aye, call Wolf and make sure they know to park soon as I press on the brake in front of the house. We going around back."

Quell did what I asked and we were all on the same page. When I turned down Verna's block, I could see a nigga coming out of her crib then getting in a black Impala that was parked right in front. Good thing we wasn't too far up the block. The game plan changed right before my eyes. Quell peeped the gameplay too.

"Tank a smart muthafucka," he laughed as I slowed down. He was on the phone soon after. "Aye, back up and park. We got company."

I put my shit in reverse and pulled into the alley. Cutting the engine, I checked my Glock making sure the silencer was intact. Getting out, Quell met me on the driver side and Wolf, Foot, and Stubs got out of the truck joining us.

"I don't know how many niggas is in the Impala, but we hitting they ass from all angles. Two on the left, two on the right, and one stay in the back. We ain't doing no muthafuckin' talking. All action. Once everything is done, y'all head back to the truck and ride out. Me and Quell will finish up."

"Noted," Foot said.

We crept up the block and it was quiet. There was no one outside so we had to act fast. As we got closer to the vehicle, the smell of weed hit me indicating the windows were down. That alone gave full access to them niggas. Me and Quell went to the left, Wolf and Foot was on the right. Stubs brought up the rear. The muthafuckas was lackin' because they didn't even see us coming.

"Damn, this nigga Kendrick ain't coming off Drake's neck!" One of them said.

"And you won't know how the beef ends, bitch."

I dumped bullets into the car before they could even figure out what was happening. Nothing was heard. The only thing that could be seen was the smoke from our tools. I took a final look and we slumped four muthafuckas at once. Mission accomplished. Me and Quell ran through the gangway to the back of Verna's crib. Picking the lock to the back door, there was a TV on in the living room. Tank's mama was sleeping in a chair facing the tube. Slipping on a pair of leather gloves, I took my hunter knife from my pocket and walked quietly behind her. Grabbing her by the top of her head, I yanked her head back and sliced her throat from ear to ear. If I wasn't worried about my DNA being on the scene, I would've pissed down the bitch throat.

Running my covered finger along the wound, I wrote "Come see me" on the front of the white gown she wore. Then left that muthafucka the same way I came in. We took the back street to the alley where I parked my whip. Jumping in, I peeled out heading to the Dungeon. My life has been in shambles since all this shit started and I was taking control so I could walk freely. I was tired of the cat and mouse games. Larisa was next then I had Cheese and Tank. After that, I could sit back and scratch my muthafuckin balls in peace.

"Nigga, why did you kill the mama?" Quell asked.

"You do know one of them muthafuckas touched the woman I call my granny, right? The bitch who means the world to them isn't exempt. It was my kill. You didn't have shit to do with it."

Quell sat back and enjoyed the ride. There was a method to my madness and I didn't give a damn what nobody thought about how I went about handling it. Shit was about to get even uglier and if my nigga had a problem with me killing bitches, he bet not follow me into the Dungeon. My phone rang and it was Scony.

"Talk to me."

"Cheno, I'm following this nigga Dro. He just came back to the Maybach he and Charlie were in."

"Where that bitch at?" I asked.

"That's the thing. She's not with him. I put a detonator on the vehicle but I don't want to hit the switch because he is probably the only one who knows where she is. We tracked the car to his restaurant. It was parked in the back. I have a bad feeling about this, fam. Charlie is locked up somewhere. We just have to find out where they are holding her. Or, she could be dead."

I thought long and hard back to when I had an out of body experience after being shot and it automatically clicked. "Them niggas got a warehouse on 27th and Kedzie. Fuck Dro for now! Beat me there."

I was pushing my whip through the streets like a madman. Everything me and Charlie went through came flowing back. I had done her wrong for years and it wasn't until the very moment, I finally had the balls to admit; I didn't deserve her love. Charlie needed to be with a man who was going to love her and only her. I wasn't him. Hell, I didn't think I would ever be able to settle down with just one woman. I'd rather let her move on with her life than hold on making her unhappy. She would always hold a place in my heart and could get whatever she desires from me. But our time was up.

Knowing she was in danger and I was talking about killing her had me feeling some type of way. Honey's words rang in my ears. She shouldn't have had to tell me something I should've already known. Charlie stood ten toes down even through the bullshit I put her through. If them niggas hurt her in anyway, I wouldn't be able to forgive myself for not tearing the city up to find her.

I focused on the road as I neared the area of the warehouse. With no idea what I would walk into, I eased down the street looking around for the building. There was only one that could've been a warehouse and it was old. The windows in the front were boarded up so I didn't know how the fuck we would be able to get inside. Waiting for Scony to pull up, I tapped my fingers on the steering wheel impatiently.

"Quell, I think this is their warehouse. I have to find a way in. Stay here and wait on Scony. If I get in, I'll hit yo' phone."

"Cheno, I'm going in with you. Ain't no telling how many niggas they got in there with her."

"Don't worry, I got it covered. Just stay here."

Getting out of the car, I walked around the building searching for any way inside. As I got to the back, there were windows with glass panels. How stupid could niggas be? Yo' shit was supposed to be locked down like Fort Knox. Especially, if you kidnapping muthafuckas. I looked around for something to break the window with and spotted a pipe. Not giving a fuck who was inside, I busted the muthafucka out. Clearing the shard pieces from the panel, I used my jacket to protect my hands from getting cut as I hoisted myself onto the sill. Access granted. Soon as my feet touched the concrete floor, I gagged. There was no way I would hold any type of meeting in such a place. The warehouse should be burned to the fuckin' ground. As a matter of fact... I thought placing a call to Scony.

"I'm almost there, fam."

"Aye, stop and get a couple cans of gas. I'm burning this shit down," I growled. "I just got inside. I have to find Charlie."

"Aight, be careful and keep yo' eyes open."

"You already know."

Standing stagnant for a few minutes as I pulled my Glock from behind my back. I wanted a muthafucka to come at me trying to save the day but it never happened. The pungent smell of mildew, dead rats, and who knew what else filled my nostrils as I crept through the building. After a while, my eyes adjusted to the semi darkness around me. I had the vision of a cat who was seeking out its prey. The deafening silence was interrupted by a woman's cries just as the thought of turning around to leave entered my mind. Swiftly, I followed the sound of her mumbles. The closer I got, the clearer her words became.

"Please, God send someone to me. I know you're not going to allow me to die in here like this," she cried. "You have to give Cheno a sign that I'm in trouble, Lord. He will come save me. I know he will because he has never let harm come my way." Charlie all but begged for her life to be spared and it touched me.

"Somebody help me!" She screamed.
As I was rounding the corner of the dimly lit room, Charlie sat bound to a chair with her head hung low. She looked so defeated and hadn't noticed anyone was in the room. I stood admiring her for a few more seconds before I made my presence known.

"I'm here, Charlie. Stop all that crying."

Charlie's head snapped in the direction of my voice and she broke down. I saw the moment the tension left her body because her shoulders relaxed instantly. I tucked my gun then pulled the knife from its holster. Charlie couldn't take her eyes off me as she cried. I could tell she wanted to react but there was nothing she could do being she was tied to the chair. I stooped low so I could cut the rope from her wrists. The moment she was released, she wrapped her arm around my neck tightly.

"Oh my God! Thank you! Thank you," she praised burying her head in the crook of my neck. I thought they were going to make it back to kill me. I'm so sorry, Cheno."

"You have nothing to be sorry about. Calm down so I can set you free."

After releasing her from the restraints, Charlie hugged me fully and in return I did the same. I sighed with relief and was glad I got to her before Cheese and his people could do any more damage to her. Stepping back, I checked her over to make sure she was alright. She was still fully dressed except the heels she had on when I saw her were no longer on her feet. Scooping her in my arms, I carried her back to the window.

Scony was there with the gas cans and Quell looked as if he was about to climb through the window. When I appeared with Charlie in my arms, both of them sprang into actions to help get her out. Once she was safely in the arms of my nigga, Quell handed me the cans.

"I'm about to torch this bitch. Give me five minutes. Take her to my car."

"You got three," Scony said walking away carrying Charlie.

Quell made his way through the window and jumped down into the warehouse. Without a word, he picked up a can and started slinging gas. I did the same with the other. Making our way throughout the dump, I made sure to douse everything I knew would burn. There was as so much paper and shit around, there was no way the warehouse would survive the fire. Going into the room Charlie was held, I threw gas everywhere. A door tucked off in the corner caught my attention. They say curiosity killed the cat but I had to see what was behind it.

"Cheno, what the hell you up to?" Quell asked.

"Something behind this door is calling my name," I said turning the knob. "Bingo! Stupid muthafucka!"

Quell came over to see what the excitement was about. There were about fifteen duffle bags stacked neatly. Only a dumb ass dope nigga would stash his shit in a place like that. The contents of the bags were either drugs or money. Unzipping one of the bags on the top of the first pile, I rubbed my hands like Birdman when I saw the rubber banded bills inside. I took my phone out of my pocket and made a call.

"What's taking y'all so long?" Scony asked irritably when he answered.

"We hit the jackpot. Pull my car to the window. This nigga Cheese got his life savings tucked away in an unlocked closet. It's ours now."

"Cheno, light the match and leave that shit. You not hurtin' for bread, fam."

"Damn right I'm not but I'd be a damn fool to burn this money. So, bring yo' ass so I can pack this shit up."

Three trips and we were officially duffle bag bandits. Scony was talking major shit but I wasn't trying to hear his ass. I hoped Cheese had insurance on that raggedy ass building because he was going to need it. Quell was about to climb back through the window but I put a stop to it. There was no need for both of us to be inside. All I had to do was start the flame. Using three of the bills I'd collected, I lit the corner and watched them burn before throwing it to the ground. I stood watching the flames dance around me before making my exist. These niggas didn't know the type of muthafucka they were playing with. they were going to find out the hard way.

***

The ride to my house with Charlie was one I wasn't used to. She rode silently without asking any questions. Instead of taking her back to the place in Downers Grove, I was taking her to my crib with me. Entering the garage, I parked and got out to escort her inside. Charlie didn't wait for me grab the food from the back seat. When I stepped into my kitchen, Charlie was nowhere in sight. Placing the bags on the counter, I went back to the trunk and retrieved the bags I'd taken from Cheese. After ten minutes of back and forth to the basement, I set out to find the woman that disappeared from my sights.

I could hear the shower running in the bathroom and knew I had found her. Knocking on the door, I opened it slightly without going inside. The scent of lavender invaded my nostrils and I missed it. My home was not a home without Charlie being there but it was something I had to get used to.

"Aye, I'm putting some clothes on the bed for you. Come down to the kitchen when you're done. We can talk while eating."

Charlie didn't respond so I closed the door and gathered one of my shirts, boxers, and a pair of socks then put them on the bed. I left the room and headed back downstairs to wait for her to join me. A few moments later, Charlie sat down looking refreshed. She played with the food in front of her before glancing in my direction.

"Cheno, I can't thank you enough for coming for me. You didn't have to, but you did and I appreciate you for doing so."

She took the initiative to start the conversation and I sat listening. I wanted to clear the air between us and it was one of the reasons I chose to bring her home with me. The main reason was to make sure she was no longer in harm's way.

"The love I have for you wouldn't allow me to turn my back knowing it was a chance you could've been killed. Actually, I know for a fact they wouldn't leave you alive to tell a soul what they had done to you. We haven't been on the greatest terms but the love we shared can't be denied," I said taking a swallow of water.

What I had to express was stuck in my throat and I had a hard time getting the words out of my mouth. Letting Charlie go completely was a tough reality for me. It wouldn't be fair to hold on after all the bullshit I'd put her through.

"If we are being honest here, my plan was to find you, beat yo' ass, then put a bullet through your head."

The look of bewilderment was Charlie's reaction to what I said. "Why the fuck would you want to do that?" She asked enraged.

"It's not how I feel now, but when I saw you come out of that nigga's crib. That shit pissed me off."

"So, you were gon' kill me because you saw me with another man? How fuckin' Sway," she chuckled.

"Nope. Seeing you with the muthafucka who tried to take out my people was the reason you almost lost yo' life. I wasn't stalking you; we were staking out that nigga's crib and you just so happened to enter the picture. All types of thoughts were running through my mind. At the time, in my mind you were out to kill me. You were the bitch feeding them information on me. So, yeah, you were about to get this work right along with them."

Nodding, Charlie finished chewing the food in her mouth. "I'll give you that. To clear the air, I didn't know him as Dro until today. I met Caesar, the successful entrepreneur who enjoyed having fun and making me smile. Why he approached me seemed very genuine. Other than him becoming upset because I wouldn't accept his gifts, he didn't come off as being shady. I guess I'll never know why he befriended me. I never want to see him again after what he did."

"You sure as fuck won't because he's about to be casket sharp with the rest of them muthafuckas," I snapped. "Enough about that. The most important issue I want to address is us. I can't even sit here and say I wasn't mad about you being with somebody outside of me. Charlie, you are any man's dream. I had you in the palm of my hand and fucked it up. I want to be a selfish nigga by demanding you stay with me, but I won't."

"Cheno—"

"Nah, ma, let me finish. I've had you out here looking like a damn fool for years and it ends now. There's someone out there who will love you unconditionally, make you smile instead of crying, hell marry your ass and knock you up. That person is not me, love. I wanted the marriage with kids but under the conditions of me doing whatever I want without you harping in my face about it. That was never fair for you to deal with. I have too much respect to put you through another day of my bullshit. I want to apologize from the bottom of my heart for the pain I've caused. I feel we should go our separate ways because overall, our friendship is forever."

For some reason, I felt Charlie was about to fight me on this one. No matter what a man put a woman through, she was going to be the one going to war for the relationship. Tears welled in her eyes and she didn't try to hide them. I reached across the table to caress her hand and she moved hers away. The tears ran down her face and she just allowed them to fall. I felt like shit for laying this shit on her after what she had been through. Charlie sniffed and wiped her face with a napkin then blew her nose.

"I'm glad you realize all the turmoil you put me through. The relationship we had started with pure love but ended up being shit in the long run. I've cried endless nights wondering caused you to treat me the way you did and I never got an answer. The past couple of months gave me time to think about why I stayed all those years despite of the foul shit you were doing. Love isn't supposed to hurt and now I understand," she said wiping her nose.

"Cheno, I did everything I was supposed to when it came to you. I cooked, cleaned, fucked on demand, helped you with your businesses, fought your bitches, listened to your lies, and most of all, I loved you when you didn't really love me in return. You loved the thought of what type of woman I was. You didn't want me, but you didn't want nobody else to reap the benefits of me either."

I sat listening to Charlie finally pour her heart out to tell me how she really felt about our relationship and every word stung. I knew what I was doing was wrong, but hearing the woman I loved say the words out loud, made me feel like a piece of shit. I had really hurt her and there was no coming back from it.

"When I walked away from you after learning about Larisa, it was the straw that broke the camel's back. I should've done it a long time ago but the love kept me in place hoping things would change. Like you, I know there's a woman who would be able to handle you and make you realize love is a beautiful thing. That woman is not me. I have to agree with you and remove myself from this toxic environment. Cheno, I will forever love you. I just hope once all of this stuff in the streets is over, you will sit back and think about all you have done in this relationship so you won't repeat the cycle with someone else."

"I want you to know you did nothing wrong, Charlie. All this is on me."

"Oh, I know."

"I will be there for you in any way I can. You can stay here until you find a place to call your own. In fact, I'm going to pay for it."

I stood and went down to the basement and came up with one of the duffle bags. Sitting it at Charlie's feet, I sat back down. I owed her more than what was in the bag, but a nigga had to start somewhere.

"That's for you. Courtesy of Cheese," I smirked. "I don't know how much is in there, but it's reparation for every tear you've ever cried behind me. You are a great woman, Charlie. I got you, ma."

"Cheno, you don't have to pay me for dealing with your bullshit. It came with being with a street nigga. You wrote a playbook I will forever live by. The next man I allow into my heart won't be able to sell me a dream thanks to you. Soon as I find a place, I'll be out of here. But don't try to sneak in the guest room at night. Go to them hoes who was crying and talking shit online. You have plenty of pussy to choose from. Not mine though."

"You a trip but I hear you." I laughed. Charlie got up to throw the food she didn't finish away. "I got that. Go rest. I love you, Charlie. Again, I'm sorry."

"Yeah, you're a sorry muthafucka. I won't remind you again," she winked leaving me in the kitchen.

Chapter 17

Tank

I woke up early to handle the bitch at the warehouse. I'd been calling Cheese to let him know what was going on and the muthafucka hasn't answered yet. He was probably laying under Honey's left titty listening to her lie about not knowing Cheno was alive. The nigga was skating on thin ice with me because I had a feeling the bitch was going to convince him to turn on my ass. If push came to shove, I would put a bullet in his head with the quickness. Cousin or not.

Cheese wasn't the only person on my shit list. That bitch Danielle was too. She ran off with my damn truck and hasn't been answering her phone either. I think her ass went back to Detroit with my shit. She was going to be in for a rude awakening when she gets pulled over for driving a stolen vehicle. I should've known better than to give her the keys anyway. I didn't even know her good pussy having ass like that.

As I got closer to the warehouse, I noticed there was more traffic than normal in the area. Turning the corner, I had to park at the gas station up the street and walk back. There were uniforms all over the place, as well as fire marshals. What surprised me was the warehouse was no more. The muthafucka had burned to the ground. That was the place Cheese kept majority of his money. The nigga was going to be pissed. I turned around and got the fuck out of there because I didn't want to be around when they discovered a dead body amongst the rubble. After getting gas and a pack of cigarettes, I sat in my car trying to get hold of Cheese. He still wasn't answering.

My nerves were all over the place and the only thing that would get me right was coke. I had to agree with Cheese, the drug had me in a chokehold and I couldn't come off of it. Before eating, shitting, going to sleep, or to calm myself down, I had to snort a line or two. Yeah, I had a problem. So what. As I put the car in drive, my phone rang and it was Miss Darlene. The last time she called, Cheno's bitch ass had my mama's house shot up. I told her if she needed anything to call me and I had her. She may have been calling to cash in on that offer.

"Hey, Miss Darlene, how you doing?"

"Issac..." she sniffled.

"What's wrong?" I asked pulling out of the gas station.

"It's your mama. The police are at her house again. There was a car parked outside and the young men inside are dead."

I hit the steering wheel hard because Meaty, Roc, Yello Boy, and Face was supposed to been protecting my mama. If they were dead, that meant them bitches were able to get in her crib. Miss Darlene was crying so shit couldn't be good and I was scared to ask the one question I needed an answer to. When I opened my mouth to ask, Miss Darlene said something that almost made me cause an accident when I swerved into the next lane.

"The coroner just picked the bodies up. Issac, somebody slashed your mother's throat and the police want to talk to you. I'm so sorry."

"Tell them muthafuckas you couldn't get me on the phone! I can't come over there. I'm about to call Cheese to come. I'll call you back."

"Wait..."

I hung up before Miss Darlene could finish. My mama was dead. There was no reason to go over there if she was no longer there. Cheno was the one who did it and that told me the bitch was no longer in the warehouse. The coke was kicking in causing my nose to run constantly. Dro had to be the one who freed the bitch unless Cheno got to his ass too. I got on the expressway and sped all the way to Downers Grove. The nigga had some explaining to do.

Pulling up to Dro's crib, I got out and made my way to the front door. I bypassed the doorbell and banged on that muthafucka hard as I could. Dro was lucky I didn't kick his shit in. I could see him walking down the stairs with a scowl on his face. His expression didn't change when he saw me on the other side. Instead, he snatched the door open aggressively.

"What happened at the warehouse?" I sneered.

"I don't know what the fuck you talking about but you better watch yo' tone when talking to me. I'm not one of them niggas that's scared of you, Tank. Now, come in and tell me what's going on."

I walked in his crib bumping his ass out of my way while doing it. Dro, chortled as he closed the door and locked it. When he came into the living room, I went in on his ass.

"The only two people who knew about what was going on at the warehouse was me and you. Oh, and the bitch we had tied up in there. How the fuck did she get out, Dro?"

He looked at me strangely. "What do you mean she got out? We were supposed to leave her there without touching her! I know damn well you not trying to say I had something to do with what happened there."

"Hell yell, I am! I didn't move the bitch and burned the building down. So, it had to be you."

"Burned down the building? Nigga, the coke you been snorting up your nose got you delusional as fuck. I didn't do none of the shit you just claimed I did. Whatever you did, own that shit because I will fuck you up in here."

"Cheese told my business?" I couldn't believe this shit.

"Tank, you got the shit all around the rim of your fuckin' nose! You told me. That's on you though. I need to find out what happened to Charlie."

"Find out what happened to her? I hope the bitch is dead! You had plans to go get her, didn't you? Snake ass, nigga. I was right, that bitch got yo' nose wide open."

"Just as bad as that coke got yours. Get the fuck out of my crib. I'm done doing business with you. All you muthafuckas messy as fuck. I'll get at them niggas G and Scony on my own. Messing around with yo' ass will have me dead before nightfall. Do not call me to do another job for you. As a matter of fact, lose my number."

If Dro thought I was about to deal with the shit he agreed to see through to the end by myself, he was crazy. Cheese wasn't answering his phone and all my other soldiers were dead. Sway came to mind and I hit his line.

"Tank, what the fuck is going on? They killed yo' mama."

"I know. I just got the call but it's too hot over there. We need to find Cheno today!"

"I'm at the crib. Come through. I'll be ready."

"Okay. Give me about an hour."

Ending the call, I turned to Dro. He was shaking his head no before I even opened my mouth. Pushing him was something I wasn't going to do because he wasn't a professional hitman for nothing. Honestly, I think Dro should retire and stick to running his restaurants because he missed his target, it's the reason we were still in the current bind. Had he hit G and Scony at the memorial, Cheno wouldn't have been shit without them.

"Can you do something for me? I won't ask for shit after this." I asked. "All I need is for you to track Cheese's phone. He's not answering like I told you before. I have to pull up on him."

Dro sat down on the couch then started typing on his laptop. After a few minutes, he got a hit.

"He's at the Marriot Marquis on 21st and Prairie. It looks like Cheese is ignoring you for pussy." Dro laughed. "Yeah, y'all priorities all fucked up. Now you have two muthafuckas to help you get revenge. You don't need me."

Dro stood then walked to the door. The nigga was putting me out like a bitch he no longer wanted to deal with. If he thought G and Scony wasn't coming for him, he was a fool. I left without saying shit else to him. He wanted me gone; I gave his ass exactly what he wanted. My next stop was to pick up Sway then head to the hotel to holla at Cheese with his missing in action ass. I called Sway when I got close and told him to be outside. When I pulled up, he was waiting as I asked.

"Man, this shit is crazy. I'm sorry about your moms. What the fuck is Cheese on?" Sway asked soon as he closed the door.

"I don't know. If his ass laid up with Honey, both of them bitches gon' die today. I've been blowing his shit up and now my mama got caught up in this shit, his ass still ain't answering."

"Cheno came back like John Wick. I know we hit everybody at his trap but damn. I didn't think he would respond this fast."

"He knew going after my mama again was going to bring me out. That's why I didn't go over there because I don't think it would've mattered how many police was out there, the nigga was going to react. He wasn't going to get at me that easy. Cheno gotta find me."

"Fuck that hiding shit. They killed yo' mama!"

"Tell me something I don't know! You want to go after Cheno, right? Where are we gon' find his ass?" Sway didn't have an answer and neither did I. "Exactly! We don't know the first place to look. But Cheese can lead us to him through Honey. She is the only way we're going to get remotely close to that nigga."

"You right." Sway agreed. "Where we going though?"

"To the Marriot on 21st. Cheese is there."

"That's why you said he was laid up." Sway shook his head. "I don't think being with Honey would make him ignore phone calls though. Especially not yours with everything going on out here. He may have just gone to the hotel to get away from Letty's jealous ass."

I never thought Cheese may have needed to get away. It was farfetched but it may render true. We were about to find out. I pulled into the parking lot and spotted Cheese whip right away. Pulling my car next to his, I got out. I checked to make sure my cousin didn't get caught lacking. He wasn't inside. Me and Sway entered the hotel heading straight to the service desk.

"Welcome to Marriot Marquis. How may I help you?" The man behind the desk asked.

"I need to know what room La'Darrius Hawkins is in," I said getting right to the point.

"Let me see if there's anyone by that name who's checked in." He typed away on the keyboard.

"He's here because his car is parked in the lot."

"Sometimes people park here and go walking to save on parking. I'm not saying that's what has taken place, but it happens more often than not," he replied. "Okay, you are correct. Mr. Hawkins is here but he should've checked out by now. Allow me to call. Maybe he needs a wakeup call."

"Man, just give me the room number," I sneered.

"I'm afraid I can't do that, sir. It's against company policy."

Joel, I learned his name by the name tag he wore, picked up the phone. He stood staring at me with a smile, but after a couple seconds, the smile fell from his face. Repeating the action, I guess Cheese still didn't answer. That shit didn't sit well with me. Joel dialed another number and told someone to do a wellness check but he turned his head whispering the room number. I wanted to put my gun his face after that. It wasn't the time to be locked up so I chilled. When the phone rang, Joel answered and the color drained from his face. He hung up the phone and picked up a walkie talkie.

"Sara, I need you to cover the front desk for a few minutes."

"On my way."

I had no clue what was going on and Joel didn't seem as if he was going to tell me either. He walked down a hall and a woman who I assumed was the Sara chick took his place behind the desk. She sat down avoiding eye contact but I wasn't standing there for decorations. I needed to know what the fuck Joel wasn't telling me.

"Aye, Sara. Where did Joel go? I need him to tell me what's up with my cousin."

"Um, someone will be down to talk to you shortly. Joel didn't disclose what the issue was before he got on the elevator. We'll just have to wait. You guys can have a seat over there for now. I'm sure he will be back momentarily."

Soon as I was about to pull my gun, police and an ambulance stopped in front of the entrance. My heart started beating fast because it was ironic how Joel looked like he had seen a ghost after he answered the call and now there was a team of EMTs rushing to the same elevators he had gone to. Something was wrong with Cheese and these muthafuckas weren't saying shit to me.

I left the hotel and took everything illegal off my person and Sway did the same. When we went back inside, there was an officer talking to Joel off to the side of the lobby. He nodded in my direction and the officer walked toward us. The grim expression told me whatever happened was not good.

"Hello, I'm Officer Hobbs. What is your relation to La'Darrius Hawkins?"

"I'm his cousin. Is he in trouble?" I asked.

"I'm sorry to be the one to inform you. Mr. Hawkins has transitioned," he said lowly.

"Transitioned where? I know muthafuckin' well you not standing here telling me my cousin is dead."

"From the information I have gathered, the hotel employees went up to do a wellness check and found Mr. Hawkins unresponsive. The EMTs didn't find a pulse. His cause of death will not be determined until an autopsy is performed. I'm sorry for your loss."

"Nah, my cousin is not dead. I need to see for myself to make sure its him."

I was fighting the tears that were threatening to fall from my eyes. I was just talking about coming to kill his ass if he was here with Honey and Cheese was already dead. My world was crashing down around me and it was all my fault. Everybody that lost their lives were gone because I stole from the wrong nigga. My mama and Cheese were all I had left and now I didn't even have them.

"That won't be possible, sir. I do have his identification card here for you to identify him with."

The officer held out the ID for me to look at. When I saw Cheese's picture, name, date of birth, and address, realization kicked in. I fell to my knees and wept like a baby. Sway walked away trying to suppress his own cries. In that moment the coroner walked in pulling a gurney with a black body bag on top of it. In all my years of witnessing someone die, I had never seen them muthafuckas come pick up a body so damn quick.

"Sir, are you going to be okay?" The officer asked.

Shaking my head I stood to my feet. I held the ID out for the officer to take because I couldn't stand around to watch them wheel my cousin out of there in a bag. It felt as if the walls were caving in on me and I couldn't breathe. Air was what I needed and fast.

"I need to gather some information from you. Have a seat and do not leave. Is that understood?"

I nodded and waited for him to round the corner. Once the coast was clear, me and Sway hauled ass out of the hotel and into my whip. More police cars pulled in as I backed out. I maneuvered past them and got the hell away from there. With nobody to call, I drove in silence.

"Do you think Cheno had anything to do with this?" Sway asked.

"I don't know. If the shit was homicide, the police would've questioned me then and there. The main question he would've wanted to know was if there was anybody who would want to hurt Cheese. That didn't happen. Honey was behind this shit. We're about to go by her funky ass shop and wait until she pulls up to open for the day. She gon' pay for the shit that happened to my cousin. I told Cheese she was going to be the death of him. He should've listened. Now he is dead."

"We gon' get them for Cheese, ya mama, and every fallen soldier who died by the hands of Cheno."

Sway wiped at his eyes as I headed to see Miss Kill a nigga, Honey.

Chapter 18

Quell

When I called for Honey to open the door after I left Cheno, she gave me a hug and went back to the bedroom. Being the kind of man I was, her actions in my mind were from the events which had taken place over the past months. So, I took a shower and got in bed with her. Honey initiated a sexual encounter and I made sure she moaned, soaked the bed, and scratched the hell out of my back so she could rest better. When she had a nigga like me, there was no need for any type of sleep aids because it was my mission to make her ass drift off like a baby every time.

I was sleeping soundly and thought I heard someone crying. Rolling over, I listened for a few seconds but I didn't hear anything. Honey was still asleep so it couldn't have been her. I snuggled closer to her body and wrapped my arms around her waist so I could go back to sleep. After closing my eyes, Honey's voice spoke out to me lowly. It was so low I thought I imagined that as well.

"Did you say something, babe?"

"I killed Cheese last night," she whispered.

Her revelation made me sit up in the bed. If I wasn't mistaken, Honey had no business being around Cheese because I asked her not to go through with the plan. Hearing her say she killed him had me hot. Things could've gone left and Cheese could've killed her. Honey turned to face me and she was indeed crying.

"I'm sorry for not listening to you. Cheese had to go and I knew if you and Cheno went after him, it would have gotten messy. Cheese still trusted me, Quell. I had to be the one to do it."

"You didn't have to do shit! We just killed all his people and on top of that, they knew Cheno wasn't dead! You as his cousin knew firsthand, he was alive. It didn't dawn on you that Cheese may have thought you were trying to set him up? He could have lured you somewhere to strangle the fuck out of you, Honey!"

"I know! Cheese was under the impression we would be together regardless of the beef he and Cheno had going on. I made him believe it could happen. When I agreed to use myself to get close to Cheese, I knew he would never hurt me. Hell, the nigga killed the bitch he was with to be with me."

"Use your head, Honey! If he could kill the woman he claimed to love, what made you believe you were exempt? Let me guess, you know him better than he knows himself."

"That's right. I do know him like that. The job is done and I'm being ridiculed for it," she said shaking her head before rolling over.

"No, you did something I asked you to allow me to handle and you did it anyway. I wouldn't call that ridiculing; It's me calling you out for not listening. Honey, the shit could've been bad and we could've been putting a missing person's report out because he did something to you. If I didn't give a fuck about you, I wouldn't be as mad as I am."

"Well, it didn't happen and Cheese is no longer amongst the living. Now, leave it alone."

"I won't just let you brush this off. If you want me to congratulate you for going against the grain, you're sadly mistaken. I'm gon' ask you this and I want the truth. Did you fuck that nigga?"

Honey sat up. Her exposed breasts heaved as she glared at me. "There you go worrying about the wrong shit. Unlike

195

the female that hurt you, I never have to fuck a nigga for anything. Especially, not Cheese." She snapped. "I'm going to tell this story one time so you better listen well. After this, I don't want to hear anything else about it."

Honey told me everything about the meet up with Cheese from start to finish. As I listened, I was truly impressed with how she carried out the shit actually. Hearing her explain how she covered her tracks made me think if she lied about why she had gone to prison. Honey sounded like a hardcore killer. When she finished, she got up, and went into the bathroom slamming the door behind her.

During the entire time of her commentary, Honey didn't have to think about anything she was saying. That alone told me she was telling the truth. It also let me know she was hurting behind what she had to do. Not to mention, she had just killed her own mother hours beforehand.

While I waited for Honey to come out of the bathroom, I turned on the news to see what was going on in the city. The first story being covered was the fire of Cheese's warehouse. I laughed because me and Cheno did that.

"This better be good. It's too fuckin' early," Cheno said groggily.

"Turn to Channel 7. They're covering the story about the warehouse fire."

I could hear Cheno shuffling around then the newscaster's voice filled his room. We were taking in everything being said. There were no leads in the case and the fire marshal suspected arson. They weren't wrong.

"We won't go down for doing that shit. It's all on Cheese's bitch ass. Maybe he needs to sit in jail like Honey had to do. This time, he would do his own muthafuckin' time."

"I don't think there's a prison where he is." I laughed.

"What you talking about?"

"I'm about to go to the shop. You should come with me and get the ink you been talking about. I'll fill you in there."

"Aight bet. I'll hit you when I'm ready."

Soon as Cheno hung up, he was calling back. I knew what he wanted because I saw the shit on the news too. Another reporter was standing outside Tank's mama's house. Honey came out of the bathroom and got back in bed.

"We famous than a muthafucka 'round these parts," Cheno gloated. "I got all them muthafuckas in the spotlight." The news segment went back to the station and the reporter had more news.

"A breaking news story just landed in front of me coming from the Marriot Marquis Hotel. La'Darrius Hawkins was found unresponsive in his suite. He was pronounced deceased on the scene. Hawkins was a well-known drug dealer who was not a stranger to Chicago Police. He is also the nephew of Verna Woodard; the woman killed in her home sometime last night. Hawkin's death is not being investigated as a homicide at this time. An autopsy will take place later today. We will share updates as we get them."

"La'Darrius Hawkins is Cheese!" Cheno yelled. "Somebody got hold of that nigga before we could. Who the fuck could've done that?"

I didn't say shit because we were on the phone. I looked over at Honey and she smirked at me. Wanting to smile but didn't because her hardheaded ass shouldn't have gone out alone. The news segment verified what she had told me and Cheese definitely died, Homicide nor foul play wasn't suspected.

"You still there?" Cheno asked.

"Yeah, I'm about to get myself together. I'll be there in thirty."

"Aight. Aye! Where's Honey?"

"Her hardheaded ass right here but let me get off this phone."

"Tell her to come over so she can keep Charlie company."

"Okay," I said ending the call. "Cheno wants you to come to his crib to be with Charlie."

197

I left her ass in the bedroom and went into the bathroom to shower. Cheese and his crew met their demise all in a matter of hours. I hadn't seen no shit like that in a minute. It was hard for me to be happy because of what Honey had done. Some would tell me to let the anger go, but fuck that. Honey was wrong as two left feet. Hearing the bathroom door open, I washed my body thoroughly and got out. As I snatched a towel off the shelf, Honey eyed my dick lustfully. Walking into the bedroom, I put on my clothes. Honey was right on my heels.

"How long are you going to be mad at me?"

"I don't know. I'll be back. I'm going to the shop."

Stepping into my shoes, I picked up my phone, wallet, and keys before walking toward her. I kissed her on the cheek then left. Honey followed me downstairs and watched while I put on my jacket.

"Put my clothes in a bag and I'll get them when I get back. Be careful going to Cheno's."

Going into my crib, Wolf was up and dressed. I went into the kitchen and grabbed an apple. "You wanna roll to the shop with me and Cheno?"

"I can do that," Wolf said. "It seems like shit has died down here. Me and the homies gon' head back to Dallas in a couple days."

"Aight. Let's go."

When we got in my truck, I backed out of the driveway. My niggas coming to Chicago to have my back meant everything to me. Before I left the crib to move, I handed the business over to them putting Wolf in charge of the operation. Cheno was ready to go full legit and put the drug game behind him. We talked about the shit the night before and I agreed with him. He had a lot of dope he was going to ship to Dallas. Being partners who are now out of the game, a percentage of the drugs would go to Cheno. Everything after that, the percentage would be mine.

"I appreciate y'all coming up here."

"Man, we wouldn't have had it any other way. Hell, y'all didn't really need us so, I'm not gon' take credit for y'all work. This shit was wild though."

"Tell me about it," I chortled. "Aye, me and Cheno getting some shit together for y'all to take back south. He plans to have it shipped so y'all can get on the plane."

"What you talkin'?"

"Seventy-five keys."

Sharing with him what Cheno and I had discussed, Wolf smiled from ear to ear. The keys were a starter pack. After that, Cheno would set up all drug deals through his plug to make sure they ate on a regular. Explaining the numbers and how shit was going to move from that day forward, Wolf was all in. We blazed up and listened to the Kendrick Lamar and Drake diss tracks all the way to the shop. With everything going on, I wasn't in the midst of the beef and a nigga had to catch up. *They Not Like Us* blared through the speakers as we mellowed out. I parked in my designated spot in front of my business.

"Is Honey opening the shop today?" Wolf asked.

"Nawl. Why?"

"There's a car parked in front like they're waiting for it to open. I could be wrong."

I looked in the direction of Honey's shop and there indeed was someone parked outside. As I studied the car, I could see the two niggas inside. Handing Wolf my keys, I got out to see what the fuck was going on. Instead of walking up to the vehicle, I went to the door of the shop and acted like I was pissed it was closed. As I was heading away, one of the niggas spoke out to me.

"Excuse me." I stopped. "What time do they usually open?"

"Nine, but since the owner loss her cousin, she's been closed. Today is supposed to be the day she opens back up for business. It's past nine so she may come in around eleven. At least I hope she does because I need an oil change."

"What's her cousin's name?" the nigga asked.

"Shid, I don't know. I didn't know nothing about her until she took over the shop. You know her?" I asked. "My bad, I'm Jerome. I own the tattoo shop a couple doors down."

"I'm Tank. I need some new ink so, I'm gon' check you out."

"That's what's up. I gotta get back to get my day started. I'll come back to check if Honey opens up. At least you'll be first in line," I laughed.

Turning to walk away, the smile fell from my face and I took my time getting back to my spot. The moment I stepped inside, I hit Cheno up. I had to catch him before he made it remotely close.

"What up?"

"Aye, where you at?" I asked.

"I'm about five minutes away."

"Tank is literally staking out Honey's shop. I talked to the nigga and he told me who he was."

"His ass is about to die," Cheno growled.

"Fam, you cannot kill that man in the parking lot. There are plenty people out here shopping. We have to lure them away. Pull close enough to see his whip, I'm about to send Wolf over there in my truck with a play for them to leave. Then, we can follow them."

"I'm about to pull in now."

"Aight." I turned to Wolf. "Go out to the truck, pull up to Honey's shop in front of that nigga. I need you to pretend you're talking to Breeze about a custom job she's been putting off. I'm about to call yo' phone so I can hear if he says something."

"I got you," he said. I called his phone and waited.

Wolf was able to pull my truck up without them seeing where he came from and got out. I could hear him cussing lowly then his voice became clearer when he took his phone out. There was silence then he put on a performance good enough for an Academy Award.

"Aye, Breeze, are you coming into the shop today?" Wolf paused. "I'm sorry about yo' loss but it's been weeks and I need the work done on my truck. This shit ain't professional at all, man. I put a deposit down and I haven't had an ounce of service done on my shit."

Wolf walked back to the truck mad as fuck. He drove out of the lot then merged into traffic and came back around by the Target. I watched as Tank and whoever was in the car with him sat talking. When I saw the brake lights come on, I told Wolf to come scoop me while I locked up the shop.

"When this nigga gets on the expressway, I don't give a fuck. We lighting his ass up from all angles," Cheno said as he followed Tank.

Wolf pulled up and drove off before I could close the door. I reached into the glove compartment to get my Glock. Handing it to Wolf, I leaned into the back seat pulling my AK-47 from under the seat. Tank was the last man standing and he was about go out looking like Swiss cheese. The way he handled Honey was the reason I was on his ass like white on rice. We never got on the expressway and was still on the street.

"Cheese, where the fuck this nigga going?" I asked.

"I don't know but I'm not letting him out of my sight."

Cheno fell back two cars and was still pretty close to Tank. We drove a little while longer before I saw his car turn off. Cheno stalled at the intersection before making the turn.

"He's going into the Wendy's drive-thru. Turn left into the Home Depot parking lot. There are three cars in front of him and two behind. The nigga's trapped. It's time to catch the rat."

The line was barely moving giving me the opportunity to mask up. Throwing Wolf a mask too, I told Cheno not to forget to put something over his face.

"Do I look like a rookie to you? Nigga, let's go."

Cocking my choppa, I got out the car and raced across the street. All three of us started blasting into Tank's vehicle. The cars in front of him sped away, the woman in the car behind him jumped out and ran around the building. Tank's horn blared as his head rested against the steering wheel. Cheno shot him in the head to make sure he wouldn't live to see another day. We raced back across the street and I got in the driver seat peeling through the parking lot.

Cheno told me to meet him at his crib before ending the call. I hoped on the expressway and cruised all the way to the south suburbs. When I pulled into Cheno's driveway, he was sitting on top of his ride smoking a blunt as if he was celebrating.

"It's finally over," I said.

"Not quite. I still have one bitch to take care of but I'm going to do that one later on tonight. Thank y'all for your help. Come in the crib with me. I got something for y'all."

We walked into Cheno's house and Charlie and Honey were sitting in the living room watching TV. I looked to see what they were looking at because Honey was crying. The young Zoe Saldana was running through the streets in the movie *Columbiana*. I was confused as to why she was crying during an action movie. Shaking my head, I walked over wrapping my arms around her neck.

"She is all alone and they are trying to kill her after killing both of her parents," she sobbed.

"It's okay, baby. It's just a movie." I kissed her on top of her head before pulling her closer into me. "I'll be right back so I can take you home."

Charlie tried her best to stifle the laugh she was holding in. "She will be alright. I promise. Go downstairs, I got her."

Stepping into Cheno's finished basement, he was telling Wolf what I'd already told him. I sat back listening to them talk business and I was glad Cheno was still looking out. Cheno got up and went to the other side of the room and opened a safe which was hidden underneath the carpet. He climbed down and came back up with one of the duffle bags. Going back down, he came up with another.

I sat up last night running this money through the counter. Cheese was making money hand over fist and I can't be a greedy muthafucka by keeping the shit to myself," Cheno said handing the bag to Wolf. "There is three mil in that bag for you, Foot, and Stubs. It's my way of saying thank you for taking over the empire. Take over Dallas and run that shit with an iron fist."

"Man, Cheno. You don't have to do that. The organization is doing damn good and that's because you were there to help us eat."

"I don't have to but I did. Accept the money and make it grow ten times over," Cheno said. "Let me know when y'all ready to head back home. Since you want to drive back, I'll make sure you have a rental truck to transport everything."

"Speaking of trucks. Quell, you gotta have Honey wrap yo' shit. I'm gon' do the same because there were too many witnesses to the mafia execution we pulled off."

"That was like a scene straight out of the movie *Godfather.* My baby gon' hook me up. Until then, I'll drive her shit."

"Honey will fuck around and go to the lot to cop a new whip for herself. Take y'all ass out of here because I need to get some sleep before G and Scony call to roll out."

"Y'all going to the club or something?" I asked.

"Nah, they going out to Downers Grove to drag Dro to the Dungeon. I'm going because I still got Larisa's bitch ass locked in that muthafucka too. Afterward, we can celebrate at G-Spot."

"Fuck that. Scoop me because I want to be there to put in work on Dro myself."

Cheno laughed and said he would hit my line when he was ready. Wolf picked up the bag and dapped Cheno up before leaving the basement. I headed for the stairs while he picked up the other duffle bag then turned off the lights.

203

Halfway up the stairs, Cheno called out to me. I turned to see what the fuck he was on.

"Don't think I didn't peep Honey doing all that damn crying when we came in. You knocked my cousin up on purpose by mistake," he laughed.

"The lies you tell. Honey is emotional because she had to pop her mama then turned around and offed Cheese."

"Wait, that was Honey's work?" Cheno whispered.

"Hell yeah, it was. I almost choked her ass because I told her to leave the shit to us."

"Man, you better get over that mad shit. Honey took care of business and I fuck with her for it. Cheese deserved everything she did to him. She was smooth with it too."

"Whatever. I'm out of here. Hit me up though."

"Wait, this bag is for Honey. Take it to her crib."

Honey was knocked out on Cheno's couch. I took the bag to her car then went back to get her. Once I had her secured in the seat to go down the street, I told Wolf to drive my truck while I got behind the wheel of Honey's. Pulling into her garage, I honked at Wolf and hit the button to lower the door. I shook her lil ass so she could walk in the house on her own. The bag alone was heavy as hell.

"Come on, Honey so you can go to bed."

She looked around and spotted the bag in my hand. "Quell, you are not about to start bringing clothes to my house. It's nothing for you to go next door to change. We not about to do that."

Honey got out and slammed the door before stomping off into the house. I took the bag upstairs where I knew she had gone and dropped it on the floor. She looked down with her face scrunched up. Honey opened her mouth to say something that would've caused me to pop her lips but I beat her ass to the punch.

"That's from Cheno. He told me to give it to you," I said kicking off my shoes.

She bent down and unzipped the bag. Her eyes grew ten times the normal size when she saw the money. "Wh-wha-what is this money for?"

"It's for you. He wiped Cheese out when we rescued Charlie from the warehouse. Put that away in the safe and I'll tell you all about it. Then maybe you can put a nigga to bed before I head out to handle some shit with Cheno tonight."

"Ohhhhh, now you wanna talk. Earlier you were so mad you barely wanted to kiss me. Now you looking for me to fuck you to sleep. Humph," she said dragging the bag across the room. "We can talk, but you will be getting acquainted with palm for that other shit."

I laughed because Honey was only lying to herself. She knew what time it was. Her attitude would change the moment my tongue glided down the crack of her ass.

Chapter 19

G

"Man. How long are we gon' sit out here?" Scony fussed. "The sun went down hours ago. These white muthafuckas done ate supper, walked the dogs, and got slapped by their kids already. We need to go in there and snatch this nigga the fuck up!"

"Scony, we got to wait for this muthafucka to go to sleep."

"Says who? Nova and those muthafuckin' kids got you forgetting who the fuck you are. Soft ass, nigga. I'm about to go kick that door down."

Soon as he opened the door his phone stopped him from getting out. He closed it back and answered the call putting it on speaker. When I heard Kenzie's voice, I knew something was going on in Atlanta.

"Kenzie, what the fuck is wrong with you?" Scony growled.

"Scony, I'm about to go the fuck to jail! Phantom think I'm boo-boo the fuckin' fool! You remember that bitch Chanel? The lawyer bitch who helped him win custody of Layla. Well, the bitch been calling his phone and this bastard talking about he can't stop her from calling. Yes, the fuck he can!"

"Where are the kids, sis?" I asked.

"They're upstairs. You better talk to this nigga."

The line went silent and me and Scony looked at one another. Kenzie was Scony's sister. She and Phantom been together four years, with three kids. Layla, who is Phantom's daughter, and a set of twins; a boy, Kannon Jr., and a girl, Kinleigh. They got married two years ago and now somebody from their past was trying to throw a monkey wrench in their lives. Scony needed to talk some sense into Phantom because if Storm emerged from the trenches, all hell was going to break loose. Then I would have to worry about her twin sister and that was a disaster waiting to happen when the two of them got together to put a muthafucka in their place.

"Scony, I got this," Phantom said when he got on the phone.

"Nigga, no you don't. Block that bitch so this shit can die down."

"I did. She keeps calling me from different apps. I block her every time. Kenzie isn't looking at the fact that I haven't talked to Chanel past five seconds. Once I hear her on the other end of the line, I hang up. I don't respond to the texts either."

"Had you allowed me to kill the bitch years ago, you wouldn't be going through this drama. I'm trying to remember I'm a mother now, but she gon' make me pull up and stomp her muthafuckin' ears together."

I laughed because Kenzie already forgot she was a mother because she was in full Storm mode and didn't realize it. "Fix this shit, Phantom. We finally got our lives on track. We don't need no more bullshit. Kenzie will calm down once she sees you are telling Chanel not to contact you anymore. Maybe if you remind her you have a wife, she will stop trying so hard."

"She knows I'm with Kenzie. We were married before making it official. I don't owe her an explanation."

"Okay. Nip it in a bud. If I get another call, I'm on the jet and it's gon' be hell in Atlanta because I'm bringing it with me. I have some business to attend to. Tell Kenzie to pipe down too. She doing all that hollering scaring my babies over there," Scony said seriously.

"Aight, bro. I'll tell her. Be careful out there."

"Fa sho."

Scony ended the call and I got out of the car pulling my gloves over my hands. While he was on the phone, I was keeping an eye on Dro's place. The lights downstairs went off as I gave a little bit of advice to Phantom. I didn't know if the nigga was watching us out the window or he actually went to bed. We were about to find out because the coast was clear and the time had come for us to handle his ass. Cheno and Quell walked up to my whip and waited for my command.

"Aight, the nigga got three ways in this house. The front, back, and patio doors. While the nigga was out earlier, I jimmied the lock on the patio so that muthafucka should still be open. Quell, you and Cheno go that route. Me and Scony will be waiting for one of y'all to unlock the front door. Then, we will ambush his ass upstairs."

"What if he has an alarm?" Quell asked.

"Did you hear me say anything about an alarm? The nigga ain't too bright or he thinks he's invincible. He doesn't have one. The muthafucka gon' wish he had installed a system once my gun is in his face."

"That's enough talking. It's time for action. Damn," Scony scoffed.

We got in position as Cheno and Quell went to the back. In no time flat, we were inside. Checking the lower level of the house to make sure the nigga wasn't trying to pull a fast one, we all headed upstairs. Leading the way, I went directly to the room I knew was his bedroom because I kept every inch of the layout in my mind.

The door was slightly open and I could see Dro sound asleep lying on his back. I pushed it open wider making my way to the side of the bed he was on. Scony purposely bumped the bed causing Dro to reach for his gun he had on the nightstand within reach. He came up empty because I had it and my Glock aimed at his head. The light from the moon shined onto his face and the nigga was scared shitless without a weapon.

"Looking for this?" I smiled waving his gun.

"Fuck y'all! You better kill me muthafucka!" Dro snapped.

"We plan on it. As a matter of fact, in due time, yo' brother and his mama gon' meet yo' pussy ass at the gate." Scony laughed. "Get up and let's go. I don't have all night to deal with this shit."

"If you think I'm about to walk out of here so y'all can kill me, somebody lied to you." He smirked.

"Have it your way." Scony grabbed his left leg and snapped the bone in one swift motion.

"Arrrrrghhhh!" Dro screamed out in agony.

"Now, we will carry your weak ass out. You ain't shit without your gun muthafucka. But you just earned yourself a slow and painful death. I've spent many years shooting niggas ending their lives fast. Go find his keys. He's going to take his final ride in his own vehicle."

Cheno left the room and I took the rope from my back pocket. Rolling Dro onto his stomach, I hogtied his ass. He squealed like a pig who was about to be slaughtered. Me and Scony took hold of the ropes and made our way to the garage. Cheno had the trunk opened as we approached then we dumped Dro inside roughly. I slammed the trunk then took the keys from Cheno. They left leaving me to climb behind the wheel of Dro's Benz. He was screaming at the top of his lungs. I used his system to look up Tupac's *Tradin' War Stories* and turned the volume up loud enough to drown out that nigga's cries and low enough so the white folks didn't call the law.

It took less than thirty minutes to arrive at the Dungeon. I pulled the car inside and went to the back to drag Dro's ass out. He had sweat running down his face and his breathing was a little choppy. What the nigga wasn't going to do was die on his own. Cheno walked over to help me get his ass out of the trunk.

"Open the hang room, Scony. We about to beat his ass like a pinata."

Entering the room, Scony was lowering the chains from the ceiling. I cut the rope from Dro's legs and arms. He laid there like a throw rug. I almost kicked his ass but I wasn't going out like that. While waiting for Scony to finish the task, he stopped midway through.

"G, I'm tired of torturing these muthafuckas. I'm ready to go home to my wife. Shoot this nigga and throw his ass in the furnace. As a matter of fact, Quell, put his ass out of his misery."

Quell didn't hesitate unloading the clip into the back of Dro's head. They picked his body up and dumbed him in the furnace. I walked down the hall and Cheno was in the white room. Standing by the door, I watched the female scratching her arms and mumbling to herself. The room would have the strongest muthafucka losing their mind if they were in there long enough.

"Larisa," Cheno called out to her.

"Daddy, is that you? I miss you daddy. Cheno is going to kill me."

Cheno cocked his head to the side as he looked at her. I thought he was about to punch her ass. Instead, he played along with her. I was glad because I wanted to hear what she had to say.

"Why is this man going to do that?"

"It's my fault. I set him up to get killed because he didn't want me."

"Did he tell you he wanted to be with you?"

"No, but he fucked me like he did. It don't matter, fuck Cheno! I wish he would've died and that ugly ass bitch too!" Larisa cried lying on the pad. "He stood there and let my sister kill mommy. I had just found her two years ago. I was in foster care after foster care because your mother took me from her after you died. She didn't even want me so why not take me back to my mama! I went through so much then I was finally able to reunite with the woman that loved me only for her to be taken away from me this time!"

My eyes darted over to Cheno and the deathly stare in his cold eyes told me what was about to happen. He pulled his gun and walked over to Larisa. She looked up realizing too late that Cheno was the person she bared her soul to. Opening her mouth, Cheno raised his tool and sent a bullet through her head then walked out. I was tired of seeing dead people so I called Scony to come into the white room.

"What's up?" He said standing next to me.

"Get rid of that shit so we can go."

"Why you didn't tell Cheno to clean up his own mess? I'm whooping his ass! What I look like, a muthafuckin' custodian?" Scony was pissed and I couldn't do nothing but laugh.

"Man, I'll help yo' grouchy ass. Cheno wasn't about to move this bitch. If she had said the shit I heard to you, yo' ass would've walked away too. Make sure you go home and nail Jade to the cross cause that's ya problem. Don't forget to strap up. You muthafuckas got enough kids running around that damn house."

"Fuck you, G! You mad because yo' lil swimmers don't flow freely no mo'. It's not my fault you allowed the white man to cut on your balls. Weak ass can't handle a couple kids."

"You tried it. I was two and done. Try that shit and see how your stress level goes down."

Scony stopped talking and we rolled the bitch up then took her to join the others in the crematorium. When I locked up the Dungeon, I had no plans of coming back to that muthafucka for a very long time. The next muthafucka who run into a problem better not come to me because I'm retired from this street shit.

211

Epilogue

Six months later

The past six months was hard on everyone. Victoria's body was found floating in the Chicago River. She was identified by her dental records and Honey was contacted. Doing what she had to do by burying her mother in a pine box. With the money Cheno had given her from Cheese's warehouse, the five million helped expand her business.

When Honey opened the shop after a month and a half of being closed, she thought it was over for her. Honey hired a Marketing manager and Alicia was a beast at what she does. People from all fifty states were coming to Chicago to get a new look for their vehicles. Honey and the crew were working hard five days a week to get that money. Two months later, she hired ten other women to work for her. Cheno had to remind Honey that she was the Boss, all she should be doing was overseeing the business without lifting a finger.

Cool Breeze was the name on the building next door to Honey's Customization. She was hooking up all the dope boys so they would be quick with the switch if the pigs were after them. Her designs were a hit and she too was making money hand over fist. Not to mention, Breeze was back selling weed too. This time around, she was selling weed in much larger quantities. She had a whole team of niggas with Coo at the top of the chain working for her.

Taz was also team Breeze and brought in money for her infamous infused drinks, food, and desserts. Breeze made sure her woman was set to make her own way in the world. Taz started sampling the edibles in their kitchen. She would bring samples to the shop for the customers then larger orders were requested. In a matter of months, TAZmanian Bliss was born. Breeze bought Taz a storefront in the very strip the shop was in and it was a hit.

The disappearance of Dawson had his people harassing Cheno and Breeze. Their aunt even sent the police saying they did something to Dawson's punk ass. It wasn't a lie but the truth would never be public information. Cleve and Shon were the only family Breeze fucked with heavy. The rest of them could kiss her ass. Cheno ignored them all and acted like he didn't know them.

Charlie was living her best life dating whoever she wanted. Being in a relationship was the furthest thing from her mind. When she wasn't working at the shop, Charlie was on a plane traveling the world. She discovered her talent was in makeup. With the help of the same Marketing manager who worked for Honey, Charlie was able to get the attention of many celebrities with her MUA skills.

She and Cheno was still friends and the relationship is a beautiful example for all the bitter men and women in the world. Who says there can't be friendships after a breakup? It takes two mature individuals who doesn't allow animosity, jealousy, or hate to destroy a lifetime connection. Cheno bought Charlie a home as promised. He even helped her move in. The two was closer than they ever were minus the sexual aspect.

Cheno on the other hand was trying hard to move on daily. Losing some of the most important people in his life was eating him up inside. He kept his feelings bottled inside while smiling broadly on the outside. Miss Pearl was the only person who would see through his bullshit. She kept him on his toes whenever he came around; which was every day.

Miss Pearl came out of the coma causing all types of hell. She recovered fully and continued opening her home to the ones she loved. Sunday was the one day everyone was together talking and laughing while eating a feast Miss Pearl cooked. Anyway, Cheno's businesses were running well, and he opened a restaurant on the Nine called Hood Burgers. His most sought-after item was the TAZmanian Bliss infused drinks.

When Cheno wasn't trying to keep busy, he spent time with his hottie of the month, Deandra. She was on the verge of getting the boot because she didn't like the bond Cheno had with Charlie. He didn't feel the need to explain anything to her because Deandra was never going to be a permanent fixture in his life. So, he stepped back and gave her the space she needed to check her feelings at the door. Amari was still around but she too was just a friend. She claimed focusing on her career was her top priority but Cheno knew something in his life scared her off.

Quell was doing his thing in the tattoo department. All of the girls in Honey's crew went to him so he could replicate the *Millie Mob* tat Breeze had. Quell stayed ready for business because the people who were waiting on their cars, went to him for tattoos to pass the time. His money was flowing with ease and there was no stopping him. With a total of seven artists, including himself, Quell was doing what he loved. Creating masterpieces for the world to see. Common, Lil Durk, and even Da Brat came through to get tatted by him. He and Honey were going strong. She finally allowed Quell to have her whole heart. The man was in heaven because Honey catered to him like a King. She just wasn't ready to pop out any babies.

The entire crew was striving in their successes. It took them a minute to get back out there to accomplished all they had once the smoke cleared. Family was everything and they

214

were all they had. It was the crew against the world. Anybody could get the smoke from a few Thugs and their Street princess.

The End

To catch up on Grant Davenport (G) and Demarius Jones (Scony), Read A Distinguished Thug Stole My Heart. Makenzie (Storm) and MaKayla (Kane) can be found in the Savage Storms Series. Get to know them.

Follow Me...

Facebook author Page: www.facebook.com/MzMeesh
Facebook: www.facebook.com/mesha.king1
Instagram: www.instagram.com/author_meesha/
Twitter: twitter.com/AuthorMeesha
Tiktok: vm.tiktok.com/TTPdkx6LEW/
Website: www.authormeesha.com

Lock Down Publications and Ca$h Presents
Assisted Publishing Packages

BASIC PACKAGE	UPGRADED PACKAGE
$499	$800
Editing	Typing
Cover Design	Editing
Formatting	Cover Design
	Formatting
ADVANCE PACKAGE	**LDP SUPREME PACKAGE**
$1,200	$1,500
Typing	Typing
Editing	Editing
Cover Design	Cover Design
Formatting	Formatting
Copyright registration	Copyright registration
Proofreading	Proofreading
Upload book to Amazon	Set up Amazon account
	Upload book to Amazon
	Advertise on LDP, Amazon and Facebook Page

***Other services available upon request.
Additional charges may apply

Lock Down Publications
P.O. Box 944
Stockbridge, GA 30281-9998
Phone: 470 303-9761

Submission Guideline

Submit the first three chapters of your completed manuscript to ldpsubmissions@gmail.com. In the subject line add **Your Book's Title**. The manuscript must be in a Word Doc file and sent as an attachment. Document should be in Times New Roman, double spaced, and in size 12 font. Also, provide your synopsis and full contact information. If sending multiple submissions, they must each be in a separate email.

Have a story but no way to send it electronically? You can still submit to LDP/Ca$h Presents. Send in the first three chapters, written or typed, of your completed manuscript to:

LDP: Submissions Dept
P.O. Box 944
Stockbridge, GA 30281-9998

DO NOT send original manuscript. Must be a duplicate.
Provide your synopsis and a cover letter containing your full contact information.

Thanks for considering LDP and Ca$h Presents.

NEW RELEASES

BLOODLINE OF A SAVAGE 1&2
THESE VICIOUS STREETS 1&2
RELENTLESS GOON
RELENTLESS GOON 2
BY PRINCE A. TAUHID

THE BUTTERFLY MAFIA 1-3
BY FUMIYA PAYNE

A THUG'S STREET PRINCESS 1&2
BY MEESHA

CITY OF SMOKE 2
BY MOLOTTI

STEPPERS 1,2&3
THE REAL BADDIES OF CHI-RAQ
BY KING RIO

THE LANE 1&2
BY KEN-KEN SPENCE

THUG OF SPADES 1&2
LOVE IN THE TRENCHES 2
CORNER BOYS
BY COREY ROBINSON

TIL DEATH 3
BY ARYANNA

THE BIRTH OF A GANGSTER 4
BY DELMONT PLAYER

PRODUCT OF THE STREETS 1&2
BY DEMOND "MONEY" ANDERSON

NO TIME FOR ERROR
BY KEESE

MONEY HUNGRY DEMONS
BY TRANAY ADAMS

Coming Soon from Lock Down Publications/Ca$h Presents

IF YOU CROSS ME ONCE 6
ANGEL V
By Anthony Fields

IMMA DIE BOUT MINE 5
By Aryanna

A THUGS STREET PRINCESS 3
By Meesha

PRODUCT OF THE STREETS 3
By Demond Money Anderson

CORNER BOYS 2
By Corey Robinson

THE MURDER QUEENS 6&7
By Michael Gallon

CITY OF SMOKE 3
By Molotti

CONFESSIONS OF A DOPE BOY
By Nicholas Lock

THA TAKEOVER
By Keith Chandler

BETRAYAL OF A G 2
By Ray Vinci

CRIME BOSS
By Playa Ray

Available Now

RESTRAINING ORDER 1 & 2
By **CA$H & Coffee**

LOVE KNOWS NO BOUNDARIES 1-3
By **Coffee**

RAISED AS A GOON I, II, III & IV
BRED BY THE SLUMS I, II, III
BLAST FOR ME I & II
ROTTEN TO THE CORE I II III
A BRONX TALE I, II, III
DUFFLE BAG CARTEL I II III IV V VI
HEARTLESS GOON I II III IV V
A SAVAGE DOPEBOY I II
DRUG LORDS I II III
CUTTHROAT MAFIA I II
KING OF THE TRENCHES
By **Ghost**

LAY IT DOWN I & II
LAST OF A DYING BREED I II
BLOOD STAINS OF A SHOTTA I & II III
By **Jamaica**

LOYAL TO THE GAME I II III
LIFE OF SIN I, II III
By **TJ & Jelissa**

IF LOVING HIM IS WRONG...I & II
LOVE ME EVEN WHEN IT HURTS I II III
By **Jelissa**

PUSH IT TO THE LIMIT
By **Bre' Hayes**

BLOODY COMMAS I & II
SKI MASK CARTEL I, II & III
KING OF NEW YORK I II, III IV V
RISE TO POWER I II III
COKE KINGS I II III IV V
BORN HEARTLESS I II III IV
KING OF THE TRAP I II
By **T.J. Edwards**

WHEN THE STREETS CLAP BACK I & II III
THE HEART OF A SAVAGE I II III IV
MONEY MAFIA I II
LOYAL TO THE SOIL I II III
By **Jibril Williams**

A DISTINGUISHED THUG STOLE MY HEART I II & III
LOVE SHOULDN'T HURT I II III IV
RENEGADE BOYS 1-4
PAID IN KARMA 1-3
SAVAGE STORMS 1-3
AN UNFORESEEN LOVE 1-3
BABY, I'M WINTERTIME COLD 1-3
A THUG'S STREET PRINCESS 1&2
By **Meesha**

A GANGSTER'S CODE 1-3
A GANGSTER'S SYN 1-3
THE SAVAGE LIFE 1-3
CHAINED TO THE STREETS 1-3
BLOOD ON THE MONEY 1-3
A GANGSTA'S PAIN 1-3
BEAUTIFUL LIES AND UGLY TRUTHS
CHURCH IN THESE STREETS
By **J-Blunt**

CUM FOR ME 1-8
An LDP Erotica Collaboration

BLOOD OF A BOSS 1-5
SHADOWS OF THE GAME
TRAP BASTARD
By **Askari**

THE STREETS BLEED MURDER 1-3
THE HEART OF A GANGSTA 1-3
By **Jerry Jackson**

WHEN A GOOD GIRL GOES BAD
By **Adrienne**

THE COST OF LOYALTY 1-3
By **Kweli**

BRIDE OF A HUSTLA 1-3
THE FETTI GIRLS 1-3
CORRUPTED BY A GANGSTA 1-4
BLINDED BY HIS LOVE
THE PRICE YOU PAY FOR LOVE 1-3
DOPE GIRL MAGIC 1-3
By **Destiny Skai**

A KINGPIN'S AMBITION
A KINGPIN'S AMBITION II
I MURDER FOR THE DOUGH
By **Ambitious**

TRUE SAVAGE 1-7
DOPE BOY MAGIC 1-3
MIDNIGHT CARTEL 1-3
CITY OF KINGZ 1&2
NIGHTMARE ON SILENT AVE
THE PLUG OF LIL MEXICO 1&2
CLASSIC CITY
By **Chris Green**

A GANGSTER'S REVENGE 1-4
THE BOSS MAN'S DAUGHTERS 1-5
A SAVAGE LOVE 1&2
BAE BELONGS TO ME 1&2
A HUSTLER'S DECEIT 1-3
WHAT BAD BITCHES DO 1-3
SOUL OF A MONSTER 1-3
KILL ZONE
A DOPE BOY'S QUEEN 1-3
TIL DEATH 1-3
IMMA DIE BOUT MINE 1-4
By **Aryanna**

A DOPEBOY'S PRAYER
By **Eddie "Wolf" Lee**

THE KING CARTEL 1-3
By **Frank Gresham**

THESE NIGGAS AIN'T LOYAL 1-3
By **Nikki Tee**

GANGSTA SHYT 1-3
By **CATO**

THE ULTIMATE BETRAYAL
By **Phoenix**

BOSS'N UP 1-3
By **Royal Nicole**

I LOVE YOU TO DEATH
By **Destiny J**

I RIDE FOR MY HITTA
I STILL RIDE FOR MY HITTA
By **Misty Holt**

LOVE & CHASIN' PAPER
By **Qay Crockett**

TO DIE IN VAIN
SINS OF A HUSTLA
By **ASAD**

BROOKLYN HUSTLAZ
By **Boogsy Morina**

BROOKLYN ON LOCK 1 & 2
By **Sonovia**

GANGSTA CITY
By **Teddy Duke**

A DRUG KING AND HIS DIAMOND 1-3
A DOPEMAN'S RICHES
HER MAN, MINE'S TOO 1&2
CASH MONEY HO'S
THE WIFEY I USED TO BE 1&2
PRETTY GIRLS DO NASTY THINGS
By **Nicole Goosby**

LIPSTICK KILLAH 1-3
CRIME OF PASSION 1-3
FRIEND OR FOE 1-3
By **Mimi**

TRAPHOUSE KING 1-3
KINGPIN KILLAZ 1-3
STREET KINGS 1&2
PAID IN BLOOD 1&2
CARTEL KILLAZ 1-3
DOPE GODS 1&2
By **Hood Rich**

THE STREETS ARE CALLING
By **Duquie Wilson**

STEADY MOBBN' 1-3
THE STREETS STAINED MY SOUL 1-3
By **Marcellus Allen**

WHO SHOT YA 1-3
SON OF A DOPE FIEND 1-4
HEAVEN GOT A GHETTO 1&2
SKI MASK MONEY 1&2
By **Renta**

GORILLAZ IN THE BAY 1-4
TEARS OF A GANGSTA 1/&2
3X KRAZY 1&2
STRAIGHT BEAST MODE 1&2
By **DE'KARI**

TRIGGADALE 1-3
MURDA WAS THE CASE 1-3
By **Elijah R. Freeman**

SLAUGHTER GANG 1-3
RUTHLESS HEART 1-3
By **Willie Slaughter**

GOD BLESS THE TRAPPERS 1-3
THESE SCANDALOUS STREETS 1-3
FEAR MY GANGSTA 1-5
THESE STREETS DON'T LOVE NOBODY 1-2
BURY ME A G 1-5
A GANGSTA'S EMPIRE 1-4
THE DOPEMAN'S BODYGAURD 1&2
THE REALEST KILLAZ 1-3
THE LAST OF THE OGS 1-3
By **Tranay Adams**

MARRIED TO A BOSS 1-3
By **Destiny Skai & Chris Green**

KINGZ OF THE GAME 1-7
CRIME BOSS 1-3
By **Playa Ray**

FUK SHYT
By **Blakk Diamond**

DON'T F#CK WITH MY HEART 1&2
By **Linnea**

ADDICTED TO THE DRAMA 1-3
IN THE ARM OF HIS BOSS
By **Jamila**

LOYALTY AIN'T PROMISED 1&2
By **Keith Williams**

YAYO 1-4
A SHOOTER'S AMBITION 1&2
BRED IN THE GAME
By **S. Allen**

TRAP GOD 1-3
RICH $AVAGE 1-3
MONEY IN THE GRAVE 1-3
CARTEL MONEY
By **Martell Troublesome Bolden**

FOREVER GANGSTA 1&2
GLOCKS ON SATIN SHEETS 1&2
By **Adrian Dulan**

TOE TAGZ 1-4
LEVELS TO THIS SHYT 1&2
IT'S JUST ME AND YOU
By **Ah'Million**

KINGPIN DREAMS 1-3
RAN OFF ON DA PLUG
By **Paper Boi Rari**

THE STREETS MADE ME 1-3
By **Larry D. Wright**

CONFESSIONS OF A GANGSTA 1-4
CONFESSIONS OF A JACKBOY 1-3
CONFESSIONS OF A HITMAN
By **Nicholas Lock**

I'M NOTHING WITHOUT HIS LOVE
SINS OF A THUG
TO THE THUG I LOVED BEFORE
A GANGSTA SAVED XMAS
IN A HUSTLER I TRUST
By **Monet Dragun**

QUIET MONEY 1-3
THUG LIFE 1-3
EXTENDED CLIP 1&2
A GANGSTA'S PARADISE
By **Trai'Quan**

CAUGHT UP IN THE LIFE 1-3
THE STREETS NEVER LET GO 1-3
By **Robert Baptiste**

NEW TO THE GAME 1-3
MONEY, MURDER & MEMORIES 1-3
By **Malik D. Rice**

CREAM 2-3
THE STREETS WILL TALK
By **Yolanda Moore**

THE STREETS WILL NEVER CLOSE 1-3
By **K'ajji**

LIFE OF A SAVAGE 1-4
A GANGSTA'S QUR'AN 1-4
MURDA SEASON 1-3
GANGLAND CARTEL 1-3
CHI'RAQ GANGSTAS 1-4
KILLERS ON ELM STREET 1-3
JACK BOYZ N DA BRONX 1-3
A DOPEBOY'S DREAM 1-3
JACK BOYS VS DOPE BOYS 1-3
COKE GIRLZ
COKE BOYS
SOSA GANG 1&2
BRONX SAVAGES
BODYMORE KINGPINS
BLOOD OF A GOON
By **Romell Tukes**

CONCRETE KILLA 1-3
VICIOUS LOYALTY 1-3
By **Kingpen**

THE ULTIMATE SACRIFICE 1-6
KHADIFI
IF YOU CROSS ME ONCE 1-3
ANGEL 1-4
IN THE BLINK OF AN EYE
By **Anthony Fields**

THE LIFE OF A HOOD STAR
By **Ca$h & Rashia Wilson**

NIGHTMARES OF A HUSTLA 1-3
BLOOD AND GAMES 1&2
By **King Dream**

GHOST MOB
By **Stilloan Robinson**

HARD AND RUTHLESS 1&2
MOB TOWN 251
THE BILLIONAIRE BENTLEYS 1-3
REAL G'S MOVE IN SILENCE
By **Von Diesel**

MOB TIES 1-7
SOUL OF A HUSTLER, HEART OF A KILLER 1-3
GORILLAZ IN THE TRENCHES
By **SayNoMore**

BODYMORE MURDERLAND 1-3
THE BIRTH OF A GANGSTER 1-4
By **Delmont Player**

FOR THE LOVE OF A BOSS 1&2
By **C. D. Blue**

KILLA KOUNTY 1-5
By **Khufu**

MOBBED UP 1-4
THE BRICK MAN 1-5
THE COCAINE PRINCESS 1-10
STEPPERS 1-3
SUPER GREMLIN 1-4
By **King Rio**

MONEY GAME 1&2
By **Smoove Dolla**

A GANGSTA'S KARMA 1-4
By **FLAME**

KING OF THE TRENCHES 1-3
By **GHOST & TRANAY ADAMS**

QUEEN OF THE ZOO 1&2
By **Black Migo**

GRIMEY WAYS 1-3
BETRAYAL OF A G
By **Ray Vinci**

XMAS WITH AN ATL SHOOTER
By **Ca$h & Destiny Skai**

KING KILLA 1&2
By **Vincent "Vitto" Holloway**

BETRAYAL OF A THUG 1&2
By **Fre$h**

THE MURDER QUEENS 1-5
By **Michael Gallon**

FOR THE LOVE OF BLOOD 1-4
By **Jamel Mitchell**

HOOD CONSIGLIERE 1&2
NO TIME FOR ERROR
By **Keese**

PROTÉGÉ OF A LEGEND 1&2
LOVE IN THE TRENCHES 1&2
By **Corey Robinson**

THE PLUG'S RUTHLESS DAUGHTER
By **Tony Daniels**

BORN IN THE GRAVE 1-3
CRIME PAYS
By **Self Made Tay**

MOAN IN MY MOUTH
By **XTASY**

TORN BETWEEN A GANGSTER AND A GENTLEMAN
By **J-BLUNT & Miss Kim**

LOYALTY IS EVERYTHING 1-3
CITY OF SMOKE 1&2
By **Molotti**

HERE TODAY GONE TOMORROW 1&2
By **Fly Rock**

WOMEN LIE MEN LIE 1-4
FIFTY SHADES OF SNOW 1-3
STACK BEFORE YOU SPLURGE
GIRLS FALL LIKE DOMINOES
NAÏVE TO THE STREETS
By **ROY MILLIGAN**

PILLOW PRINCESS
By **S. Hawkins**

THE BUTTERFLY MAFIA 1-3
SALUTE MY SAVAGERY 1&2
By **Fumiya Payne**

THE LANE 1&2
By Ken-Ken Spence

THE PUSSY TRAP 1-5
By **Nene Capri**

DIRTY DNA
By **Blaque**

SANCTIFIED AND HORNY
by **XTASY**

BOOKS BY LDP'S CEO, CA$H

TRUST IN NO MAN
TRUST IN NO MAN 2
TRUST IN NO MAN 3
BONDED BY BLOOD
SHORTY GOT A THUG
THUGS CRY
THUGS CRY 2
THUGS CRY 3
TRUST NO BITCH
TRUST NO BITCH 2
TRUST NO BITCH 3
TIL MY CASKET DROPS
RESTRAINING ORDER
RESTRAINING ORDER 2
IN LOVE WITH A CONVICT
LIFE OF A HOOD STAR
XMAS WITH AN ATL SHOOTER

www.ingramcontent.com/pod-product-compliance
Lightning Source LLC
Chambersburg PA
CBHW071149260626
47162CB00003B/971